KELLZ KIMBERLY

NAME KEY

Jacelyn: Jay-suh-lyn
 Nazari: Nuh-aaa-ree
 Aidan: Aye-den
 Creedence: Kree-dence
 Rhea: Ray-uh
 Dionne: Dee-yown
 Sariah: Shuh-rye-uh
 Tara: Tar-uh
 Bryn: Br-in

PREVIOUSLY JACELYN

As I DROVE OUT of the school's parking lot, I chewed my bottom lip like it was a piece of gum. Nerves had been getting the best of me lately. Aidan hadn't returned home, but he was riding the hell out of my coattail. Since I really wasn't answering his calls, he would constantly call Rhea's iPad. They would talk, but her iPad always ended up in my face with her father faking like we were some kind of happy family. I mean I faked it too, but at least I wasn't in denial.

In the few days Aidan had been gone, he'd brought up us renewing our vows and even having another kid all while in the presence of our daughter. Rhea was happy about possibly having a sibling, but I was pissed. For one, I was adamant about keeping my marital problems away from Rhea. I didn't include her in conversations that were meant for adults. Aidan was well aware of that, but I wasn't dumb. He did that on purpose, trying to manipulate the situation. I didn't know what I was going to do about my husband and his antics. The longer he stayed gone, the better. It gave me time to decide my next moves, but it also gave me time to end this thing with Nazari.

The way Sariah walked up on me questioning me about Rhea was inappropriate. My daughter wasn't her concern. Rhea had a father and it damn sure wasn't Nazari. Sariah asking me questions did make me wonder if Nazari was thinking the same. Avoiding that conversation altogether would've been ideal but, I knew if I was going to leave Nazari alone, I also had to ease his mind.

Coming to a red light, I glanced at Rhea, trying to find a drop of Nazari in her, but I didn't see him. Nothing about Rhea reminded me of him. My daughter couldn't have been his, I was certain.

"Baby, put your headphones on please. Mommy has to make a call."

Rhea was listening to her YouTube videos louder than necessary.

"Okay Mommy."

I made sure Rhea had her headphones on and opened IG, found Nazari, and called him through the app. I felt odd calling this man through social media, but I didn't have any other choice.

"Yo." His lazy tone oozed through the phone, speeding up the knocks against my chest. "Yo, who the fuck is this?"

"Can you not curse? I have my daughter in the car," I spat back, finding my voice.

"Man, who the fuck is this? You called my phone I'ma talk however the fuck I wanna talk."

Nazari was so damn arrogant, it was nauseating but sexy.

"Aye, you gon' speak or—"

Hurriedly, I blurted, "It's Jacelyn. I know you saw my screen name when you answered the call."

I smacked my lips, ready for whatever outlandish thing he was going to say next. What I didn't expect was the phone going silent. Not even the wisp of our breathing was heard.

"Uh hello?"

"Whatchu want?" The nastiness in his tone was back.

"We need to talk," I snapped.

"Man, I'm busy right now. I'll see you when I see you."

"Wrong. We need to talk, and we need to talk now. Tell me where you are, and I'll come to you."

"Hello," I sang out, tired of hearing only his breathing.

"I'll send you the address."

"Goo—"

The call ended, and I rolled my eyes while letting out a heavy sigh. Going to see Nazari, especially with Rhea, was playing with fire, but I had to clear the air. I couldn't risk another run-in with Sariah and someone overhearing our conversation, then running to tell Aidan. In the midst of me driving, a notification popped up with an address that was two blocks over from Nunu's house. I grinned, happy that I wouldn't have to bring Rhea along for this awkward conversation.

"Okay Nunu, I'll be back in a few. Rhea is out back with Gramps. I'm leaving my car and walking to meet with a friend."

I tried my best to walk as fast as I could past the kitchen, but Nunu was not having it.

"Jacelyn, sit down."

"Nunu, I really have to—"

Nunu gave me one look, and I was sitting my ass down at the table.

"I know I said I would stay out of your marriage and Lord knows I've been trying. What I can't ignore is your husband calling your grandfather and snitching on you."

"What?" I gasped.

"Pick up that heavy bottom lip because you heard me. I had to listen to your gramps go on and on about how you were out all night with another man that wasn't your husband."

"Why would Aidan call Gramps when Gramps doesn't even like him?"

"That's a part of the game sweetheart. Gramps doesn't have to like Aidan for him to be made aware of his granddaughter exhibiting whorish behavior. Aidan can't get through to you, so he wants to use Gramps to do so."

"Then, why didn't Gramps say anything?"

"I told him not to. What you do in your marriage is your business Jayce, but you need to be careful. I don't condone any woman stepping out of their marriage but, if that's what you're choosing to do, make sure the other guy is worth it and willing to take care of you and Rhea."

"I'll handle it Nunu," I sighed.

"Handle it? You need to divorce it. I know you think you're doing what's right for Rhea by staying with that man, but you're not. What are you going to do? Stay with Aidan until Rhea turns 18 then leave?"

Nunu allowed her heavy breathing to take over the conversation, and I knew she was looking for an answer.

"Not 18 exactly but when she gets a little old."

"And what's going to be your explanation for leaving? Huh? How are you going to explain to your daughter who looks towards you as aspiration that you're leaving her father because you've been unhappy for years? Jayce, I understand you want to give Rhea what you didn't have, but at what cost? Staying with Aidan is only teaching Rhea it's okay to stay with a man even when you're not happy. That's not a lesson you ought to teach her."

Nunu stood up from the table with her arms stretched out in my direction. Like a child needing a warm embrace, I fell into her arms. My eyes burned with sadness because everything Nunu said was true.

"Alright, now, put your big girl draws on and handle business."

"I will."

Smiling, Nunu wiped my eyes and walked me to the door. I gave her one last hug, then headed towards Nazari. As I walked, I called Aidan.

"Hello, wife, how are you to—"

"Stop calling Gramps with your bullshit Aidan. I'm grown; my grandparents aren't going to chastise me for you."

"I wanted to give the people you admire the opportunity to reel you in before I have to. Jacelyn, you are my wife and I love you. The last thing I want to do is start keeping tabs on you because you can't hop off dick long enough to make it home."

"You have to stop with your bullshit. I messed up that night, but you've been messing up for years Aidan!"

Aidan let out a heavy breath, softening his tone. "I know and I want to fix that."

"How, by telling on me to my grandfather?" I was annoyed and had been sucked in one too many times by Aidan's *I want to change* speeches.

"I was wrong and I apologize, okay. We've both been operating from a place of anger, and it isn't helping. When I get back on Monday, Rhea can stay with my mother for the week and it'll give us a chance to reconnect. We can even go back to couples' therapy."

"I'll think about."

"That's all I ask. I love you, Jacelyn, and I'm sorry for not showing it more."

"Okay. Me too. I have to go."

As I approached the address Nazari gave me, I rushed off the phone with Aidan. Nothing he said held any weight, and I wasn't in the mood to fix us.

"Ashes 2 Ashes."

I mouthed the store name, dropped my phone into my purse and pressed the bell. Through the intercom, Nazari barked, "Who?"

I replied as nicely as I could, "Jacelyn."

A crisp breeze brushed against my face and then another before a buzz was heard and Nazari instructed me to step onto the threshold. I did like I was told, jumping slightly when a heavy mist sprayed down on me.

"Ahh!" my shriek shattered the stillness.

"Chill," Nazari chortled, appearing in front of me. "It's just a special sanitizer."

"Are you a germaphobe or something?"

I entered the shop pursing my lips towards my nose and looking at Nazari through slanted eyes. His laughter surrounded me, as I waited for an explanation.

"Well?"

"I grow my own weed. It's a sensitive process. Contamination of any kind can compromise the integrity of my weed. Business is too good for that, so a nigga can't take chances."

A lazy grin and his tongue lightly flickering across his juicy lips clued me to Nazari being high. His darkened orbs lingering over me brought on an unexplainable heat that spread throughout my cheeks. I turned away from him saying, "Didn't anyone tell you not to get high off your own supply?"

Nazari laughed, and I allowed his chuckle to fade as my eyes wandered around the shop. There really wasn't much in the front area. A few chairs were in the corner and there was a random ass counter blocking off the back part of the shop. Taking it all in, I wondered what Nazari planned on doing with all this empty potential.

"Jacelyn." His smooth voice guided my gaze back towards his. "I thought you wanted to talk."

Nazari leaned against the wall with one leg propped up and his hands placed in front of him. He looked so damn fine in his stance, even while wearing a slight frown. Nazari's attractiveness was undeniable. Even when doing the least, I found myself swooning.

His teeth dragged his bottom lip into his mouth, then slowly let it slip from its grasp. I swallowed hard, feeling hot between my legs. Parting my lips, all words and sounds were lost upon me. Everything inside of me slowed, including my thoughts the longer Nazari looked at me. It was as if his smoldering squinted gaze had slowed time.

"Jacelyn."

Again, his gritty silky tone commanded me. Unintentionally, I began moving towards him. I reached him, yet he didn't move. He didn't reach out for me like he'd done on so many other occasions to bring our bodies together. He just remained in his stance eyeing me questionably. Feeling foolish for thinking he'd wanted me in his orbit, I took a step back laughing awkwardly and asking, "Besides growing weed, what else do you do here?"

In such a brute and cocky manner, he chuckled gravelly, tugging at his beard. "Why are you here Jayce?"

The nickname only my grandparents called me escaped him and ran straight into my beating heart. It fluttered, growing warm with each of his exhales lightly brushing against my cheeks.

"I came to talk about... Sariah came to me while at the kids school and I—"

I knew exactly what I wanted to say. I needed to tell Nazari that Rhea wasn't his and how it would be better for everyone if he just left me alone. I wanted to scream for him to never talk to me again because him simply uttering my name would cause confusion in my life. Everything I needed to say to Nazari was at the tip of my tongue and, still, all words were lost the longer I peered into his eyes.

"Sariah came to you saying what?" Nazari's brows squinched in confusion. He had no clue about Sariah's intentions regarding Rhea.

"Um, never mind. I thought you were the reason she asked about—"

"Rhea."

Nazari's whole demeanor changed when he spoke my daughter's name. His bushy brows peeked with his low resting lids opening wider than I'd ever seen. His shoulders even relaxed a bit with the rise and fall of his chest quieting.

"Is she... she—"

Like me, all words were lost on Nazari. I didn't know why either of us were having a hard time getting to the point but we were.

"Is she mine?" Hurt flickered in his eyes. His jaw tightened, sharpening his jawline.

"No, she's not."

"You did a DNA test?"

"No because I didn't have to. Rhea as the same unique color eyes as her—"

Throaty laughter spewed from Nazari's mouth. With my lips pursed together, they scrunched towards my nose. Nazari ignored my displeasure and continued laughing. After a while, I stopped trying to find the joke and decided to find the door instead.

"Ugh!" I spat after trying to push the door open with no luck. Kicking the door, I let out a frustrated groan when a sharp pain shot through my foot. "Can you please open the fucking—"

A hand at my waist and faint tickles of hair against my neck shut me right up. I swallowed hard. Asthmatic like exhales escaped once I felt his words graze my cheek.

"Where the fuck you think your goin' Jayce?"

NAZARI CADDEL

I WASN'T EVEN TRYING to be funny by laughing at what Jacelyn said, but she was definitely talking bullshit. I mean what she said about Aidan made sense, but that nigga wasn't the only one with eyes the same hue as Rhea's. If her ass stopped running, she could get to know me. She would realize my eyes weren't as dark as they looked.

I wasn't ready to fill her in on the family trauma I carried with me. I needed time to see where her head was at without all the drama because when the truth came out, she was gon' like what happened next. Rhea being mine meant it was a wrap for her and that nigga Aidan. Another nigga wasn't gon' raise my daughter and my bm wasn't about to be married to a nigga that wasn't me.

Lowkey, I wanted a family, even with my fear of falling in love just to fall out of it. A nigga wanted all the sweet corny shit. Matching Christmas pajamas, sending out corny ass Christmas cards, and whatever else came along with being in love. I wanted to experience it all, I wanted it with her. Before any of that could happen, I was trying to spend time with shawty, ease my crazy into her life on some chill shit.

"Where the fuck you think you're going Jayce?"

Her response was nothing more than faint cooing. I smirked to myself. As much as I didn't want her to leave, she wasn't ready to leave either.

Bzzzt! Bzzzt! Bzzzt!

The doorbell to the shop rang but, with the kind of door I had, you couldn't see out or in. Still holding on to Jayce by the waist, I shuffled our bodies towards the intercom.

"Who?" I spoke, holding the listening button.

"Mr. Smyth."

I buzzed him, then noticed Jacelyn trying to squirm away from me.

"Aye, whatchu doing?"

"I gotta go."

"Man, I already told ya ass that you ain't—"

"Nazari, you don't understand. I have to go because—"

The door to the shop opened and the sanitizer sprayed down a smiling Mr. Smyth. Quickly, Jacelyn turned, burying her face in my chest.

"Jacelyn?" Mr. Smyth quizzed.

"Fuck." Her curse was almost inaudible. Nervously, she faced Mr. Smyth. "Hey Gramps."

"Jacelyn, what are you... matter of fact, never mind. Nazari, you and I need to talk."

"Gramps, it's okay, we can just—"

"Jacelyn, stop talking," he told her sternly.

Impulsively, my jaw locked. The tone Mr. Smyth used wasn't pleasing to me, but I fucked with dude.

"Go through that door to your right and chill. There's some snacks in there and shit. Be easy, most of it is infused." Jacelyn's eyes darted between me and her gramps.

"Fine but I'm only giving y'all five minutes."

Huffing, Jacelyn poked her juicy ass bottom lip out and walked off, following my directions. With her back towards me, I licked my lips, loving the view of the sway in his hips and her fat ass.

"Ah shit!"

Mr. Smyth's open palm slid across the back of my neck. I flinched, then balled my hands into fists.

"I wish you would," he challenged. "Lay your light bright ass out on this here floor," he grumbled.

I stifled my laugh, releasing my clamped fists. "No need for that. I respect my elders... long as they respect me," I warned.

Mr. Smyth was a good dude. He'd been copping weed and edibles from me for a few years now. Stayed in a good mood and spoke with wisdom. I'd never had an issue with dude and I wanted to keep it that way.

"I hear you; now, you understand me. I do not play about my grandbaby, Nazari."

"Shit, neither do I."

Nodding, Mr. Smyth still wore a tight expression.

"Look, I know Jacelyn got a nigga at home. I also know she's not happy with dude. I like her and I haven't liked a bit—"

Mr. Smyth dipped his brows, causing me to laugh.

"I haven't liked a woman in a while, but I like her. I wanted to leave her alone her, but her annoying ass stays on my mind. She got a hold on me, you know?"

Mr. Smyth chuckled and moved closer to me, putting a firm hand on my shoulder. "I know all too well about meeting someone and feeling instantly connected to them."

"Yeah, it's som' like that."

"Don't hurt my baby. She has a lot going on and deals with it because of Rhea. I don't like it, but Jacelyn is grown. She has to figure out life on her own, but that doesn't mean I won't two-piece biscuit a nigga if he hurts my baby girl."

"I get it and I got her."

Proudly, Mr. Smyth smiled. He squeezed my shoulder in appreciation, and I felt good 'bout the shit.

"Let me go get ya pack," I told him.

He tapped my shoulder one last time, still smiling. I moved away from him and headed where I told Jacelyn to chill out. Reaching for the knob, I twisted and gently pushed the door open, knowing Jacelyn's ear was probably pressed against it.

"Oh shit!" Her nosey ass tried scurrying away.

I guffawed, closing the door behind me. Propping my foot up and leaning against the door, I told Jacelyn, "Come here goofy ass."

She looked hesitant but eventually moved her feet in my direction. Once in reach, I pulled her body into mine. Wrapping my arms tightly around her, I held her. I took all of her in, mentally memorizing every little detail about her that I could see. More than anything I wanted to know Jacelyn, but I yearned to remember her.

"What are you doing?" she asked.

"Nothing."

"You sure? It feels like you're never going to see me again."

"Am I?"

I moved Jacelyn back, watching her subtle movements. Her gaze was fleeting, and her lip trembled slightly.

"Jacelyn." I pinched her chin between my two fingers, bringing her attention where I needed it to be. "Am I going to see you again?"

"I don't... I can't... I—"

All words were lost on her, and I wasn't mad. I'd been there before. I had every intention of leaving Jacelyn the fuck alone. Who she was married to hit too close to home. Like everything in my life, Aidan managed to snatch what I wanted, leaving me with a void in my heart. I used to think Charlotte's ass would come around to seeing her life wasn't shit without me. The void her absence left behind had been filled with hate. I was cool with that. Jacelyn, tho, I couldn't ever see myself hating someone so beautiful. That shit scared me because without hate to fill the loss of her in my life, I would just be empty.

"Nazari, I—"

Her words were whispers, ones I didn't care to hear. I didn't need confirming that when she left out of shop today, she'd also be walking out of my life.

"Nazari—"

Slowly, my lips pressed against her cloud-like softness. I took my time with her, savoring the taste of her mouth out of fear of never being able to kiss my peace again.

"Nazari," she whimpered.

The airy breeze of my name leaving her mouth, I swallowed. I became possessive.

"Say it again." A low growl escaped me and was met with her repeating my name in the same breathless manner as before. My fingers dug deep into the sides of her waist. If I had it my way, they would've pierced her skin, traveling upward, across her upper body until they reached the heightened pace of what I was craving to make my home.

"Fuck."

I was falling, and this shit didn't feel like a quick trip. Sucking on her bottom lip, I pecked her a few more times, then pulled away but kept her close. Her eyes fluttered open and the innocent flustered expression she wore was so fucking sexy. Smirking, I swiped my thumb across the corner of her mouth, cleaning her up.

"Spend the next 48 hours with me."

"Nazari, I can't."

"Why not?"

"You know why. I have a husband."

"What that nigga gotta do with me? Matter fact, what that nigga gotta do with you when he can't do somethin' as simple as keeping a smile on ya face? Marry me, Jacelyn, and you won't go a day without a smile spread across them juicy ass lips."

Like I knew she would, Jacelyn smiled, then let it fade as her bottom lip got caught between her teeth.

"See, just like that."

Jacelyn was blushing, but her eyes squinted and fell inward.

"I can't Nazari, it's wrong—"

"Y'all better not be in there making whoopie with my shit in there. Those cookie and cream edibles are for Nunu, Jayce."

Mr. Smyth was knocking hard as hell on the door and popping shit.

"Can you open the door, so I can get him out of here?" Jacelyn giggled.

"Only if you say you'll fuck with me for the next 48."

"What if I don't?"

"You might as well get comfortable. There's food and water, we'll survive." I shrugged.

For Jacelyn, this might've seemed like I just wanted to fuck, but I didn't. I wanted more from her and, if she agreed, these next 48 would tell me if all the little shit I was feeling around her actually meant something. I could think it was love but, at the end of the day, that shit was just a thought. I needed to feel it was love before I jumped out the window and really closed the curtain on her situation with Aidan.

"You can't keep me in here."

"Who's gon' stop me? Gramps? I fucks with dude, but his old ass ain't getting in here."

Jacelyn let out a few heavy breaths, blowing all that hot ass air in my face. I ain't mind cause her shit didn't stink.

"Fine. Let me see what I can do. Okay?"

Wrinkling my brows, my sight became narrowed.

"I'm forreal. I'll talk to Gramps about keeping Rhea and I'll let you know."

"Ight." I stepped out the way, letting Jacelyn open the door.

"What were y'all doing?" he grumbled to Jacelyn but kept his focus on me.

"Nothing Gramps," Jacelyn answered.

I laughed inwardly and grabbed Mr. Smyth's stuff. Handing it to him, I locked eyes with the old man.

"We're good?" he asked sternly.

"We're straight."

I nodded and Mr. Smyth did the same.

"Okay, let me get you out of here. Nazari, I'll be back."

"Don't make me come find you. I don't mind being the cat chasing the mouse, just know I always get mine."

Jacelyn flashed me a weary smile and guided Gramps from the room. I followed behind, unlocking the front entrance for them. The door closed and my chest tightened. The air Jacelyn left behind felt toxic. It felt like when she left, she snatched the freshness out the air, leaving all the bad shit behind. If breathing with ease was the gift of being around her, then I planned to pay that tax ten times over. A nigga wasn't trying to breathe if it wasn't Jacelyn's air I was inhaling.

JACELYN SMYTH-KLEIN

MAKING IT OUTSIDE THE shop, I finally felt the coolness of the air circulating around me. Being within distance of Nazari always felt like the air was being sucked out of the room and me along with it. He was magnetic.

"Jayce, you okay?" Gramps asked, coming closer to where I stood.

I forced a smile and nodded, but he wasn't buying it. He outstretched his arms and, at first, I thought he wanted a hug. As I moved in, his hand palmed my chest.

"Your heart is racing," he smirked, then moved his hand.

"So?"

"It's okay to like someone other than your husband."

"What?" I frowned, embarrassed Gramps could tell another man had me flustered.

"You heard me, Jayce. It doesn't take much to put the pieces together baby girl."

"So, you would be okay with Nunu liking someone else?"

"Fuck no!" he groused, making me laugh. "I wish Nunu lopsided wig ass would step out on me. Knock her wig back straight she ever play with me like that."

The way Gramps was carrying on had me doubled over in laughter. His whole face was scrunched in anger as if Nunu actually had a little side piece.

"Relax, I was just asking."

"Ask one mo' question like that again and your Nunu is gonna have to find a new place to lay that big ole head of hers."

"Gramps," I chuckled some more. "If it's not okay for Nunu, then why can I do it?"

"I know Nunu's worth, and I add tax to that muthafucka as the young people say. I uphold my wife in the highest esteem. Nancy knows she's the baddest woman on this earth because I instill that in her. I encourage that type of confidence in my wife. Can you say your husband does the same?"

I dropped my head, silently answering his question.

"And that right there is my point. I by no means condone cheating. I think the act is despicable. With that being said, what I just witnessed between the two of you was loud. Everything Nazari feels for you I felt when speaking to him, and he only said a few words."

"Nazari doesn't feel anything for me."

"That husband of yours has done a number on you if you can't see what I see. When I spoke to you, Nazari inserted himself by encouraging you to leave the room, do you know why?"

I shook my head no.

"He was stating his dominance while being protective. He wanted me to know my tonality was out of line when speaking to you. Only a man who feels something for a young lady would step in the line of fire, especially when it's her grandfather doing the shooting. If you know what I mean."

"He wants me to spend two days with him, but I don't know if I should."

I finally let go of the wall I was so desperately trying to uphold when it came to my undeniable attraction to Nazari. What I felt was morally wrong. I was married and, even though Aidan and I were far from perfect, he didn't deserve my heart being swept away by another man. Still, that didn't stop the excitement from rushing through my entire being whenever Nazari claimed me as his own. Never did I want a man to look at me as a possession because I didn't belong to anyone. Nazari made me feel comfortable enough to appreciate his dominance over my person.

"Where is Aidan?"

"We got into a little tiff, and he went away on business. I spoke to him today and he said he would be back on Monday."

"We'll keep Rhea."

"Gramps, no, you don't—"

"Jayce, if I wasn't sure about that young man in there, I wouldn't be entertaining this conversation. I've known Nazari for some time. Not personally but enough to get a good sense of his character. He seems like a good man, a good man who is willing to cherish all that you are. Spend time with the young man and see what happens."

"I'm scared Gramps."

"Fear is the cost for the chance to experience an all-encompassing love. The richest form of love brings out the heaviest emotions because of its capability to shatter you."

"Then, what's the point?"

"Experiencing life, love, and spirituality with a person who's the interlocking pieces to your soul is the point. Finding your person, the one who has been created imperfectly for you is the point because even though he'll have flaws and make mistake, Jacelyn, he'll still feel like home."

Flicking my gaze upwards, I sniffled and held back the tears. What Gramps described was exactly what I wanted in life and in death. A person who was mine and that I could find across any and every lifetime.

"Go ahead, take him up on his offer."

"What about Rhea? This change could effect—"

"Rhea is a smart girl who understands more than you give her credit for. She knows you're not happy and she'll understand you deserve happiness. Now, stop with all the excuses and go."

Laughing while still sniffling, I threw my arms around Gramps, hugging him tight. Gently, he kissed my forehead, then got in his car and waited to pull off until I was back in the shop.

"I almost thought I was gon' have to strap up a pair of Timbs and come searching for ya ass," Nazari said.

Before the shop doors could close, Nazari had me back in his arms, where my body melted into his thanks to the warm vanilla bourbon scent of his cologne. I inhaled deeply, letting my eyes flutter shut and the sweet, yet masculine scent influence all five of my senses.

"You weren't about to do nothing," I joked.

"Yeah ight. Play with me and you gon' see how I'm comin'."

I giggled a little and, once I stopped, nothing was heard but a lot was felt. We both held on to each other speaking silently about the way we felt. No words were exchanged, but the beats of our hearts matched the slothfulness of our breaths. We were in sync. It was eerie to feel this close to a stranger since I'd never felt this close to Aidan.

"Wassup tho, you gon' fuck with me for the next 48?"

Breaking the silence, Nazari lifted my head from his chest and bowed his, so we were eye to eye. My lips parted to speak, but Nazari's tongue grazing my lips swiped all words. To answer him, I nodded.

"Nah Jayce, baby, I need you to use them words. Speak that you're gon' be mine for the next two days, so I know how to treat you. How to eat you. How to fuck you." In between each of his *hows*, Nazari tenderly pressed his thick lips against mine. I shuddered after each one, wishfully hoping for another.

"I have work tomorrow morning but, yes, after that I'm—" I swallowed hard. The pound of my heart echoed in my ears, leaving me mute.

"Whose are you, Jacelyn?" he spoke gravelly.

"Yours," I answered in a honeyed tone.

"Fucking right!"

Without warning, Nazari grabbed a hand full of my ass, bringing me to my toes. He squeezed, then parted my lips with his tongue. Fighting to keep up with him, I tongued him down the best I could.

"Ight, that's enough. Come on, let me give you a tour."

I never got a chance to answer, thanks to Nazari grabbing my hand and pulling me along with him. I followed him happily yet anxious about what he had planned for our 48 hours together.

"Jacelyn Klein, please come to the nurse's station."

Hearing my name over the loudspeaker in the clinic, I looked towards my right at Devin, the nurse I'd just walked into work with.

"Do you know what's that about?"

"Nope but go find out, then let me know."

She closed her locker and patted me on the shoulder as a sign of support. I finished putting my stuff away, then grabbed my badge and attached it to the neckline of my scrubs. I walked to the nurses' station with my mind running rampant, trying to figure out if there was anything I'd done that would cause me to be summoned.

Being a nurse and following in Nunu's footsteps was all I cared about. As a kid, she used to bring me to work with her after I got out of school. I would sit behind the nurse's desk watching her work. What I loved most were the moments when she allowed me to come into the rooms with her. She was a labor and delivery nurse, and watching how she brought a sense of peace to the new mothers was beautiful. When they doubted their mothering capabilities, she reminded them they'd just delivered a human and, if they could do that, the rest would be like riding a bike. Hard to learn, even a little scary but, once you got it, you got it. Just watching her speak confidence and positivity into people she didn't know was enlightening, and I wanted to do the same. I did a year in labor and delivery then switched to a clinic that was dedicated to ensuring black woman received the health care they deserved. I loved my job and couldn't see myself working anywhere else.

"Hey Melody, I was called," I spoke to the woman sitting behind the desk.

"Hey yeah, you got a delivery and Dr. Jameson wanted me to let you know."

Smiling, I asked, "Where's the package?"

"It's not a package but it's in the break room. Your husband sent a hell of an apology gift," she smirked.

"Aidan?" I was confused.

"I didn't wanna be nosy and read the card, but I assume so. He really showed out. Dr. Jameson told everyone not to touch anything unless you say it's okay. I'm hungry, so be a doll and feed the needy."

We both laughed at her joke.

"I'll be back."

As I walked towards the break room, I checked my phone, but there wasn't a missed call or text from Aidan. He'd never really been into surprises, so I was confused as to why he was starting now. Maybe he really wanted to change.

Pushing open the break room's door, I stood in the threshold with a heavy heart. My eyes wandered throughout the room in awe of the arrangement of breakfast foods that were neatly set up on the table. A bouquet of orange, cream, and brown balloons were tied around the legs of the table in a true celebratory fashion. Sheer happiness spread from within, eventually oozing to the surface. My lips spread wide, and my eyes bulged in excitement.

I walked further into the break room and immediately spotted the huge boutique of orange and cream roses. They were gorgeous. I grabbed them, instantly catching a whiff of Nazari's vanilla and bourbon cologne. Inhaling deeply, I filled my lungs with the remnants of him.

"See, your husband must love you if he did all of this for you."

"He just might," I smiled. "You can tell everyone they can eat whatever they like."

"You don't want any?" Melody asked.

"Nope."

Still smiling, I walked around Melody carrying the bouquet of flowers out to my car. I placed them on the passenger seat, then got settled and opened IG on my phone to call Nazari.

"Damn, you look good as fuck. I'ma have to step my shit up if you walking around looking like that throughout the day." His heavy sluggish tone was so fucking sexy to me, my skin tingled. "Wassup tho?"

"You ask like you don't know what you did." I grabbed the flowers from the passenger seat and held them into the camera frame for him to see."

"Yo, who you got buying you flowers?" His voice hardened and was no longer sluggish and sexy. His face even perked up in anguish.

"Huh? You got me these."

"Nah, it wasn't me. Who's the nigga Jayce?"

At this point, my mouth was floored because I knew I wasn't bugging. "There is no other nigga."

"Who the fuck is he?" The growl in his voice was felt, even with him being on the phone. I became panicked, unsure of what to say.

"I... I... my husband got me these."

"You fucking right he did. That's who I better be to you."

That irresistible cocky smirk glided across his face but, this time, it didn't cause my blood to heat; it actually did the opposite.

"What the fuck is wrong with you? I called to thank you for my surprise and you decide to play in my face for your own amusement?"

"Fuck you got an attitude for?"

I narrowed my vision. "Bye Nazari," I told him in a flattened tone.

"Hol' up Jayce, damn, I was playing ight."

"I didn't find it funny."

"How you know I was the one who did all that?"

Rolling my eyes, I shook my head then answered, "The roses smell just like you."

"You better know what ya man smells like." He flashed that handsome grin, and I couldn't help but to become hot.

"Whatever. I just wanted to say thank you."

"You're welcome. You get off at six, right?"

"Yup."

"Ight bet. I'ma have my sister with me, so she can park ya car at my Pops' house. You with me the next couple days, you don't need it."

I started to fight Nazari on it but decided to let him control the flow of things. "Okay. I'll see you later."

"You can bet on it."

The call ended and I took another whiff of the flowers, relishing his scent. I hopped out the car and went back into work, hoping the hours went by faster than normal.

NAZARI

I WAS SMILING HARD as fuck once Jayce ended the call. If I was more in touch with my emotions, probably would've fucked around and told Jayce she had a nigga feeling like he was drifting on a cloud. All the grinning her ass was doing had me imitating the same. Shawty fucked with a nigga, that meant something to me. It meant the most.

Before her call, I was chilling at Pops' crib on edge wondering if I did too much or did too little with her surprise. I wasn't used to going the extra mile for a woman. I kept it simple with any woman I allowed into my space. We fucked, grabbed something to eat and, if the pussy was good, we were fucking again. I made sure to never overstep to avoid blurring lines. I didn't want to be attached to any woman who wasn't kin. Tara was as close as it got to being in a real relationship, and that situation wasn't nothing more than fucking, sharing a meal and her keeping up with my braids. There was no real pressure from Tara to come correct. Jacelyn wasn't pressing me to do anything and, still, I wanted to be extra for her. I knew how I wanted Jayce to feel when she arrived at her job. To make shit happen, I had to shoot blindly in the dark.

While touring *Ashes 2 Ashes* yesterday, I let Jacelyn lead the conversation. I wanted her to feel comfortable around me and shit. A lot of what she said was brief, which was expected. I was a random ass nigga to her. The only time she allowed herself to get excited was when she was talking about her job. Her whole face lit up, with her cheeks turning as red as her mahogany complexion would allow. The shit was adorable to me, and I wanted to know more.

Jayce filled me in about how becoming a nurse was a way for her to honor her Nunu. She wanted to have the same positive effect on her patients that her grandma did. Hearing how happiness and fulfillment coated that conversation had my wheels turning. Most people hated what they did for work but sucked it up because bills still had to be paid. Jayce loved what she did and was doing it for all the right reasons. In my eyes, that was to be celebrated.

She let it slip that she didn't often eat breakfast because her mornings were always hectic. Cooking wasn't my ministry, but I knew all the bomb lowkey places to eat. I hit up the owner of my favorite breakfast spot and asked if she could pull something together last minute. Her weary ass started to say no until I told her the kind of money I was trying to throw her way. A few thousand had her singing a different tune and asking me about flowers and balloons. Getting all the extra stuff never crossed my mind but, if shawty was recommending it, then it had to be the way to go.

I told her the colors I wanted the balloons and ordered five dozen peach roses since that was as close to Jayce's favorite color as I was going to get. Shawty made shit happen. Jacelyn got on the phone showing all thirty-two. Visually seeing her excitement felt good, it felt better than good. The twinkle that hit her eye when I came on the phone and that juicy ass smile stroked my ego better than getting pussy ever could.

"Why you smiling big head? Tara done did more than fuck and braid you up?"

Sariah flopped her ass on the couch laughing at her own corny ass joke.

"You stay in my business. You might wanna fuck around and find some of your own."

Her face fell flat, and I knew I pinched a nerve. "I didn't mean it like—"

"It's fine Nazari," she interrupted.

"Nah, Sariah, it's not. I shouldn't have went there."

I got up from the stool Pops liked to keep in the corner of the living room as Cree's time out chair and walked over to the couch. Grabbing Sariah's wrist, I pulled her up, forcing her into a hug.

"I love you, ight."

"Yeah, I love your ugly ass too."

"Man, you buggin'!" I mushed her ass for playing in my face like I wasn't the handsomest nigga moving throughout the four boroughs.

"Stop playing Nazari. You know I'll fuck you up."

I stuffed my phone in my pocket and mushed her again. "What was all that shit you were... ah shit!"

Sariah moved from my reach and swiftly threw a quick jab, hitting my ribs. Her punch wasn't shit other than unexpected.

"Chill Nazari. I told you I'll fuck you up."

"Bullshit. Throw 'em up."

Sariah grinned then got in her stance, and I did the same. Fuck her ass thought? She wasn't about to punk me. To test the waters, I extended my hand, tapped her cheek lightly, then pulled my arm back.

I caught her a few more times moving in with taps and redrawing with quick movements.

"Stop cheating," she complained in a whiny ass tone. It was the same shit she used to do when we slap-boxed as kids.

"No one's cheating, your hands are just trash." I chuckled, pissing Sariah off. She swung, almost nicking my eye if I hadn't moved quick enough.

"Man, chill, I didn't mean no harm. I'm just saying it's good for me to know, so I don't tell a bitch my sister will fuck you up."

Sariah's face scrunched into a menacing glare. Still laughing, I pulled her grumpy ass into me, hugging her tight.

"Get off me, Nazari." She pushed against my chest, trying to free herself. Her baby ass force did nothing but make me laugh harder.

"Get off me, Nazari, or I'ma tell Pops you have a daughter."

Her voice was muffled, but I got the message loud and clear.

"You always startin' some shit, then get mad when I finish it."

"Whatever. Keep your hands to yourself buddy," she smirked.

"What are the two of you in here bickering about now?" Pops entered the living room eyeing the both of us.

"Nothing," I answered before Sariah had a chance.

Sucking her teeth, she went and took a seat on the couch right next to Pops. I took that as my sign to hurry up and say what I came here to say. Clearing my throat, I stood before them both feeling awkward as fuck. I never really asked my people for nothing. I got whatever I needed on my own. What I needed from them now, I couldn't do myself. I needed to figure out if all the intense and loss of breath commotion I felt around Jayce's pretty ass was something real or me being on some nigga shit and wanting to fuck again. A part of me knew it wasn't the latter, but I had to make sure. Once I figured that out it was important for Pops and Sariah to catch a vibe from shawty.

They were the people who knew me the best and could tell if a woman wasn't the right fit. Lastly, I wanted to see if Cree took a liking to Jayce. My lil man's opinion meant more to me than anything else. If Cree wasn't with the shits, then I couldn't be either.

"Nazari, do you have something to say?" Pops eyed me oddly.

I let out a low chuckle, still unsure of how I was gon' present this to my family without them doing the most. "I need y'all to do me a favor."

They both stared with their brows crinkled, probably shocked I even said y'all and favor in the same sentence. Slightly, my lips parted once Pops and I locked eyes. Sariah would probably be cool with what I had to say, Pops might've been a different story. Jacelyn's roots ran a lil too deep into his history, the same history he fought hard as fuck to come back from. Pops considered himself healed from Charlotte's bullshit, but a healed wound was only a slice away from being re-opened.

"Um, we're not getting any younger Nazari, what's the favor?" Sariah smacked her dry ass lips, annoying the fuck out of me.

"Yo, shut the fuck up!"

Soon as that shit went out into the air, I felt bad. Before I could take it back, Sariah pursed her lips together and shot me the finger.

"Nazari—"

"I know," I spoke before Pops could get at me. "My bad. I didn't mean for it to come out the way it did. I was thinkin' bout some shit and you rushing me put me on the spot."

"Yeah, okay, just watch your mouth next time."

Sariah laughed, breaking the tension in the room. I agreed with a nod, then hung my head while running my hand back and forth across the back of my neck.

"Your sister was rude in what she said but she was right, we're not getting any younger," Pops said.

I brought my head up, and the first pair of eyes I caught were his. A part of me wondered why I couldn't have chestnut colored eyes like his. Shit might've been easier that way.

"Nazari, what's the favor?" His question was riddled with worry, matching the worried lines on his forehead.

Clearing my throat, I shrugged and said, "I need y'all to cook family dinner on Sunday."

"Boy, I should go upside your big ass head for asking me that foolishness. We cook *every* Sunday in this house. Got me worrying for nothing."

"This ain't the same kind of thing. I need y'all to go all out. Set the dining table with the good stuff and shit. I might bring company and I want y'all to feel her out."

Jacelyn didn't come off like the high-strung bougie type. She seemed chill as fuck, but I still wanted to impress her. Aidan had money, and I wanted to show Jacelyn my family fucked with fancy shit on occasion too.

Goofy grins spread across both their faces.

"Man, y'all gotta relax. I don't even know if shawty gon' come through but, if she does, I wanna make sure shit is good."

"I've been waiting for a moment like this since I made the vow to get clean. I thought you bringing a woman home would never happen. I even blamed myself as the reason why. Thought you were ashamed of your old man." Pops' shoulders lowered as his normal strong, deepened baritone voice cracked.

"Aw Pops!" Sariah moved in to comfort him while I stood silent as fuck.

"Let me get this out." Gently, Pops pushed Sariah's open arms from moving in on him.

"Opp!" She smacked, shuffling back and giving Pops space.

Whatever Pops had to say, he wanted to stand on it. My old man wasn't looking for sympathy. I appreciated that.

"Y'all both know I've fucked up in more ways than one. I allowed you to grow up suffering and feeling unloved."

Pops' regretful stare burned with an overwhelming amount of emotions. I bowed my head, unable to stand the discomfort.

"I had a good thing going with your mom, Sariah, then fucked that up because I couldn't let go of love and pain. A lot of things have gone wrong in my life, but the best thing I've done outside of creating the two of you is put that bottle down. Had I done it sooner, Nazari wouldn't have had to run with who he was runnin' with and—"

"It's cool."

My tone was dry and brash, and Pops took it for what it was, letting me know he understood with a simple nod. The life he was referencing had been put to rest. I wasn't that nigga anymore. For me, it was a figment of my imagination.

"All I'm trying to say is, I thought being a great Papa to Cree would change all the mistakes I've made with the two of you. That getting it right with Cree meant I didn't have to make it right with the two of you, and I was wrong. All of my mistakes have cost the both of you the most precious thing life has to offer, love. I couldn't get past my own heartbreak for a long time. Nazari, you took my pain and internalized it. You masked love with fear. Neither love nor heartbreak should be feared. Both are beautiful. One gives you an experience and the other blesses you with lessons."

"Pops, stop, you're going to make me cry." Sariah tilted her head and began fanning her eyes with her hands.

"Cry if that's what's needed. Lord knows I've cried many of nights out of anger with myself, my ex, and just the world in general. Through my troubles, I've learned sometimes you need to fall when jumping over a hurdle to learn how to get back up. So, please don't let my failed attempts at relationships and love be the blueprint for your experiences. Go out, date, fall in and out love, cry because the person took what seems like the best parts of you when they left and cry when you feel the person brings out the best parts of you. Find your person."

Both Pops and Sariah had misty eyes and ashy cheeks. They embraced in a hug, holding each other tight while I stood off to the side. I was happy Pops was able to get that off his chest, but I wasn't emotional because of it. Pops' issues weren't the foundation of mine. They played a part, but it was really the abandonment that had me saying fuck love. I couldn't see myself giving everything I had to a person just to watch them walk out of my life.

Shit was crazy. Never getting an explanation on the matter from Charlotte only further sealed my disdain for that four letter word in regard to a significant other. I loved my family and that had always been enough until it wasn't. Seeing how a simple gesture brought out what I assumed to be genuine happiness in Jacelyn had me wondering if the love my family provided was enough. Shit was starting feel different and, before I fully acted on those feelings, I had to be sure.

"Well, if it's looking like you might be finding a Mrs., then I'ma do whatever to make sure you secure shawty." Sariah smiled in my direction.

"All I said is shawty might be coming through. Ain't no Mrs."

"Nazari, please. If you're even considering bringing her around us, then this won't be a girlfriend/boyfriend situation for long. But I hear you... baby steps," she giggled. "Anything specific you want us to make?

"Nah, do y'all, I was just givin' a heads up."

"We got you, son." Pops leaned forward, giving me a quick dap.

"Ight, I'm out," I told them.

"Okay, be safe out there."

"Always and love you too," I assured Pops.

"I'ma leave out with you," Sariah chimed in.

"What was the point in y'all coming over just to leave so soon?"

"I don't know why she showed up, but I came for breakfast and that favor," I answered.

"I came for the food too, but Nazari messed up my appetite with his news. I'm too nervous to eat now."

"Man, shut ya goofy ass up," I told Sariah and snatched her ass up, placing her in a gentle headlock.

"Alright, move outta my house with the nonsense. Love y'all."

I let Sariah go, then told Pops I loved him as I walked towards the door. Sariah followed behind me telling Pops she'd be back later with Cree. Proudly, Pops watched us as we headed out the door. I walked towards my whip and noticed Sariah was still walking closely even after she had passed her car.

"What?"

"Is Jacelyn the company you're bringing?"

"She told me 'bout you pulling up on her asking about Rhea," I answered instead.

"We need to know. If Rhea is your daughter, we should be in her life. Not to mention, Cree will die of happiness," she laughed.

"I'ma figure that part out. For now, I need you to chill. Let me figure out her and I first."

"Okay, but do you really think she's going to leave Aidan for you? She might be the type who loves a comfy life."

Sariah had a point, but that didn't stop the tension in my jaw from building.

"Did I say something wrong?"

"Jayce isn't like that. She don't love that nigga."

"Then, why does she stay?"

"Rhea. Some niggas don't know how to be a parent from outside of the home."

"You really think Aidan will skip out on his responsibilities?"

"He was raised by the bitch who skipped out on hers, so you tell me." I shrugged.

"What are you gonna do about Tara?"

"What about her?"

The way Sariah glanced up at me with hopeful eyes, I knew I was missing what she was silently trying to get across.

"You don't think you owe her a conversation?"

"Bout what? I already told her I'm off her."

"And what was her response?"

"She ain't have much of one."

"That's exactly why you need to have a conversation with her. Tara isn't taking you seriously because for the first time, you're taking *you* seriously."

"Yo, what are you talking about right now?"

I felt slighted by Sariah. My whole life, I had to take myself seriously. The slightest slip up would've left me in the last place I wanted to be.

"Can you relax? I'm not coming at you. I'm trying to show you a different perspective... Tara's perspective."

Tugging at my beard, I leaned against my whip. "Wassup?"

"Whatever you said to Tara isn't sticking because she knows how you move. She understands you don't fuck with love and relationships. She's accepted that. The same way she accepts your habits of fucking on other girls then getting right back. What you got with Tara is as close to a relationship as it gets, even if you don't see it as such. She's the one you keep running back to. In her mind, it can't just be because her pussy is good."

I frowned. Sariah was putting extra sauce on dry ass wings that would never taste good.

"Am I lying?" She huffed in disbelief.

"You puttin' extra on the situation for sure. I fucks with Tara because fuckin' her comes without the headache. Whatever happens is at my discretion, not hers. That's not to be confused with building foundations in hopes of when we get to the top, love is waiting on us."

"You might feel that way, but I can almost guarantee Tara doesn't see it the same. I don't care what she tells you, no woman is okay being pussy to a nigga for almost two years without catching feelings. You don't have to listen to me, but I'm telling you she deserves a conversation. No one should be left wondering what they did wrong or why you were able to change for a random woman but not the woman who's been by your side accepting you for who you are."

Leaning up, Sariah gave me a quick kiss on the cheek and walked towards her car. I hopped inside of my car, sitting for a moment. What Sariah said hadn't fallen on deaf ears. If anything, her words stung. The picture Sariah painted was similar to how I painted Charlotte as the villain in my story. Charlotte was around one minute, then up and vanished in the next. No explanation came with her absence. So, I got what Sariah was trying to say, but the shit wasn't the same. I never agreed to the terms of my situation with Charlotte. Tara and I both agreed keeping our situation fun and light was better for the both of us. Neither one of us wanted anything serious at the time and, for me, that hadn't changed. What I was trying to explore with Jacelyn was apples and oranges to what Tara and I could ever be.

JACELYN

"You sure you wanna go away with him for two days? I mean, he's fine, but to disappear with a stranger is crazy."

Pulling the phone away from my ear, I glanced at the screen to make sure I was talking to Ms. *leave your husband and move Nazari in.* There was no way Dionne was changing her tune after all the shit she'd talked about this man being my daughter's step daddy.

"What do you mean am I sure? Wasn't you the one telling me how I needed to leave Aidan for him?"

"Yeah, but that was jokes. I knew you weren't going to leave Aidan's trifling ass, so what I said didn't matter. This is different tho, Jacelyn. Aidan already thinks you were out creeping when you were supposed to be with me. Messing with Nazari again this soon is only gonna add more stress to the situation."

"I know Dionne, but what am I supposed to do? I've tried to ignore Nazari. When I went to his shop, it was to tell him to leave me alone."

"Then, what happened because agreeing to a baecation doesn't sound nothing like *nigga, leave me alone*?"

For a second, I sighed and looked out the window towards the night sky. The stars were definitely out tonight, and they looked beautiful illuminating the sky.

"Have you ever just looked up at the sky and watched the stars?"

"Yeah, but what does that gotta do with you running off with Nazari?"

"Everything, and I'm not running off."

"Yeah, okay, but explain."

"When you look towards the night sky, your intentions are usually to glance then look away. It's not meant to be a lasting moment, but then something catches your eye. Something you haven't seen before, but it shines as bright as a star. The radiance sucks you in, holding your focus for ransom. Payment is your smile. Soon, the rays warm the surface of your skin. The soothing eventually goes beneath the surface and, before you know it, your body is tingling with fervor. Breathing no longer seems easy or natural, it's labored and forced because you know the *something* you saw in the sky is capable of sucking the essence out of you. And, of course, you're not afraid because in an odd way, it's exactly what you want. To be consumed by the person who inhales you, so you're able to exhale a greater version of yourself. You know?"

Silence took over the call for a while, and I almost thought Dionne hung up.

"Jacelyn," Dionne sniffled mixed with a soft chuckle. "I don't have a clue what you're talking about but when I say that was beautiful." Randomly, Dionne began clapping and cheering.

I laughed, thinking *this girl is too fucking silly*. "Can you stop and get serious?"

"I am being serious. Man, answer my FaceTime because you think this is a game."

My phone vibrated, alerting me to Dionne's video-call. I switched the call over and, sure enough, Dionne's eyes were misty the moment she came on the screen.

"You are too much," I told her.

"I'm not but I don't think you understand how profound what you explained was. What you described is a feeling many women may not get the chance to experience. I mean, I haven't, and I have a nigga who I don't love but we're in like heavily."

"I don't love Nazari," I blurted, feeling the need to make that clear. What I felt for Nazari was strong, but I knew in my heart it wasn't love.

"No one said you do, but how you feel is a hell of an indicator of where it can go and, baby, love is definitely the direction."

"You don't think I'm crazy for feeling this strongly about a stranger?"

"Is he really a stranger tho?" Dionne laughed.

"Girl yes! I don't even know this man's last name."

"You know that dick and mouth tho!" She cackled, sticking her tongue out.

"I promise I'm not telling you nothing else." I stifled my laugh.

"Who else you gonna tell? Aidan?"

"That's not even funny." The blank look I gave gathered Dionne together.

"Listen, I don't judge and I'm not about to condemn you for leading with your heart or your pussy after you've led with your mind for so long."

"Advice. Any real serious advice would be nice."

"You want my advice, fine. Another person's influence over our feelings is the one thing we cannot control. How we respond to said influence is completely on us. It's no secret Nazari has some kind of hold on you. You also have one on him because why else is he running around making speeches threatening niggas over his *wife*?"

"Girl, what's the advice," I chortled lightly.

"The connection the two of you have is purposeful. I don't know what the reason is, but it's not to be ignored. Go into these next two days with a clear mind. Let your guard down and give in. See what happiness feels like with Nazari as the provider. Oh, and share your location so I know where you are at all times. That nigga might be fine and suave, but that don't make him exempt from crazy."

"You are so fucking unserious." Playfully, I rolled my eyes, wondering what the hell was wrong with my friend. She gave great advice but wouldn't be her if she didn't sprinkle in the funny.

"I'm serious as hell. I don't put nothing past a nigga, especially a fine one."

"I feel you."

My phone binged with a notification from IG popping up. I swiped my thumb from the top of my screen to see what the notification said.

NazariSRT: I'm out front where you parked?

Nervous tingles ran rampant through my fingers as I typed my location.

"Bitch, he's here?" I gasped.

"Why you acting nervous?"

"Because I am. It's not like I'm going on a date as a single woman, Dionne. I'm married and sneaking around while my husband is out of town for work."

For the first time, guilt set in, and I didn't even know if it was actual guilt.

"Don't start that marriage bullshit because we both know you checked out a long time ago. You're bringing him up now as an excuse. Enjoy yourself and remember what I told you, be open."

"Okay."

"Send that location too. Bye girl."

Dionne hung up just as Nazari's navy blue SRT slowly pulled into the spot next to me. I shifted in my seat, glancing towards the tinted window. I couldn't see through Nazari's tints the same way he couldn't see through mine, yet that didn't stop the heat only his stare could stir from rising into my throat. I swallowed hard, still glancing towards Nazari's car.

This man is too fine.

I licked my lips, as he coolly stepped out and leaned against the driver's door. He was dressed casually in light gray Nike tech sweats, the matching hoodie, and a pair of white forces. Nazari's braids weren't freshly done like I was used to seeing, but the crisscross design was cute. My eyes traveled along his face, taking in his strong and prominent features. When I got to his lips surrounded by his thick nicely lined beard, I quivered. His lips latching on to my clit was a memory I didn't mind recreating right here and right now.

"Come get out the car and stop fetishizing a nigga."

The taps against my window and the light humor in his voice was the cue I needed to hop my ass out the car. I turned the engine off and grabbed my bag from the passenger seat before sliding out the door Nazari was now holding open.

"You look good," he complimented.

Before I could give him one back, Nazari closed the car door and pulled me into him. I hiccupped silently, startled by the gesture. Closing my eyes, I memorized his scent, not wanting to forget it or him. If these were our last days together, I wanted to remember everything from this moment 'til our last.

"You ight?" he asked calmly but with a worried glower.

"Uh yeah. You just smell good, and I was trying to pinpoint the notes."

"Why, so you can have your other nigga smelling like me?"

"No. You just smell amazing."

"Good fucking answer. You smell good too. What you wearin'?"

"Why, so you can have your bitches smelling like me?" I shot back.

Smirking, Nazari bobbed his head, trying to find an opening to my neck. I placed my hands on his chest, fighting to keep him back. While laughing, Nazari's hands slipped from my waist to my ass, lifting me on my toes and bringing me in closer.

"Nazari, sto—"

My words faltered. The hair from his beard tickled my neck as he inhaled starting at my collarbone and dragging the whispers of his breath up to my jaw where he planted the softest of kisses.

"I wanna know what you're wearin' so I can make sure you have it in abundance. Whatever the scent, it's the only one I want you to wear when you're with me."

Going back towards my neck, Nazari feathered his lips against my skin.

"Nazari."

His name left my lips and fell against his immediately. In his embrace, I unraveled, completely falling under his control, his lips guiding mine. I was completely free in this moment with him. In the parking lot of my job for anyone to see, I allowed Nazari to take his time kissing me with ardor and intention. Everything about how he took his time exploring my mouth seemed intentional. If I tried to speed up, he pulled back, forcing me to slow down. He made sure to let me know he was in control, yet didn't mind being attentive to what I liked in a kiss. Pecking me a few more times before taking my lip between his teeth, Nazari freed me but in mouth only. His kept me pinned to him with his hand on my ass and the other pinching my chin. Looking down, he smirked. I blushed, unable to hide how the giddiness ruptured from within.

"You ready to go?"

Reaching up, I wiped the corners of his mouth and swiped my thumb across his bottom lip, clearing it of my lip gloss. Nodding, he leaned towards me.

"That was cute, but I'ma man, Jayce. I don't gotta problem wearin' you on my lips. Lip gloss from them lips..." With his fingers, Nazari traced my lips and dropped his hand below my waist, placing it at the drawstring of my scrubs. "Or these lips. It's whatever to me, beautiful."

A surge of warmth burst from my middle. I just knew these panties weren't going to last long around this man.

"Bet you say that to all your hoes," I teased, just to see if there were any. Nazari knew about my husband and my situation, but I knew nothing about him. I refused to fight for my life behind dick I hadn't had in almost six years. Now, Nazari's mouth action could get a hoe cursed out in a hot minute.

"If you the hoe, then hell yeah," he chortled loudly.

I smacked my lips, clicking my tongue with each word I spoke. "Nigga, don't get smacked up. A hoe ain't ever been me."

"Ight... which you like better, beautiful or bae?"

"What happened to *wife*?"

"You didn't like that shit, so I'm tryin' to switch it up."

"Oh. Beautiful is fine I guess," I answered dryly.

"Ight and turn that frown upside down. The thought to add my name to yours still stands. I gotta prove to you I deserve the right to call you my wife. Something like that takes time."

"Did your friend come to drive my car?"

Changing the conversation was more for my excitement than anything else. I never realized how much words of affirmation and words obscured in purpose meant to me. I knew Aidan lacked in that area, but I told myself it was fine since it wasn't the way I wanted to be loved. I was wrong. Each time Nazari spoke, he did so with confidence and a defiance which made me believe whatever he said was the truth. The assurance he was instilling in me was spooky because he was doing it with only his words. I didn't have to see action in order to believe him, a part of me knew if he said it, then he meant it.

"Yeah."

Nazari knocked his knuckles against the back window a few times, then turned back to look at me.

"You had someone in your car the whole time?"

"Yeah, why?"

"Nazari, you were basically fucking my mouth. Whoever you had in there could've been watching."

Nazari dipped his face towards my neck. "Ya mouth wasn't getting fucked. I ain't feel that lil shit in the back of ya throat."

Catching on to what he said, I slapped his shoulder while laughing. Nazari's croons painted my skin as his lips pressed deeply into my spot. I pressed further into him, trying my best to become an extra layer of skin.

"You want me in you?"

Nudging Nazari's face from my neck, I cradled his beard, bringing our faces together. My lips feathered his as I answered, "Yes."

Nazari's gaze spoke loudly, and my wish was his command. He tugged at my drawstring until the string untied and he was able to slip a hand inside.

"Ah," I hummed, feeling his fingers separate my lips.

"Damn, am I interrupting?" The passenger door to Nazari's car opened, ending our moment. "I tried to give y'all a minute after you knocked. It was looking like a moment out here. Like a scene at the end of a romcom when the nigga who been pining finally gets his bitch," Mitch spoke.

For the first time since I stepped out of my car, Nazari and I broke eye contact.

"Nah, not a romcom," Nazari joked loudly. "What bitch got you open like that my G?"

"Dionne. She talk hella shit but loves all the sappy love movies." They laughed, sounding all full and hearty. Smacking my lips, I moved out of Nazari's reach, walking towards Mitch.

"Aye, Nazari, come get ya girl."

"When somebody refers to my girl as a bitch, it's your job to correct them, joking or not." Dionne was my girl; I would always ride for her.

"My bad," Mitch chortled. "Aye nigga, watch ya mouth referring to my girl as a bitch."

Nazari laughed while he held his hands up in acknowledgment of what was being said.

"Love to see you got Dionne's back," Mitch said to me.

"Always, that's my girl. Fuck with her, you fucking with me."

"And fuck with her," Nazari's arm slumped over my shoulder, bringing us back together, back where I felt safe, "you fucking with me and fucking with me means—"

Nazari stuck his hands out with his finger motioning like he was pulling a trigger. I found it odd but said nothing. Most dudes like

Nazari kept a gun on 'em. I wasn't bothered by that. It was the far off daze Nazari's eyes fell into. His left one was nearly shut like he was actually lining up the shot. The way his face went into the choreography of a kill was too skillful. Almost second nature.

"Man, stop playin' 'cause you know I got a few—"

"Chill." Nazari's jaw stiffened. His eyes slashed with thick brows blanketing over them.

"Ight." Mitch shrugged his shoulders, and Nazari's face went back to his natural scowl.

"Toss Mitch your keys. He's gon' park ya whip at *Ashes 2 Ashes*."

Digging in my purse, I handed my keys over, warning Mitch about what would happen if he fucked up my car.

"I don't want beef with you; trust, ya whip gon' be good."

"It better be." I bucked towards Mitch, making him flinch.

"Man, bring ya punk ass on."

Nazari held the passenger door open, helping me inside. Once I was fully in, Nazari closed the door, said a few words to Mitch, and hopped in the car. Quick and uneasy breaths heaved my chest, as Nazari pulled out of the parking lot. I kept my focus on the side mirror, watching as my car pulled out in the opposite direction. This was actually happening. All the flirting Nazari and I did was just fun in my mind. Our little routine was easy to fall into because it never felt real. There was no doubt what was happening between us was actually happening. I could physically feel all the ways his thumb massaged the small of my back or how his lips masked mine. All of that was real. What seemed fake were the feelings between us. I hated how cliche it all sounded, but it was true. The magic, the sparks, the magnetic pull were all invisible to the eye but recognizable to the heart. Everything about Nazari felt familiar, and that seemed so damn unreal.

"You good over there?"

His eyes drifted from the road meeting my gaze, as I turned to face him. The need for me to be *good* burned in his orbs.

"I'm good." My answer put out the flames and brought his hand to my thigh. His fingers plunged, squeezing possessively.

"You good on the aux?" he asked, swerving into the lane next to us.

"I like to think so."

"Hook ya shit up and don't disappoint. This is your moment."

Feeling challenged, I reached forward, pressing a few buttons on the dash and connecting my phone to the Bluetooth. I remembered what he'd said about this being my moment and found the perfect song.

"Make sure you have an apology sitting on ice for doubting me."

Piano keys blared from the speakers, setting the mood. Nazari came to a red light and turned to pinch my chin just as Victoria Monet began to sing.

"I'll always have an apology on reserve for you. My intentions are never to use 'em but, on the rare occasion I hurt your feelings by mistake, you'll always be given the apology you deserve."

Slyly, Nazari licked his lips and mouthed along with the song. "It's your muthafuckin' moment."

I was taken aback that he knew the song but pleased that he did. From my peripheral, I caught the light changing. Feeling drawn in by him mixed with the vibes of the song, I smashed my lips into his. Rhythmically, I matched the haziness of the song with my kiss.

Slowly.

Selfishly.

Savagely.

Nazari took all of my emotions. Aggravated drivers cursed and blared their horns as they swerved around us. The road was a straight shot. I ached for the thrill, the exhilaration of danger ripping through me, as Nazari's outpour of affection stitched me back together.

"Move your seat back," I hummed against his lips.

Without question, just trusting what I said, Nazari moved his seat back as I restarted the song. Carefully, I climbed into his lap, making sure my legs were far enough away from the shifter. The position wasn't comfortable, but comfortability didn't matter. Locking eyes with Nazari, he read the daring expression on my face and lust for excitement in my eyes. Placing my hand on top of his, I wedged my fingers in between his, taking control of the shifter. His leg moved slightly, switching his foot from the brake to the gas.

"Drive," I mouthed as the light turned green.

Nazari's SRT sped through the street leaving nothing but the sound of his tires impacting the road and my inhibitions in the distance.

"You an adrenaline junkie?" Nazari slowed, pulling over before we made it onto the Ave.

"Not really," I giggled. "I just wanted to feel free for once you know. Let all the things that hold me back go."

"You wasn't worried about me crashing?"

"Nope, I trust you."

My words came out in pants, choked up by the way this man was able to stir a frenzy from within with nothing more than a smoldering stare, a handsome face, and the sexiest rasp.

"Good to know." He winked, then placed me back on my seat. "Don't think you got outta ya aux duties. Play some else."

"Fine but let's get some food and drive around."

"You don't wanna go in somewhere to eat? I wanna date you, Jayce, not just treat you like my homegirl."

"A date can happen anywhere, with us doing anything. Driving around with the streetlights as the ambiance, some bomb ass food and good tunes is a vibe."

His eyes widened, then quickly rested.

"The girls you date love it when you spend money huh?" I laughed.

"I ain't never date a bitch forreal. I'm used to fucking and moving around."

"Wait, you've never dated anyone? Like, not even as a teenager?"

"I had a lil girlfriend back then, but that wasn't 'bout nothing forreal. Shawty wasn't tryin' to give up the pussy and kept talkin' about marriage like we weren't sixteen and seventeen."

"Wow!"

"Right," he chuckled. "I was too young to be thinkin' about forever and moved on."

"What about now?"

"What about now?" he shot with his eyebrows raised.

Nazari knew exactly what I was hinting at but wanted me to spell it out. In our own ways, we kept testing one another, trying to see just how serious the other actually was.

"How do you feel about marriage now?" I clarified.

"Why you wanna marry me, Jayce? Become Mrs. Caddel and live happily ever after?"

"I'm already someone's wife. Why would I want to marry you?"

Normally, I welcomed Nazari's humor but, in this moment, I couldn't. The part of me hoping something great came out of this was now saddened. What I needed in this moment was an answer which showed me Nazari wasn't on the same timing he once was. Seventeen was too young for him to get married but, at his big age now, he should've been going on dates, falling in and out of love.

"Ask the nigga you married."

"Huh?"

It didn't take long for my confusion to be met with an explanation. Swiftly, Nazari reached for the dashboard, answering Aidan's call.

NAZARI

I watched Jacelyn, waiting to see how she was gon' get herself out of this one. Her forehead rippled with lines caused by the furrow of her brows. Her talking to Aidan in my presence wouldn't have happened in any other situation. I was a man. A selfish, stingy man who never had to share in the past and had no plans of sharing in the present. My time with Jayce was mine. Any other nigga she thought about having in her life had to wait 'til my turn was over. Thanks to the slick shit she'd said, time was up in this muthafucka.

"Hello Jacelyn? You there? Baby?" Aidan rambled off, waiting on Jacelyn to say something. Her eyes shifted from the dash towards me. I greeted them with a nod, encouraging her to speak to her *husband*.

"You gon' talk?"

Quickly, she muted the call.

"Why would you answer the phone?" she asked.

The anger decorating her face was cute. Her eyes were squinted with her lips poked out looking kissable as fuck. Had she not pissed me off, I would've leaned in, taking her bottom lip into my mouth, tonguing her sexy ass slowly. Unfortunately, what she said rubbed me the wrong way and, now, I wanted to see her squirm.

"Talk to that nigga or I can talk to 'em for you. You wanna divorce, right? I'll let that nigga—"

"Okay," she gritted, flickering her gaze upward.

"What the hell is wrong with my phone? Jacelyn, can you—"

"Hello Aidan, I'm here. My phone was on mute, and I didn't know. Wassup?"

"I was checking on you. I spoke to Rhea a few minutes ago. She said she was with Nunu for the weekend."

"She is." Jacelyn's responses to this nigga were short and dry as fuck.

"I knew you were going to forget," Aidan let out an exaggerated breath, muffling the call. "How many times do I have to tell you to write things down so you can remember them? Rhea was supposed to be with my mother this weekend for the event at Wellington Prep."

"Aidan, I don't know what you're talking about. I never agreed to let Rhea attend any event, especially for a school she isn't attending."

"You didn't agree to it, I did."

"Since when did you start making decisions without me?" Even with the rise in her tone, Jacelyn still sounded dry while speaking to this nigga.

"When you left dinner, lied and fucking disappeared for the night," Aidan bickered, sounding just like a bitch begging her nigga to come home.

"I don't care what I did. When it comes to my daughter, you don't make decisions without me. Had you not acted all bent out of shape when I came home, we could've talked about Rhea spending the weekend with your mother. Since we didn't, Rhea will stay where she's at."

"Rhea is my daughter too, Jacelyn. I'm allowed to make decisions on her behalf without your consent. Unless there's something you want to tell me."

It wasn't hard to figure out what Aidan was alluding to or how much it bothered Jacelyn. Without knowing much about her, I was able to pick up on a few things when it came to her. Jayce wore every emotion on her face. When pleasured, her lip curled between her teeth with her lashes fluttered, giving her a blurred view. When happy, her cheeks rose until her normally round eyes fell into feathery slits. Fear caved her chest, interrupting the normal rhythmic percussion of her heart's pitter patter. Sadness seemed to present itself as defeat in Jacelyn. Her chin rested in her chest, leaving her head to hang and her eyes to dance amongst the floor.

Without Aidan visibly being able to see Jayce, he should've known what her silence meant. Shit, maybe he did know and didn't care enough to shut the fuck up for two seconds and realize he was losing his wife.

"Aye nigga, if you gon' speak to Jayce, do so with some fuckin' respect," I spoke. Jacelyn turned her head so fast in my direction, I almost choked concealing my laughter brought on by her panicked and flushed expression. "Bitchin' won't bring ya wife home nigga."

Throwing her hands up, Jacelyn leaned all the way back in her seat, rolling her head from side to side. Inwardly, I chuckled. Aidan was acting like a bitch and not telling him so would've made me less of a man.

"Who the fuck are you? Jacelyn, who the fuck is that?"

"Don't worry about who I am, take heed to what I said. Show ya wife some fuckin' respect and watch ya mouth."

"Jacelyn, you're going to let him speak to me that way? Jacelyn! Jacelyn!"

Tired of hearing this nigga whine, I ended the call from the dash and took Jacelyn's phone from her lap. I tapped the screen and angled the phone towards her face for it to unlock.

"I have a code on my phone," she giggled while typing in her code.

Looking at her screen, I went through her contacts, blocking the one labeled *husband* then deleting it along with the text thread.

"What did you do?" Jacelyn took her phone back and immediately started scrolling. "You blocked and deleted him?"

"You with me for the next two days. I don't need no bad vibes trying to fuck up what I'm tryin' to build with you."

"My husband is a bad vibe?" she smacked.

The question was rhetorical, but I was still gon' answer it to make sure Jacelyn knew where I was coming from. "Yeah, that nigga been a bad vibe since the day I met you."

"Oh yeah, how you know?"

"Look at how I met you. Sad and drunk in the club 'cause ya husband didn't know how to 'preciate all that you are. If that's not a bad vibe, then maybe I got my definitions fucked up. I'm well-read tho, so you might wanna check in with ya heart to figure out why you can't see just how bad that nigga is for you."

The car got quiet, and I welcomed the silence. We weren't even two hours into our forty-eight and shit was popping off faster than I intended. Aidan calling Jacelyn never crossed my mind. That nigga wasn't a factor until he was. Before he interrupted the flow of things, Jacelyn was in her feelings over whatever I said about marriage. Going into this, I was thinking selfishly. I didn't consider Jacelyn having as much to lose as I did. I was focused on protecting myself when I should've been focusing on protecting us.

"Before we enjoy the rest of the night, I need you to promise me something."

"Depends," she smirked.

"Promise to be honest throughout your time with me. I'm not the easiest to get along with and, like I said earlier, I don't know how this date shit works forreal. All I know is how I'm trying to make you feel while you're with me. So, if I say or do some shit you don't like, speak on it and I'll do the same."

"I can do that. The joke you made about me wanting to marry you rubbed me the wrong way. Trust me when I say I can take a joke. I actually love to laugh and play around. But this..." Jacelyn paused, swaying her fingers between the both of us, "has the potential to destroy my life or add meaning to it. This can't be a power trip for you. I can't be another notch on your belt or a trophy you put up in your room for stealing me from my husband. Your lack of experience in all of this scares me, Nazari. I won't mention love because we're far from that, but I can't date for fun; it has to be for a purpose. I promised you forty-eight hours. We can have all the fun we want during that time but, after, if you're not ready for more, then you have to let me go and I'll do the same."

"I gotchu. I 'preciate the honesty."

I paused, wanting to express exactly what I was looking for when it came to Jacelyn. I was inexperienced but I was eager to learn if it meant I could have her. Telling her all that now would be setting us up to fail. Before I told her the good, I had to introduce her to the bad. There was a lot about me Jacelyn had to wrap her mind around. Until I knew for a fact she could digest my past, there was no need to speak on the future. We both just had to make the most of the present.

"Okay, can we please go get some food and finish our little vibe session?"

Her childlike smile took the mood from what it was and made it brighter. I slipped my arm across her shoulders, bringing her closer to the middle console.

"We can do whatever you like. That's my word. All the corny couple shit I see muthafuckas on the gram doing, we doing."

"Even the matching outfits?"

"Especially the matching fits."

Jacelyn squealed in excitement. I kissed her on the forehead, then mushed her silly ass. She fussed a little, then got back to playing music. Driving down the Ave, we vibed to R&B with a few hip hop songs in between. Each song that played, Jacelyn sang with her chest. She kept her hands in my beard, tugging my face in her direction whenever her part came on and she wanted to sing to me. Jacelyn couldn't sing for shit, but the gesture was cute enough for me to feel something I'd never experienced before.

Cruising the Ave listening to music with a woman in the passenger seat was shit I'd done before. That's why I didn't consider something like this a date. Tara been in the same position as Jayce, where I had her on the aux to curate the vibes. Tara and I vibed, but it was nothing like this. Jayce's antics hit different. Her energy wasn't only being felt, I was immersed in it. The high she was on, I matched, singing along with her like she was Keke and I was Avant. The intimacy without being body to body was crazy. It was the greatest high I'd ever known.

JACELYN

WAKING UP, I MUMBLED a few words to a song that was humming throughout the room. Since I was fully awake, I didn't think much of the song actually playing; I assumed it was nothing more than a melody playing repeatedly in my head. I churned the covers from my body, sat up and grabbed my phone from the nightstand. Normally, I didn't rush to be on my phone as soon as I woke up. I loved to lie in bed gathering my thoughts for the day, say a quick prayer, and spend a little time with Rhea before the rush of the morning happened.

This morning was different. The sun seemed brighter as it heated the left side of my body. The floor to ceiling windows were gorgeous and had the perfect view of the Hudson River mixed with the rest of the city. This morning I woke up feeling lighter, the stresses of my marriage didn't matter, and Aidan hadn't been a thought since Nazari blocked him. It was a new day and a fresh start.

Before checking any texts, I called Rhea to make sure she was okay. I wasn't worried about her wellbeing while with my grandparents. They loved her probably more than they loved me. I was more concerned with Aidan trying to pull a fast one in the name of his mommy. The control she had over her son was nauseating.

"Mommy!" Rhea's cheerfulness blared through my phone thanks to how close she was holding her iPad to her face.

"Rhea, you have to move back from the screen. Mommy can only see your eyes and nose."

I laughed, as Rhea fussed about wanting to stay close. After a few minutes and a *girl move back from that screen before you need bifocals* from Nunu, I was able to see the gorgeous child I and her titty milk still on the tongue ass daddy created.

"How was your night?"

"Mommy, it was so good. I talked to Cree last night and guess what!"

"What baby?" I asked, matching her excitement.

"We're going to race cars today!"

"Race cars?"

"Yes mommy. Nunu said we could go, and Cree mommy said we could go."

Rhea's little adventure immediately got the wheels turning in my head. Was this a set up? I didn't want to believe Nazari would go as far as getting me out the way, so he could sneak and have his sister do a DNA test on my baby, but that was the only thought running through my mind.

"Oh no," Rhea cooed, poking her bottom lip out.

I couldn't stand when Rhea put on her pouting face. My kid was adorable but, when she started to pout, it was impossible to tell her no.

"Mommy, are you mad I see Cree?" Her voice was baby like. Her brows dipped and her dimples softened, playing into her pout.

"No, I'm not sad. I—"

"Good mommy. I no like when you're sad." She smiled.

"Baby, give the iPad to Nunu."

"Okay mommy."

Rhea disappeared from the screen as she shuffled across her bed to go find Nunu. While I waited to hear my grandmother's loud boisterous voice, I continued to mumble the words to the song that I now knew wasn't just playing in my head.

Feel the energy in this room.

"Rhea, baby, you be careful shoving that thing in my face like that," she fussed.

I looked towards the screen, and Nunu looked just as grumpy as she sounded.

"That girl won't be happy until she buss me in the face with this damn iPad."

"She doesn't mean no harm, Nunu."

"Harm doesn't have to be intentional for it to hurt. Now, what do you want? Gramps told me a fine ass man done swept you up for the weekend."

"He did not say that," I laughed. Nunu was known to add sauce to what she considered a dry ass story.

"Yes, he did, I swear for—"

"Nunu."

"Fine, he said the nice gentleman who owns *Ashes to Ashes* wanted some of your time. I asked him why he would allow that when you're married. Tell me why he said the gentleman didn't give a damn about you being married and even bucked up to him because of how stern Gramps was talking to you."

Nunu was all giddy as she recalled the conversation between her and Gramps. I really wasn't trying to entertain her foolishness, but her ass was just so animated.

"Jacelyn Smyth, when I tell you my little hot numbers got to getting moist when Gramps told me that. I almost ran down to the shop and bust it wide open for that young man."

"Nunu!" I cried, swiping my finger under my lashes.

"Don't Nunu me. I just knew I was about to give that tenderoni all this good cougar cat."

"I'ma tell Gramps on your nasty ass."

"Tell him, he knows what this snatch do. Snatched his handsome self-right on up and pussy only gets better with time. You remember that Jayce."

"I cannot," I laughed harder. "Snatch and hot numbers is too much for me."

"I don't see why. Snatch is pussy and hot numbers is the panties I wear when I want your Gramps to make my knees touch my ears. What y'all call that position? The *trap a nigga position?*"

"Nunu, who do you be talking to? No one calls that the *trap a nigga position.*"

Besides laughing, all I could do was shake my head. This old lady was too much, but it was clear well into her old age she still found herself needing Gramps in that way. I never put much thought into how Aidan and I would be in old age. Listening to how Nunu spoke, with lust gracefully coating her words, made me want the same thing.

"It needs to be. Gramps lucky all my eggs done dried up. His dick get to knocking on my spot, and I can just feel the baby being conceived."

"Okay, that's enough," I choked on my spit.

"I don't see why you're making a big fuss. You'll be acting the same with your gentleman friend because babyyyy, that man is blessed. I don't know who his mommy and pappy is, but you need to thank the lord twice for them people. Whew!" Nunu was doing the most, fanning herself and biting her lip all in the name of Nazari.

"Can you stop getting hot and bothered by my man before I snitch on you to Gramps?"

"Oh please, Gramps knows I only have a hunger for him. But these eyes see very well and Nazari needs to be seen. Why you think Gramps goes and gets my stuff from him? I was doing a little too much looking."

"I can't believe you. I don't even know you at this point."

"Jayce, you know me, so stop it. I'm the same woman who raised you after your mother passed away. I'm the woman who's always wanted nothing but happiness for you. I'm the same woman who told you not to marry that husband of yours. I will always be the one to give you the hard and sometimes hurtful truths. That's never going to change."

"I appreciate and love you for that Nunu. Do you have any advice for what I'm dealing with now?"

It was abundantly clear Aidan and I were never going to work. The evidence had been piling up for years and, with each new fact, I turned a blind eye. I allowed myself to believe loving him was enough to hold on. And when it wasn't enough and I was ready to walk out the door, guilt brought me back. Then, Rhea became the reason I stayed. Everything kept me with Aidan except for what should've kept me.

"Follow your heart. The only advice I can give is for you to do what feels right. You've always been such a logical person who put the needs of others before her own. Operating like that isn't necessary, it never was. Yes, Rhea depends on you. Her having her father in her life is a priority but, if Aidan can't be a father without being with you, then that's not for you to internalize. Rhea will always be okay and know the love of a man, Gramps will make sure of it."

"You damn right I will," Gramps added. "I heard you talking about that boy too. Don't make me fuck you up in here in, Nancy."

"Okay daddy," Nunu purred.

"Can y'all not with me on the phone?"

"You see how he checked me." Nunu's widespread smile was so hard to ignore, her eyes were even twinkling with the same happiness her grin gave off. "Anyway, baby, that's my advice. Follow your heart and know that we got your back. No need to stay with a man who doesn't know your heart or care enough to learn it."

"I love you, Nunu."

"I love you too. Go enjoy your time."

Nunu was about to end the call when I called out to her, remembering why I wanted to speak in the first place.

"What now child? I'm all out of advice."

"How did Rhea speak to Cree?"

"Oh, his momma walked up to me talking about a play date with the kids. I told her to put Cree's info into Rhea's iPad and we could figure something out. They figured it out too. They wanted to do the arcade, so I agreed to take them."

"Oh okay."

"Nothing for you to worry about. Now, get off this phone."

I rolled my eyes, ended the call and fell back onto the bed. The melody to the song was still looming over the room. By this time, it should've stopped playing. The song wasn't long, so it had to be on a loop. I grabbed my phone, opened IG, and went to my DMs.

This nigga.

I shook my head seeing Aidan's name at the top of my message list. I swiped left, deleting the thread. His bitching had to wait until I was back at home on my wifely duties. I tapped on Nazari's thread and typed up a quick message.

SooJayce: Hey you up?

I started to close the message until I saw he was typing.

NazariSRT: Yeah.

Cheesing for a reason unbeknownst to me, I started typing. I typed, deleted, then typed again. I was trying to think of something funny to say since our means of communication was the DMs. There had to be a joke somewhere in there.

Knock! Knock! Knock!

Nazari's knocks rapped against the bedroom door followed by his rasp paralyzing my fingers.

"You good? Can I come in?"

"Uh... yeah sure... come in."

Swallowing hard, I fluffed my hair out as quickly as I could, then tried to act normal. I kept my phone in my hand, faking like I was scrolling my timeline when, really, I was enamored by his presence. My fingers were sliding upward on the screen but, from the corner of my eye, I was digesting just how ruggedly handsome Nazari was. His facial features were hardened but in the sexiest of ways. His obsidian hues were tempting, pulling me in each time they flashed in my direction.

The tattoos his upper adorned only added to his attractiveness, to the mystery of what kind of man he was. As he leaned against the door frame, my gaze traveled south. The Ralph Lauren pajama pants hung slightly off his waist, showing off his crazily defined v-cuts. Nazari's brawny stature could've gave any Calvin Klein model a long fucking day. That went without question. The man was exquisitely built.

"Good morning beautiful."

A sentence so simple should've never sounded as good as it did. Shivers were left behind from his tenor awakening my nerves.

"Good morning han... Nazari."

"It's ight for you to call me handsome. I'ma good lookin' ass nigga."

Chuckling lightly, Nazari stepped further into the room. I held my breath waiting to see where he would find comfort. He glanced at the bed but opted for the bean bag at the foot of the bed. Watching his tall ass fall into the circular bag was comical. He looked so damn uncomfortable.

"You could've just sat on the bed. It's yours and I'm not going to bite." I wanted to say more, my pussy screamed for me to say more. Last night after our drive, all I wanted was to feel Nazari next to me. The way we vibed out to the music was orgasmic.

Nazari was so damn stoic, I didn't peg him to be such an R&B fan, especially when a lot of what I was playing was from artists who didn't have mainstream success. It was clear to see Nazari had been hardened by whatever troubles life had brought his way. With me, I didn't want those troubles to exist. I played music that felt sensual, where the bass hitting vibrated against your skin and the crooning voice pierced the sensitive parts we all tried to hide in order to protect ourselves. Music was my love language. Through the voice of others, I was able to show him my needs, the cravings brought on by my sexual appetite. Last night's music was Nazari's introduction to how my soul desired to be not only loved but cared for. I wasn't sure if he caught on but I was hopeful.

"Even if I told you to?"

"Told? What happened to ask?"

Exhaling, Nazari smirked. "Jayce, when I'm in you, I'm not asking shit. What I tell you is what I want."

"Well, okay then, Mr. I make demands!"

Shaking my head, I turned away from Nazari, so he wouldn't see the red hues bursting in my cheeks.

"Anyway," I clicked my tongue, "about you being handsome. It seems you made an impression on my Nunu."

"Why you say that?"

"I talked to her this morning, and she had nothing but good things to say about you."

"Cause I'm a good dude."

"She also said I need to thank the Lord twice for your parents." I giggled, thinking it was a cute joke to make. The joke fell on deaf ears in regards to Nazari. His jaw clenched, sculpting his bone structure. Quivers swept my stomach as I scrambled to find the words to say.

"I didn't mean to—"

"Thank the Lord for my pops when it comes to me. The man I am today is because of the man he is. Deadbeats don't deserve prayers, just first class seats and gasoline drawers on their way to hell."

Deadpan and dry was Nazari's voice. It was eerie. Ghostlike, leaving chills in its trail. No emotion was spoken, yet so much was felt.

"I'll make sure to thank the Lord a hundred times over, then for your Pops."

"You do that 'cause I'll be thanking him for a lifetime for my introduction to you."

This time, I couldn't hide the fever in my cheeks. A way with words was what Nazari had. Too many times when he spoke to me, his words communicated beyond what my ears could hear.

"Do you *always* know what to say to make a girl smile?" I would be foolish to think Nazari was this smooth with only the likes of me.

"I know what to say to *you* because I'm speaking from within. I don't care enough about other bitches to even try and speak a language they understand."

"So, you care about me?"

"I care for you in a way that makes me want to be selfish with you. Never wanna see you hurt or in the arms or vicinity of another nigga, especially your husband. I care enough to want to explore and figure out what these feelings I feel for you mean. Find some understanding to why I know I need to leave ya ass alone but can't. I don't know if that's the type of *care* you mean, but that's all I have to offer. Is that cool for you?"

The hopefulness I always saw when Nazari wanted me to answer in his favor was so hard to deny. It reminded me of Rhea's pout but an adult masculine one.

"That's cool with me.

Easing up from the bean bag, Nazari made his way on to the bed. I shuffled my body back, only stopping once the cushioned headboard stopped me from going further. Casually, like he'd done this before, Nazari stripped the blanket from around me. He went to push my legs apart and stopped when I leaned forward, palming his chest.

"Nazari, no. I only have on your t-shirt."

Nazari was the perfect gentleman while I was ready to be a heathen. He showed me to the guest room, carrying my spending the night bag and me the whole way. When I pulled out my pajamas, Nazari asked would I be more comfortable in one of his t-shirts. My heart fluttered at the consideration. I told him yeah and, after, he left the room after giving me one of his. After he was gone, I slipped out of my panties. I hadn't thought about putting them back on until now.

"You're good. I won't do nothing you don't want me to."

We stayed fixated on one another, exchanging breaths until his forearm was separating my legs and his frame became my blanket.

"I also care about all the ways your body can be pleasured by me."

Kisses raining from my neck ignited the wick I was yearning to watch go up in flames. Stopping at my breasts, Nazari smudged them together tenderly, biting on my nipples through the cotton of the t-shirt.

"Nazariiiii."

Floating across my lips, his name became a part of the whispering of music that was still playing amongst us.

"Where is that music coming from?" I asked.

Nazari lifted his head, grimacing.

"What?"

"You just now realizing music is playing?"

"No but I thought to ask now."

Shaking his head, Nazari lifted the t-shirt, pulling it over my head.

"I—"

Lost in lust, Nazari wandered my body. I squirmed, unsure if he was pleased or displeased. I reached for the comforter and, before I could pull, Nazari was yanking it away from.

"I have speakers throughout my crib. Last night you said some 'bout wanting to wake up on a beach with *Rather Be* playing low enough for you to hear but loud enough for it to become part of the ambiance. My crib ain't a beach, but I figured this was a good start."

"I said that? That weed must've been stronger than I thought." I was shocked because I'd never told anyone how my dream wedding was on the sands of Jamacia. Each morning leading up to the wedding, I wanted a song my future husband believed reminded him of me to play on repeat.

"I only grow the best. It was after we smoked and, then, you had those cookie crisp infused lemon pepper wings."

"They were good, can we get more?"

Nazari knew a good spot out in Harlem who had a secret menu of infused foods made with his weed. The food, both infused and not, was bomb as hell.

"We can do whatever you want, long as you make a promise to me."

"Okay."

"Never try to hide yourself from me. Ya body is fuckin' perfect."

I nodded, unable to speak. Nazari smirked, lowering his body on top of mine. Once again, the wick in the center of my heart was flamed, crackling with each kiss Nazari trailed towards my pussy. With his head planted right where it needed to be, he flicked his gaze upward. Hunger fueled his vision, demanding that my pussy quench his thirst.

"You know what to do."

The growl of his demand yanked my legs from the bed, making my freshly polished toes his shoulder jewelry. Wetness awarded from his tongue slapped against my clit. Inhaling me like a deep hearty breath, Nazari appreciated the pussy singing its praises each time I masked his beard and lips with my juice. Nut after nut, I creamed, feeling as if my last time was indeed my last time. Nazari wasn't satisfied until I'd accomplished four.

"Ight, come on so you can eat shower and hit the mall." Nazari laid next to me on the bed, then pulled me close to him as if my pussy juices weren't glistening on his face against the sunlight.

"Mall? Can't we just eat in bed and chill?" I yawned.

"I already ate in bed," he chuckled, caressing his fingers along my silky fold.

"Shut up because you know what I mean."

"I do, but you gotta get up. I'm tryin' to do the matchin' outfit thing with you. And we gotta get you fitted for a dress for dinner."

"Dress for dinner?"

"Are you gonna frown and question everything I say? Yeah, a dinner Jacelyn. I'm not tryin' to eat pussy all day or do casual shit."

"Then, what are you trying to do?"

"Date you. I only got until tomorrow night. Then, I gotta return you to your bitch ass husband."

"Mhm. Fine but only if you promise to fuck me."

"Aye yo," he coughed, choking on his laugh. "Where that come from?"

"I want dick. If this is just a two-day thing, then I want you to fuck me. The head is amazing." Leaning up, I kissed his lips, enjoying the taste of my pleasure. "But I want to feel—"

"This dick in ya womb," he finished.

"If that's how you want to put it."

"I got you."

"Good." I kissed him again. "Now, let's go get some food."

Jumping up from the bed, I grabbed the t-shirt Nazari took of me and put it back on. Nazari got up behind me, tugging at the shirt and pulling me into him. Playfully, I rolled my eyes, but I enjoyed having him this close to me. Together, with his arms wrapped around me, we headed downstairs and into the kitchen.

"Good morning Jacelyn. I hope you find this breakfast spread to your liking," a woman dressed in a chef's outfit said.

Instantly, I felt naked in front of her, embarrassed that I was only wearing a t-shirt and Nazari. "I'm sure I will. Thank you."

The chef smiled, then walked passed us.

"Why wouldn't you tell me someone was here? Oh, my God, do you think she heard us?"

"Nah, she didn't," he laughed, embarrassing me even more. "I promise you she didn't hear anything and, if she did, she probably jealous she not getting swallowed up."

"That doesn't make it better."

"Chill, ight. She didn't hear shit. Make your plate and enjoy. I gotta go pay shawty."

Nazari went in for a kiss and, as I turned, I noticed all the food the chef cooked was my favorites.

"Wait, how did you know these were my favorite?"

"I asked Gramps."

"You called him?"

"Don't worry 'bout how, just know I did."

I smiled. Nazari smiled back, then went in for the kiss I'd previously denied. We kissed longer than necessary, only ending when we heard the chef.

"I have another appointment Nazari."

Giggling, I wiped his mouth and freed him. While he handled his dealings with the chef, I started making our plates. The chef had really outdone herself. Everything looked and smelled amazing. Cheese eggs, turkey sausage links, grits topped with shrimp, biscuits, sausage gravy, and brioche French toast topped with strawberries and powder sugar. The way I piled all of the food onto our plates was definitely me eating with my eyes. I placed both of our plates at the place settings, made sure we had all the utensils we would need and grabbed a few extra paper towels. I was a girl who loved to eat and didn't care about eating pretty. I wasn't a messy bitch, but I wasn't above digging in forreal either.

Grabbing two glasses, I filled both with some champagne and added a splash of orange juice to one and a splash of cran-grape in the other. I was allergic to oranges. Gramps must've told Nazari, and he opted for my favorite juice. My heart was full seeing how far this man was willing to go to ensure I kept the smile he promised to always make sure graced my lips.

"Damn, you made me a plate? I wasn't expecting that. I'm full Jayce. That pussy was enough to satisfy my hunger and thirst."

"Nazari, shut up and sit down. You need food. What's between my legs isn't enough for you to survive off of."

"Bullshit. You must not know how satiating your pussy is?"

"How good is it?" I asked for shits and giggles.

Nazari licked his, then flashed that boyishly handsome grin. "Good enough to make a nigga become a pussytarian."

The sip of mimosa I had just taken into my mouth went flying out when he said that goofy shit.

"Yo, you good?" Nazari laughed, knowing damn well I wasn't.

"Pussytarian? What the hell is wrong with you?"

"You. You let me taste between them thick ass thighs and, now, that's all I want in terms of nourishment. What's food when ya pussy fuels me. Straight up, ya pussy might be to me what stress is to Bruce Benner."

"What?" I felt like I knew what Nazari was hinting at, but I wasn't sure.

"Stress triggers that nigga into becoming the hulk. The taste of your pussy turns me into the pussy monster. I can't wait to see what feeling that sweet pussy does to me." Nazari closed his eyes and a shiver swept through him.

"You are crazy but, for someone who doesn't date, you damn sure know how to make a woman feel special."

Nazari finally took his seat. He placed a napkin on his lap and grabbed my hand. His thumb rubbed across my knuckles as his stare devoured me.

"I told you I know how I want you to feel when you're with me. That stutter in your breathing, the extra beat of your heart and the way your smile burns because of how often it's happening is all that I want. Long as that's happening, I know I'm doing right by you."

"But why? We were a one-night stand. You don't think this is a bit much?" The way I could see myself falling for Nazari was something straight out of a fairytale. We met and there was an instant connection. I'd never in my life felt so drawn to someone that I was contemplating uprooting my life. Not for a man but because a man showed me while barely knowing me that I deserved more.

"Shit, it might be. I'm questioning shit just like you. I don't even know what I'm doing with you 'cause on ya left hand, you wear that band. You're not mine, but I want you to be."

Our silence was loud. We both wanted to throw caution to the wind and dive in. Explore the sparks and fight through the tribulation they might cause. We wanted to be that one for one another but wasn't sure if either of us were actually ready for that.

"Let's eat tho," he said. "You not getting out of the matching drip. Bless the food beautiful."

We bowed our heads, and I said a quick grace thanking God for the food and doing what my Nunu said and thanking God for Nazari's father twice. Whoever the man was, he raised a gentleman. As for his mother, she was a sorry ass bitch. One I might've felt the need to slap if I ever came across her.

While we ate, I filled Nazari in on Cree and Rhea's playdate. He responded just as confused as me but thought it was a good idea since Cree had been asking for Rhea to come over. I asked a few questions about Cree and Sariah, not prying but looking for a better understanding of his family dynamic. Nazari told me Cree's dad passed and he stepped up. Nazari was proving to be an admiral guy, making it harder to believe he didn't have someone lurking in the shadows.

TARA

"BITCH, I'M TELLING YOU what I saw. That nigga is not fucking with you the way you think he is. Him and ole girl were hugged up outside of *Ashes 2 Ashes* looking into each other's eyes and shit," Kim smacked loudly for everybody in *Auntie Anne's* line to hear.

"Can you lower your voice please?" I looked behind us to see if anyone was listening; thankfully, they weren't. A mall wasn't my first choice to have this conversation, but Kim called asking if I wanted to go shopping. I agreed since I didn't have any appointments and Nazari had went ghost.

"My bad girl, you know my tone doesn't change whether I'm in public or in the house," Kim laughed.

"All I know is niggas hug hoes every day, that doesn't mean he loves her or even wants a relationship with her. You of all people should know that."

Kim was one of those people who couldn't keep a man to save her life. Niggas were running through her like the A train running through Manhattan. Still, I loved my girl. She held it down when it came to keeping me informed about the hoes Nazari fucked with. The way this bitch snooped was unmatched. No stone went unturned with Kim. I loved her nosey ass for that. Bringing up any bitch Nazari might've been fucking with was a conversation he refused to have. Who he fucked was his business and he made it clear I had no right to speak on it.

So, I had Kim do deep dives on anyone Nazari could've been linked too and brought the drama to that hoe. I meddled in her life until they left my man alone. I even went as far as pulling up their old controversial tweets and getting them fired. Nazari wasn't doing much other than fucking those hoes, but I still wanted his dick for myself.

"Don't try and throw shots because you don't like what I have to say."

"I'm not, I'm just saying—"

"Hey, *welcome to Auntie Anne's,* how can I help you?" The cashier smiled.

"I'll take cinnamon pretzel bites. You want anything?" I asked Kim.

"Pizza nuggets."

The cashier put in our orders; I paid and stood off to the side waiting.

"I wasn't throwing shots, but you know these niggas will say and do anything to fuck a bitch."

Kim's loud and boisterous laughter garnered a shit load of stares, including those from the people behind the counter at *Auntie Anne's.* Unaware of the dramatic scene her laughter was causing, she continued talking.

"Now girl," she smacked, humor still erupting. "You know damn well Nazari's fine ass never had to do much to get some pussy. Hoes would leap into the air naked in hopes of landing on Nazari's dick if that nigga wasn't so menacing. I'm trying to tell your delusional ass; the way he was hugging ole girl with his hands all over her ass, it was looking like he might've found the one. Her ass was fat and sitting too. She might give Ari a run for her money. I ain't never seen an ass that fat with the thighs matching in my life."

"Bitch, do you wanna fuck her?" I snarled.

"Shit, if I went that way, I might bump coochies with the hoes," Kim joked.

"Uh, here is your order—"

I snatched the bag from the cashier who also found what Kim said funny. Walking off, I rambled through the bag, grabbing my nuggets and roughly passing the bag to Kim.

"Damn, bitch, you ain't have to shove it in my chest like that," she complained.

"Whatever," I smacked.

"Tara, I didn't mean to hurt your feelings. I'm just telling you what I think. I've seen Nazari around a few hoes and never did I think he might've been feeling the hoe. This was different."

"She's not special. She's not even that fucking pretty."

"Not you salty and lying. I showed you the picture he put on the big screen at Mitch's party like it was summer jam. That nigga made it clear she was not to be fucked with. If I'm being honest, the picture didn't do her justice. She's prettier in person."

"I'ma ask you again because all this capping you're doing for this hoe is nauseating. Do you want to fuck her because we can arrange something, and it'll solve both our problems?"

The constant praise of this bitch from Kim was really getting under my skin.

"Just because I give a woman a compliment doesn't mean I want to fuck her. That first little jokey joke you got off was cute. Don't let your jealousy be the reason I whoop your ass in this mall."

I knew better than to push Kim's buttons. She was a nosey bitch who talked too much, but she was also a nosey bitch who talked too much and kept a blade under her tongue at all times.

"You act like bigging this hoe up isn't supposed to bother me."

"What happened to Ms. *a bitch could never have me bothered*?"

"I'm not bothered, but it's annoying to hear. You never gassed anyone else Nazari fucked, so why start now?"

"None of them hoes had Nazari the way *this* one does."

"She doesn't have Nazari like nothing and she doesn't know what she's doing with dude."

"Oh yeah, how so?" Kim pinched her brows waiting on my answer.

"Nazari isn't the type to be hugged up with no bitch. Everyone knows that. So, whatever he's feeding her, she's eating up and walking through a door that doesn't lead to anything but a wet ass and a broken heart."

Clicking my tongue, I smirked, knowing I'd ate that explanation up. His little stunt at the kickback had the streets whispering. Everyone swore he was about to be a changed man, and I was going out sad claiming a nigga who'd never claimed me. I laughed at all the gossip because none of these hoes knew Nazari the way I did. I knew all of Nazari's boundaries. Love and relationships were at the top of the list. Most women wouldn't be okay with attaching themselves to a man who didn't commit; I wasn't most woman. Any man who swore off relationships always settled down at one point or another. I was willing to wait Nazari out for however long it took. No man wanted to be alone in life, Nazari included; it was just a matter of when he would figure that out on his own.

"Yeah, you might be right. If anyone knows what Nazari wouldn't do, it's you." Kim shrugged. She thought she was throwing shade when, really, she was making my point.

"Right! So, there's no way Nazari would meet some random hoe and fall head over heels in love. It's fucking impossible. If he was to choose anyone, it would be me."

"Girl, I hope so."

"No need to hope because I know. He told me himself," I lied.

"Okay," Kim smacked, trying to lighten the mood.

We continued walking through the mall, and the subject changed to Kim's plans for the weekend. There was a party going on that she wanted to attended. I was thinking about going too but needed an outfit. We went into a few stores, grabbing a few things. Nothing really stuck out, so I was ready to go. On our way out, Kim spotted a pop-up boutique that was only in town for the next few days.

"Hopefully you find something in here."

"I should be able to. They have some cute stuff from what I can see."

I looked through a rack that was to the left of the entrance.

"Mhmm, they have good looking men in here too," Kim smacked.

I turned around just to see who the good looking man was and blushed, realizing the man was my man. Nazari was a few feet away standing by the dressing rooms.

"Damn, my man's fine," I murmured. "I'ma go speak."

Handing my nuggets to Kim, I adjusted the black leggings, pulling them a little bit above my waist. I flipped the curly ends of my braids over my shoulder and stepped forward.

What the fuck?

The confusion etched on my face could've been spotted a mile away. The way this bitch sauntered out of the dressing room, floating on the tips of her toes angered me because who did she think she was? She hit all angles, showing Nazari the way the chocolate crocodile textured dress not only hugged her curves but emphasized them. Kim wasn't lying. Shawty's ass was fat. All she did was sway to the right and her ass rippled as much as it could in the painted-on dress. I was feeling like Kim with the way I was gawking. Had I been into woman, she would've been the first person I wanted to bump coochies with.

"Look at how he's looking at her, Tara. I'm telling you this is more than him wanting to fuck. The nigga is smitten, and I don't even know what smitten means forreal."

I eyed Kim stupidly, wondering how she could be so smart and dumb at the same damn time. "Will you shut the... oh shit!"

I grabbed Kim's wrist and pulled her closer to me, so it looked like we were both strumming through the clothes on the rack. I watched Nazari from the corner of my eye walk past and leave out of the store with his phone pressed against his ear.

"I'm going over there to say something," I told Kim in a hushed tone.

"Please do not start no shit in here," Kim sighed, but it was too late. I was already heading towards the register and grabbing a purse on my way over.

"This dress was made for you, you hear me," the sales associate gushed. "I probably don't have to tell you this, but your man was practically salivating at the mouth when he saw you in this."

"He was not," she giggled, cheeks turning red.

"I have 20/20 vision so, trust me, that man was eye fucking you. Just licking his lips like he still had a taste of you on 'em."

"He might."

The two laughed at that childish ass joke, taking my annoyance level from a five to an eight. Not only was my presence being disregarded but my place in Nazari's life was being disrespected. Clearing my throat, I slammed the purse on the counter, gaining the attention of both ladies. With a forced smile, I said, "I'm ready to pay."

Matching my unpleasant glare, the sales associate peeked over her shoulder while telling me, "Okay, give me a second. I'm ringing her up. When I'm done, I'll be right with you."

"Oh, you can take her. It seems she has somewhere to be, and my friend is the one buying my things. He stepped out to take a business call and could be a while."

What she said sounded polite, but I was well versed in the art of *bitch*. That comment about me having somewhere to be was a dig and her saying Nazari was paying for her things was a stunt. I looked towards Kim, hoping she caught the shade but all she did was shrug.

"I hate when a broke bitch has to spend a nigga's money to know luxury."

The sales associate looked nervously between me and Nazari's little friend.

"I hate when a bitch tries to act like it's beef behind a nigga she can't lock down," she shot back.

"What did you say?" I frowned.

"You heard me. This little attitude you have is clearly about Nazari and whatever spot you *think* you hold in his life."

"Bitch, please. You think you're the first one Nazari took shopping? He does this with all of his slides. He likes for his hoes to look up to par, so he has a pretty canvas to smear his nut on," I chortled loudly, thinking I had the final word.

"Sweetheart—" the bitch chuckled, bringing her hand to her chest and letting out a quick *whew*, "whatever you're trying to paint this to be, it's not. The only one who's getting cummed on is Nazari. That nigga be nose deep in this pussy and my ass."

"Liar!" I yelled like a spoiled child.

"What reason do I have to lie? I don't owe you anything, but Nazari does. It's clear whatever y'all have means more to you than it does him. All this—"

As she waved her hand in front of me, I moved back in case she tried to sneak me.

"Is exactly what I wanted to avoid. Handle your business, whatever it may be with Nazari, and leave me the fuck alone," she scoffed, swinging her curls inches from my face as she turned her back to me.

Her disrespect was so blatant yet calm that it triggered me. Everything I said was supposed to anger her. The lies Nazari told were supposed to come flooding back, blinding her with rage until she put hands on me, making me the damsel in distress. Instead, I was the one blinded by rage and it didn't take long for me to act on it. I lunged forward, gripping her curls and yanking her body back.

"Oh shit!"

She came crashing into me, knocking us both off balance. Even in that tight dress, she recovered quickly. My hands were now free of her curls and were swinging with no real direction. Her, on the other hand, was punching with purpose. Anywhere she aimed, her fists connected.

"Kim!" I screamed.

Finally, her punches ceased, which should've happened prior to me calling for help. Kim should've stepped in the moment I started getting beat up. Struggling to stand, I made it to my feet and saw Kim was now having a hard time with her. Having already got my ass beat, I decided to leave that alone.

"I'm calling security!"

"Bitch, shut up! Where was security when that hoe was beating my ass?" I challenged.

She looked at me nervously, placing the store phone back onto its receiver.

"Slice that bitch up and let's get the fuck outta here Ki—"

"Let a blade touch any part of her, and your blood gon' be the new decor in this bitch."

A voice as calm as an afternoon day but heavy as thunder crackling through the night sky silenced the room and parted Kim from that bitch like the Red Sea. Not a single hiss of air entered my body when I felt Nazari's presence loom over me. Holding the swell in my chest, I waited to feel the cold steel of a nine pressed against the back of my neck. The chill was absent from my skin, and I knew that was his way of giving me grace.

"Get the fuck outta here Tara."

His command loosened the tightness of my body. Slowly, I inched to the right, too afraid to step back and possibly bump into him. Kim parted her lips in what looked like an attempt to apologize, completely underestimating the person in front of her. I blinked twice, and Kim was on the sales floor holding her leaking nose. My eyes widened in shock.

Who the fuck is she, she hulk?

"Jacelyn!" Nazari called out, stifling a laugh.

She ignored him, and I became the focus of her threat.

"I'm not the bitch you want to fuck with. Play with your pussy, not me," she snarled.

"Jacelyn!" Nazari called after her again.

She walked into the dressing room, acting as if she'd never heard the name Jacelyn in her life.

"Give me a second," he told the sales associate who still hadn't called security, but I wished she would've.

"O... oo... okay." Stuttering, she hurried into the dressing room.

"I'm sorry!" I blurted the second Nazari brought his menacing glare my way, chills creeping down my spine.

"Get ya bitch and get the fuck up outta here."

"Okay, but can we talk about this? It didn't happen like you think. I was just trying to buy a purse and—"

"Tara!" he gritted. "I'll see you. Get that bitch up and get out of here."

I nodded, scurrying over to Kim. I helped her and lent her my body to use as a crutch.

"I should beat ya fucking ass for getting me into that mess." Kim's threat fell on deaf ears because there wasn't much she could do that Jacelyn hadn't already done. My whole face ached and throbbed, along with my head.

"How many times do you want me to say I'm sorry? I apologize, okay. I didn't know the bitch was Rocky," I said, helping Kim into her car.

"Maybe that's the problem, you never think about shit. You just do. You do the most thinking because a nigga fucks you and lets you play in his hair that y'all have some type of special bond."

"We do!"

"No, y'all don't. That nigga treats you like a cum rag every chance he gets, and your stupid ass gobbles it up every time. Nazari does not love you. He threatened to kill you over that bitch. Do you hear me, Tara? He threatened to kill you, the bitch he's been fucking for two years over a bitch he seemingly just met."

"So," I smacked, waiting for her to get to the point.

"So!" She heaved with bug-like eyes. "Bitch, if you can't read what's in front of you, then fuck I look like trying to give you insight. Keep acting like Stevie Wonder and that nigga's gon' be the one to show you a whole new world."

"I know you're hurt but—"

"Hurt? This look fucking hurt to you?" Kim moved her left hand from her nose, and I winched. Her nose was definitely out of alignment in regard to the rest of her face. "My nose doesn't hurt bitch, it's fucking broke!"

Scoffing, Kim slammed the car door and sped off, nearly running over my foot. If Kim was upset, that was her business. I apologized; there wasn't any more I could do. In a few days, I would send her an edible arrangement and all would be forgiven. I hopped in my car that was parked a few spots down and started it up. Before leaving, I grabbed my phone, opening IG and going straight to Nazari's page from my burner account. I scrolled through the people he followed until I found what I was looking for.

Clicking on Jacelyn's page, my heart sunk to the pits of hell. The little girl that took up most of her feed was the same little girl Nazari showed me and claimed was his daughter. Rapidly, I swallowed until my throat burned. My eyes tightened in angst, glued to the little girl who'd single handedly ruined my life. Nazari wasn't leaving me for some random; he was leaving me for his baby momma, a bitch I didn't even believe existed until today.

NAZARI

WOMEN FIGHTING WASN'T SOME shit I was a fan of. If the situation warranted it, then by all means get ya shit off; other than that, I didn't care for it. Sariah loved throwing hands, and that's where my distaste for it came from. I couldn't stand seeing someone I loved in that type of position, especially when I buried bodies for a living. Fighting seemed minuscule in the grand scheme of things when I could just kill a muthafucka. Sariah learned that quick, and Tara was gon' learn. Her ass backed up spooked 'cause she knew fucking better. Luckily, that little tussle hadn't left nothing but a few scratches on Jayce from what I could see.

I knew leaving the boutique without Jacelyn saying much was setting the tone for the rest of the day. She was pissed and had every right to be. Shit, I was pissed Tara had the fucking balls to even step to Jayce. Her ass wasn't no fucking fighter. I guess this was the reason for the conversation Sariah was talking about. I fucked up not having it before, but Tara and I was gon' speck soon. Real fucking soon.

"Jacelyn!"

Testing the waters, I called out to her. She gave me the same response as before: silence with a heavy roll of her big ass eyes. Shit was cute when we were in the mall, and I was picking out our matching fits and sneakers. It was even cute when she pouted in the *Newbury Comics* after being forced to walk inside and pick out a few vinyls for her collection. The attitude and poutiness stopped being cute when we got back in the car and I was trying to speak on the situation, and she still chose to ignore me. I'd seen way too many people allow the unsaid to cause a rift in all they deemed good. Jayce was the good in my life, and I wasn't trying to have that on shaky waters.

"Jacelyn."

Silence.

Shaking my head, I pulled over, put the car in park and grabbed my phone. I smirked, knowing I was about to do some corny shit. Ruben Studdard's *Sorry 2004* began to play, and Jayce smirked and quickly went back to being stoned face. I didn't know the words to this shit, so I hit the button to pull up the lyrics.

"Nazari, leave me alone."

Jayce swatted my hand away when I went to grab the sides of her face like she'd done to me when she was singing to me the night prior.

"Nazari, I'm not playing," she fussed some more.

Tired of her shit, I reached for her neck. Gently, my fingers squeezed at her throat, tugging her closer to me.

"Girl, this is my sorry for 2004, and I ain't gonna mess up no more, this year."

Singing to Jayce I thought I would at least get a laugh out of her, but she frowned even more.

"What's wrong you?" I asked in frustration while letting her go.

"Nothing, just bring me home."

"Home? Unless you talking about my crib, ya ass ain't going home."

"You can't hold me hostage Nazari!"

"Fuck if I can't. Who's coming for you, Jayce? What nigga gon' risk his life to try and save you from me?" I gritted my teeth to keep from raising my voice.

"I don't need a man to save me and fuck you, Nazari!"

Sucking her teeth, Jayce jumped out the car and started walking. Being the dumbass I was, I got out and started following her stupid ass.

"Jacelyn!"

"Leave me alone Nazari!"

"Jacelyn!"

"Leave me the fuck alone!"

Walking down the block going back in forth dressed in matching cargo pants, fear of God hoodies and dunks had us looking crazy forreal. I let Jayce get to the end of the block 'fore I got tired of this bullshit. I jogged up to her and grabbed by the arm. Like a whiny child, she fought as I dragged her ass back to the car.

"Chill the fuck out. Someone gon' think this a DV situation."

I pinned her body to my car, leaning my frame against hers. I kept one hand at her waist and brought the other below her chin, angling our faces so we had no choice but to see the other.

"Why won't you leave me alone Nazari? I'm married."

That *married* word had to be a nigga's kryptonite. Cold were the shivers that blanketed my nerves. Stiff was the tension of every muscle I possessed clenching as hard as it could.

"I don't give a fuck about ya marriage or the bitch ass nigga you married. Stop bringing that shit up. I'm not letting you run from me or ya feelings behind a piece of paper you don't give a fuck about."

Glaring down, I took in the message from her fleeting gaze. Jayce was a woman of emotions. When she spoke, she did so with strength, hardly ever allowing her words to present as weak or afraid. Her emotions hidden in plain sight as the brown in her eyes spoke differently. Had I been a nigga who never had to be meticulous, I would've missed it. I was able to read the hurt sparkling under the disappointment she held for me. Inhaling slowly, I counted to five, exhaling my stiffened state along with my frustrations.

"What did I do? How did I hurt you?"

"Nazari, just leave it alone. It doesn't matter."

Her passiveness reminded me so much of the torment I walked with for the majority of my life. It was my safe spot; Jayce's passiveness was hers.

"How much longer are you gonna allow the shit niggas do to be acceptable?"

"What?"

"You heard me. How many more niggas are you gonna let walk all over your feelings, thoughts, and opinions?"

A snarl plagued Jacelyn's face.

"Nigga, you don't know me to say I let anyone walk all over me. Don't let eating pussy have you misconstrued."

I chuckled cockily. "I don't have to know you to read you, Jayce. You've been ignored for so long, you can't even see when a nigga is trying to understand you. You're not in this alone."

"Never said I was but, if I don't want to speak on something, then I don't have to."

"You're right, you don't, but keeping how you feel to yourself after someone hurt you is selfish as fuck."

"So, now I'm selfish because I don't want to talk about what's bothering me? Nazari, move with your bullshit." Jayce tried waving me off, but I wasn't her husband; it wasn't going to be that easy.

"Why is it bullshit 'cause you've never had a nigga care enough? Hurt isn't yours to carry or yours to solve. Keeping it to yourself is selfish as fuck Jayce, especially when you have someone who's trying to right his wrongs."

I paused, moving in close to make sure I was heard by Jayce. "Get it out ya head that when someone hurts you, it's for you to fix. It's not. When I hurt you, I'ma correct it. Any other nigga hurt you, I'ma correct that shit too."

The curve in Jayce's lips puffing her cheeks up and squinting her eyes finally appeared. Knocks against my chest warmed the chill upon my skin.

"You lied to me, and that's what hurt. We both said we were going to be honest."

"I didn't lie. You asked if I have someone, I don't. I fucked with Tara for two years. It wasn't anything more than fucking, a few events we chilled at together and she braids my hair. When you popped up, I eased off shawty. Then, I told her I was trying to fuck with someone else and we were done."

"So, why was she telling me you blow bags on all your hoes?"

"Gotta ask her." I shrugged. "Sariah told me I needed to speak to her and make things clear, but I didn't. I apologize for that. If I had, things wouldn't have happened. But from the looks of it, you held your own."

Using her chin, I angled her face, looking for any war wounds.

"Boy, stop. I don't know why hoes love to fight when they can't."

"Me either. You pretty as fuck." The complaint was intended for my mind only.

"You're handsome as fuck."

I wasn't a blushing ass nigga, but that brought it out of me. "I 'preciate that. You still wanna go home?"

"Nope. I wanna go to the carnival on the next block over. I saw a flyer for it before you snatched me up."

"Ight, we can do whatever you want, long as I can get you every stuffed animal in that bitch."

"If you can win 'em, I'll take 'em."

Giggling, Jayce leaned forward, sealing our promise with a kiss. Her perfume clouded my head. It was easily becoming my favorite scent. Jayce slipped her hands into mine, then placed them at her hips. Them shapely ass hips. I massaged her fullness with my thoughts drifting to how good Jayce would look on all fours, ass in the air bouncing against my pelvis. The thought alone lengthened my dick. I pressed it against her thigh and brought my lips to her ear.

"You still wanna get fucked?"

Shivering, her hands glided against my thigh. A tight squeeze from her soft hands choked the head.

"Mhmm," drifted from her mouth breezing against my lobe.

"I wanna be fucked in every way. Treat this pussy like it's ya first day out. I can handle it."

Pulling away from Jayce, I checked to see just how serious she was. Lust and temptation coated her brown eyes.

"Man, bring ya horny ass on."

Grabbing Jayce up, we laughed and headed towards the carnival. With how Jayce was talking, I wasn't worried about her taking dick; I was on the fence about how laced the pussy was gon' have me. Jayce's personality was top tier without the sexual tension. That little quickie we had back in the day was straight. Pussy was wet like a faucet, tight and warm. Somethin' like that was only gon' get better with time. The years had definitely treated Jacelyn like she was a favorite, so the pussy had to be pristine. Pristine pussy, gorgeous face, and bomb personality was the recipe for the world's worst drug.

JACELYN

BEYONCE WAS WRONG AS hell when she asked *who wants that hero love anyway?* Because I sure as fuck did. Nazari wasn't the perfect image of what a hero might look like and our situation was far from a fairytale. But the way he made me feel was like I'd been thrown from a building. Free falling in fear until I was inches from the ground and he's standing there waiting to catch me. In his arms, I caught my breath and the scent of vanilla and bourbon calmed me, bringing my breathing to the pattern of his choice. Just putty in his. Completely free of judgement, embracing who I was no matter how silly was the kind of comfortability his presence awarded. Nazari was who I thought I would marry. He reminded me so much of my Gramps with how safe I felt and the amount of attention he supplied me.

Our carnival date was one of the cutest things I'd ever done. Had I not gotten a few pictures on my phone and dragged Nazari into every photobooth, I wouldn't have believed all the fun we had. Nazari was so stoic when, truly, he was a big ass kid at heart.

Every ride at the carnival, we rode it. Every game, we played it until Nazari won me the prize I wanted. He wasn't lying about getting every big ass stuff animal either. I looked crazy trying to carry all ten animals that were almost the same size as me. It got so bad Nazari gave all but one away to the kids running around.

By the time we left, I was so damn tired and wanted to chill in the house for the rest of the night. Nazari wasn't going for it. He drove us back to his house, made me get in the shower and basically dressed me for the surprise he had tonight. I acted like a brat the whole time too. I refused to lotion myself, and Nazari wasted no time massaging lotion all over me and topping it with my favorite body oil. His firm hands kneaded into my body, leaving me to feel doughy. And when it was time to lotion the inside of my thighs, his lips magnetized my clit.

Swollen.

Throbbing.

Twitching.

Nazari took my pussy through emotions until his beard was coated in my love. Thinking about it, I clamped my legs tightly.

"You good over there?"

"Uh yeah, fine," I giggled.

"Yeah ight," he laughed, placing his hand on my exposed thigh.

The dress I wore left little to the imagination, and I loved it. The chocolate crocodile print was gorgeous. It wasn't too short, stopping just above my knees but, when I sat down, my shapely hips scrunched it up to mid-thigh. A laced pattern held my boobs up in the halter sweetheart neckline. The back of the dress was probably the sexiest part of the outfit. Most people would say my ass was my best asset when, truly, it was my back. The width of my shoulders were wide enough to add emphasis to how cinched my waist became as your eyes traveled south. From my shoulders to the nape of my ass was free of the crocodile material. Tonight, I was feeling myself and felt the best I'd felt in a while.

"I love ya hair like that."

"Thank you."

I blushed under his quick glance and twirled one of the lose curls I had framing my face. I wanted to keep my look simple, so I opted for a natural no make-up, makeup look and piled my curls into a slicked up messy bun. Well defined curls cascaded down in every direction but neatly. Since I didn't know we were going anywhere special, I didn't wear much jewelry besides the gold letter R that I wore daily and my diamond earrings Nunu gave me when I was sixteen.

To my surprise, Nazari picked out my shoes and they were actually a good match. After seeing the dress and when I thought Nazari was handling a business call, he snuck away and purchased me a pair of Rena Caovilla Omega snake spiral-wrap stiletto heels. The shoe was so damn pretty that I wasn't mad, but he would be carrying me around by the end of the night. I loved a good heel, but heels were not as fond of me.

"How did you get reservations for *Duluchi's*?"

As Nazari pulled in front of the restaurant, my whole face lit up. *Duluchi's* was the one restaurant in town that I'd been dying to go to for the last year. Anytime I called to set a reservation, they told me they were booked out for the year. Aidan, with all of his celebrity connections, couldn't even swing a table.

"Does it really matter how?" He smirked.

"Hell no!" I answered.

Too excited, I opened my car door, ready to step out and eat the night away.

"Whatchu doing Jayce?" Nazari asked, stopping me from getting out the car.

"Getting out."

"Not like that. Close the door."

Flustered, I did what Nazari said. He opened his door, got out, said a few words to the valet, and came to my side of the car.

"When I'm in the car, you don't touch a door. I let you jump out earlier cause that shit caught me off guard. From this point on, I got you."

I swear fucking with Nazari was going to cause my cheeks to break. I wasn't sure if that was possible, but how hard he kept me smiling was definitely going to test the theory. With my hand in his, Nazari helped me out the car and stood in front of me, shielding me as I fixed my dress. Together, we walked towards the door, bypassing the disgruntled people who seemed to be bickering amongst themselves.

"What's going on? Are they closed?"

With all the people who were standing outside, it was hard to not think the worst.

"You trust me?"

It was a simple question. I knew he was only asking if I trusted him in this moment, but I couldn't stop myself from applying it to every part of my life.

Do I trust him with me? Yes.

Do I trust him with my happiness? Yes.

Do I trust him with my heart? Yes.

No matter what I applied the question to, the answer was yes. I trusted Nazari in an unwavering manner, which was both scary yet comforting.

"I do."

"You better," he chuckled softly. "Come on then."

Nazari led the way with my hand clasped in his. Feeling a slight chill, I snuggled the leather trench coat I wore closer to my body.

"Excuse me, my man."

While Nazari spoke to the man who was attempting to clear out the front of the restaurant, I looked around smiling at a few people who were looking at me snobbishly.

"Isn't that Aidan's wife?"

"Looks like her but that's not Aidan."

An older couple's conversation had caught my attention once I heard my husband's name.

"I'm not surprised. Charlotte did say Aidan was struggling in his marriage for some time now. Charlotte even told me the wife put hands on her."

"Aidan is a better man than me. I would've sent her packing and shipped her right back to the projects she came from."

Hearing how the couple and Charlotte talked about me hurt. Not because I gave a fuck but because I'd put my life on hold just to be disrespected in private by those who were supposed be family.

"Jacelyn, what happened?"

One sniffle was all it took for Nazari to pause his conversation and look in my direction. I almost shook my head and mouthed *nothing* until I remembered what Nazari said about holding in my feelings.

"You see that couple over there?"

"Yeah."

"I overheard them talking about me and the things my mother in-law said about me."

"What she say?"

"That I put hands on her and how my husband should've sent me back to the projects."

Nazari said nothing as he wiped the few tears that spilled from my eyes. I smiled, and he outlined my lips with his thumb before kissing me. When he pulled away, I was still smiling. He told the guy he was talking to, to give him a minute, then led the way over to the couple. The walk was short, but Nazari still made sure I didn't trip or stumble in my heels by holding me close.

"Apologize." The way Nazari spoke sternly without raising his voice was a true gift. What most men had to get irritated to accomplish, Nazari did simply with his presence.

"What?" he grumbled, stepping in front of his wife as a way to protect her.

"I said apologize for that fucked up shit you said about my lady."

"Your lady?" His brows dipped suspiciously. "I thought Jacelyn was Aidan's wife."

"She is. That nigga won't check you tho. That's apparent from how comfortable you were flappin' your wattle. Since he's too much of a bitch to check you about his, I'm checkin' you about mine."

Nazari stepped in front of me, but him doing so had a very different outcome than when this guy did it with his wife.

"Oh... ahh... I... see. I, um, I'm sorry," the gut stammered, eyes bouncing all around Nazari's stature. His chunky short self was no match for Nazari's stocky frame.

"Nigga, you weren't jugglin' ya wattle 'bout me. Apologize to my lady."

Nazari stepped back to my side, then shifted me in front of him. His arm draped over my shoulder and his hand resting on my titty garnered strange stares from him and his wife. I knew this was crazy for them to see because it was crazy for me.

"I apologize," he said.

"I apologize too. I normally do not partake in gossip, but Charlotte was going on and on about you. You seem like a wonderful woman. If anything, you should leave Aidan since he has that—"

"Ight, that's enough," Nazari cut in. "I shouldn't have to tell you this, but I will. Run ya fuckin' mouth to her husband or his momma, and that wattle won't be the only flab of skin that's where it shouldn't be, feel me?"

Nodding frantically, the guy murmured *yes* and whisked his wife away.

"What the hell is a wattle?" I asked, turning to face Nazari.

"That extra skin on a turkey's neck. That nigga looked like he was carrying a ball sack without the balls under his chin. Shit was crazy."

"Nazari!" I laughed.

"Tell me I'm lying."

"I'm not saying anything."

"Exactly. Now, bring ya fine ass on."

"Why? They're turning everyone away at the door. The fact you were able to get reservations is enough."

Nazari laughed, and it was a hefty laugh too. I frowned because why would this nigga laugh at me trying to have a cute moment?

"Niggas getting turned away at the door 'cause they ain't me."

"Oh, and you're special?"

"I might be extraordinary, an urban legend of the sorts."

"Yeah, okay."

"Let me make you a believer."

I allowed Nazari to lead me to the restaurant and, as people were getting turned away, the guy he was previously speaking to stepped aside, allowing us to walk in.

"How did you—" I started to whisper.

"I rented out the spot."

"You didn't? I heard the owner doesn't close down for no one."

"He did for me." Pulling me into him, I melted. "Ya man is some-thin' like an urban legend," he smirked.

I smiled back, rolling my eyes at his arrogance. Planting a kiss on my forehead, he clung to me as we followed the hostess into a private area past where the normal patrons would've sat. As the hostess slid open the velvet cushioned door, Nazari placed his hand on the small of my back, gesturing for me to walk in first. The room could've easily seated a party of fifty but, tonight, it was set for two.

The navy-blue upholstered tuft that lined the walls reminded me so much of Nazari. The color and style was that of his guest room. It was so pretty and elegant under the illuminance of the candles. The pillars in the room all held vases of white roses which made me smile. White roses weren't my favorite, but Nunu loved them and I loved her. The subtle detail was Nazari's way of letting me know he heard me when I spoke. The ambiance of the room was giving grown and sexy.

"The two of you can have a seat and the first course will be out shortly."

"Thank you," Nazari said, taking my coat and handing it to the hostess, then did the same with his suit jacket.

This man is too damn fine.

Dressed up or dressed down, Nazari was handsome. His cream buttoned up shirt fit just right with the top three buttons undone, showing off his gold chain. It was tucked into his tapered, dark-brown dress pants that stopped perfectly at his ankles, showing just a slither of his honeyed complexion before his Dior loafers stole the show. Nazari dressed up was a whole other level of sexy. Even with his slightly messy braids and tattoos, he didn't possess that thug semblance. He looked every bit of the boss he was proving himself to be.

"What happened to me fucking you?" he asked randomly.

"Huh?"

"You said you wanted me to fuck."

"I do."

"You sure? The way you're eyeing me is saying different."

"Oh yeah?"

Grabbing at my hips, Nazari brought me to him. Soft music began to play.

"Do you dance?" I asked. *Under The Moonlight* was playing, and it was one of my favorites.

"I'll do whatever for you."

So much certainty was in his words, I would be a fool to disagree. Our bodies swayed to *Trey Forever* crooning about making love under the moonlight.

"What were you saying before?" I asked.

"I was saying how you want me to fuck you, but ya body language is saying you need love. To be loved and be made love to. Fucking is cool, I can give you that, but is it really what you need?"

I laid my head on his chest, letting my silence be all the answer he needed.

NAZARI

IN LIFE, THERE WERE only a few things I was afraid of or actually felt hesitant about. Death was one. For something to be so final, it left too many unanswered questions. I wasn't scared of dying cause we were all gon' do that. In my life, I'd done a lot of shit I wasn't proud of. Ended lives of those who probably weren't the scums of the earth, but they crossed the wrong nigga. All of my sins had to be paid for in one way or another. I feared having to pay those sins in death.

Second on the list was love and heartbreak. Both were synonymous to each other and, as beautiful as they could be, there was an ugly side. Lastly, Jacelyn was the only person I actually feared on this earth. In my eyes, Jacelyn was dangerous. She had the ability to reach parts of me that I'd locked up for years. A smile and her eyes lingering on mine was all it took for her to have me like putty in her hands. I was ready to do whatever I needed to have her, to breathe her when I needed to satisfy an inhale that regular air couldn't quench.

Love was how I never wanted to fall. My footing hadn't been stable since meeting her. This time together only made it worse. I was tripping, and Jacelyn not being the one to catch me put me in a dangerous place mentally. A place I hadn't been since my last kill. She was the comfort I didn't realize was lacking in my life. Death, love, heartbreak and Jacelyn were the only things I feared. Each one had the possibility to lead into the others, depending on how this shit played out.

"I can't believe you were able to rent out *Duluchi's*. The food was so good. I'm feening to go to sleep and wake up, just so I can eat my leftovers."

I laughed because without her saying it, I could've guessed that she enjoyed the food. Jacelyn couldn't get enough of the Italian cuisine at *Duluchi's*. I told her she could order whatever from the menu I helped to create for tonight, and her ass took full advantage. Jacelyn nibbled on everything we both ordered, never making it to dessert. Whatever she didn't finish, I had wrapped up for her to take back to the crib.

"Tell me how you did it?"

"The owner Kass is a business partner of mine. We used to run together back in the day."

"Wow!" she gushed. The look of approval she wore gave me a boost in confidence. I already knew I was that nigga, but she made it feel real. "You are definitely a lot different than how I thought you were?"

"How did you think I was?"

"It doesn't matter." She waved me off.

"Nah, tell me." Coming to a red light, I glanced at her and smirked. "Tell me. My feelings won't be hurt."

"Okay." She shifted in her seat, so she was looking at me. The light changed and I drove off, breath hiccupping in my chest.

"I thought you were the typical hood nigga. You know, selling drugs, dogging woman, mean and emotionally immature."

"Damn," I chuckled. "That's what I had you thinking?"

"Not the night we met at the club. But, after, at the spades game. The way you pushed up on me was a lot. Telling a stranger they're your wife came off like you were running game."

"You weren't a stranger, and I wasn't gaming you. I don't gotta do that shit for pussy. A woman gon' either come up off it 'cause she wants to or I'ma move to the next. I've never been pressed for pussy."

"I know. Well, I know that now. I'm not used to a man being interested the way you were, so it surprised me."

"Emotionally immature tho?"

"Yeah. Most men are."

"But, I'm not?"

"You've done a lot of subtle things that show me you take how I feel into account. You listen when I speak and force me to speak when I'm feeling away. Those things might be meaningless or little to sum, but it means a lot to me. The little things matter when you're not used to receiving them."

"I feel you."

"So yeah that's what I thought before but not anymore. Now, I think you're perfect, a little too perfect."

"I'm far from perfect."

Jacelyn didn't know all the fucked up shit I'd done in the name of money, protection, and revenge. Purposely, I kept her talking about herself. I asked all the questions a woman would usually ask a man she was interested in. The more she talked about her life, the less I had to speak about mine.

Woo-woo! Woo-woo!

Blue and red lights flashed behind us, signaling for me to pull over. I did what was expected, then reached across Jayce to grab my registration from the glove compartment. I reached in the middle compartment for my license and sat both on my lap.

"You good?" I asked Jayce.

"With you?" She frowned but couldn't hold it for long. "Always." Her laughter was so vibrant, I chuckled too, just to feel like I was a part of her.

Knock! Knock! Knock!

A heavy fist rapped against my window. I placed my hand on Jayce's thigh and rolled the window down.

"Nazari Caddel, I need you to step out the car."

"For what?" I gritted.

"Sir, step out the car or—"

"Back the fuck up and I will."

The cop chortled, stepping back with a smug expression.

"What is going on?" Jacelyn asked as a knocked appeared on her window.

"Just remain calm," the other officer told her.

"Jayce!" I called out.

The moment she glanced in my direction, I pinched her chin and kissed her deeply. Her panicked breaths slowed. I was now able to get out the car without worrying about her.

"Man, what the fuck y'all want? My shit right here."

Stepping out, I waved my shit in dude's face. If his intent was to arrest me, he was gon' do that shit regardless of how I conducted myself.

"Mr. Caddel, we meet again." That stupid ass grin helped to put a name to face.

"The fuck you want?" I barked.

"Nothing from you... this time. Mr. Klein wanted to speak to his wife. He so kindly provided us with your plates, and we did the rest."

I glanced over my shoulder, looking into the car. Jayce was visibly upset as she held a phone to her ear. Pissed Aidan was able to get to Jayce, I turned my back towards Officer Jones and leaned into the car.

"Mr. Caddel, turn back—"

Ignoring the nigga, I asked Jayce, "You good?"

When she looked towards me, tears were pooling at the brim of her bottom eyelid. Heat overwhelmed me seeing her saddened expression. Without thought, I reached inside, snatching the phone from her hand and ending the call.

"Mr. Caddel, you shouldn't have done that. You're playing a dangerous game," Officer Jones said.

His partner came from around the car standing at his side like the good bitch he was. I gritted my teeth to keep from telling these punk ass cops they could end up on that hit list, right under the bitch they were taking orders from.

"Dangerous ain't shit I haven't fucked with before. Tell whoever sent you, I'll be seeing them."

I couldn't get my shit off forreal 'cause Jacelyn was listening. Soon as I took the phone from her, she leaned towards the driver's seat being nosey.

"I'll be sure to relay the message. Hopefully, our mutual friend does not take that as a threat. If so we'll be seeing you under different circumstances," Officer Jones smirked.

"My phone," Officer Tucker said. He stepped forward with his hand out.

"Oh this?" I showed him the phone.

"That's the one," he answered.

"This a burner. You're not 'posed to have this, so let me do you a favor."

I dropped the phone and stomped on it, shattering the screen. "I'm sure ya boy can fetch you a new one. Y'all be safe."

Getting back in my car, I pulled off, not giving a fuck if I hit one of them niggas or not. Doing eighty on an empty street, I couldn't see shit beyond the streetlights. All that mushy shit I was feeling moments before I got pulled over had been smothered in hatred.

"Nazari!" Panic trembled in Jayce's voice, but it wasn't enough. I swerved to the left and back to the right, bypassing the car that was now in my rearview.

"Nazari!"

Breathe!

"Nazari!"

Fucking breathe!

"Nazari, please talk to me. What was that back there?"

I tried. I tried drawing in slow and steady breaths to numb the violent torment of my heart pounding against my chest.. Death was calling. Pounding against the door to unleash the man I used to be.

"Nazari!"

"What did he say to you?"

"Who?" Jayce trembled.

"Your husband. That's who was on the phone, right?"

"Yeah, how did you—"

"What did he say?" I barked.

"He knows I'm cheating on him. He said he memorized your tags from when you dropped me off at home. He made it clear that if I don't come home tonight, he's going to take my daughter from me."

The need to kill intensified. I had no words. Mentally, I was on a rant. Physically, I couldn't find the strength to speak. There was so much to explain, mad shit to tell, but I couldn't find the words.

"Nazari, tell me what's going on. Keeping it to yourself is selfish. That's what you told me, right? I'm already hurting, don't hurt me even more."

That was it.

The red and black streaks began to fade. I was able to see clearly and knew exactly what I needed to do. If I couldn't tell Jayce what I was feeling, I had to show her. Wondering if this thing between us was real wasn't a thought that could've been based on our chemistry anymore. She needed to know the truth. She needed to know the story behind the man.

JACELYN

I SAT NERVOUSLY, TRYING to figure out how I became so comfortable with destroying my life. Everything good I'd ever know was being threatened and, instead of going to my Nunu's house, grabbing Rhea, and running away, I was sitting in a parking lot of a park with the man who was the cause of my head and heart ache.

"Nazari," I whispered.

His focus was glued to the swing set that it seemed like he purposefully parked in front of. Without touching him, I could see how tense he was. His jaw line was well defined, and the veins were apparent in his clenched hands. Nazari was hurting.

"Nazari, please talk to me."

I reached over, grabbing a hold of his beard. Tugging gently, I directed his face towards mine. Our gazes met. His normally dark eyes seemed darker than normal. A lot darker with a misty tint.

"Na—" My throat tightened, muting me instantly.

"You ever pull up to a spot where something fucked up happened to you?"

I nodded, making note of his mellow deepened tenor.

"That's what this place means to me. I used to think the day the bitch who birthed me left and never came back was the worst day of my life. It wasn't. That shit hurt, but it had nothing on the hurt I felt at ten when I saw her pushing a little boy who was about two years younger than me. That shit was like being stabbed a thousand times over in the heart. From that day forward, I believed love wasn't nothing but a way to torment a muthafucka. It reels you in by making you think the person you love will love and protect you forever. Put you above their own selfish needs. You know, be selfless with you. Once you believe that and get comfortable, it's swept from underneath you. Unfortunately, for me, I learned that lesson at a young age."

Listening to how Nazari spoke so disgustingly about love crumbled my heart. What he experienced as a kid not only jaded him but tainted his heart.

"Fucked up part is when I got about high school age, I did my homework on her and her bitch ass son. He was her perfect little boy. I guess that's why she chose to be his mother and not mine. He was perfect and I was damaged."

"That's not true."

"How would you know? 'Cause I took you on a date and made you feel special? Yeah, I did that 'cause I like you. I might even love you, if I knew what that shit felt like. But I did all that to keep you from asking about me. Up until this point, I've told you only surface-level shit."

"That's not true."

And it wasn't. The night of Mitch's party, we had a moment.

"It is. I told you about my family and how I see Cree as my son, but you don't know why."

"Because his dad died."

"Right but who killed him?" Nazari scoffed.

"I don't know."

"Ask me."

"Why does it matter—"

"Ask me!" The low growl when his voice erupted gave him exactly what he wanted.

"Who killed him?"

"Me."

Since our conversation started, Nazari had been looking at me, but it felt like he was looking past me. His orbs saw right through me as if I was made of glass. That feeling was gone. I was now solid, a firm piece of wood, and Nazari's shadowy glare was the match waiting to set me ablaze.

"Oh."

The tightness of my stomach hallowed my breathing.

"See, that's the shit you don't know, the shit you don't want to know. That hood nigga you thought I was is exactly who I am. I fuck bitches 'cause I'm scared of love. Scared because I watched my Pops nearly die from drowning his heartache in alcohol. Became the hood's clean-up man 'cause I had to provide when my Pops was too fucked up to do so. I let the darkness motivate me into pulling the trigger repeatedly. Ain't shit lovable about me, Jayce. Love don't exist in my world. Any time I might feel that shit sneaking up on me, some shit happens to remind me, a nigga like me isn't built for love."

Never had I heard a heart cry. It was without sound. A heart crying wasn't something meant to hear, it was to be felt. Nazari was pouring his inner most thoughts out to me and leaving a lasting impression.

Swing after swing, my gut was bombarded with blows. My insides churned listening to the hand Nazari was dealt. Where love should've flourished, fear and pain thrived.

Fear of being broken.

Fear of being unlovable.

Fear of needing anyone.

Fear of loving.

It was all Nazari knew, so he found comfort. In the name of survival, he did unforgivable things. I didn't condone them, but I understood... a little too well.

"You better off finding another nigga who can be the nigga you need. Not ya husband tho but someone else. That nigga don't deserve you."

"You're not the only one who's done something they're not proud of Nazari."

"This ain't about shit I'm not proud of Jacelyn—"

"It is!" I blurted. "I get it. You think you don't deserve things because of how life chose to handle you, but you do. If I can find someone to love me after... I... I—"

Getting choked up, I turned away from Nazari and covered my face with my hands, tears streaming my cheeks. Inhaling so deep, air filled my throat. I exhaled and wiped my eyes. I still wasn't able to look at Nazari, but that was fine; he couldn't look at me either.

"A year or so after Aidan and I got married, I got pregnant. At first, I wasn't happy. I was young and focused on school. Plus, my husband had this thing about me having kids and being a stay-at-home mom. Anyway, it took me a while to get used to the thought of having a child. I never fully came to grips with it, but I was accepting. At the time, I was working as a nurse extern in the emergency room. One of the patients became irate when I went to draw blood. He ended up swinging his arm, hitting me in my stomach and knocking me to the floor."

Sniffling, I stopped talking as the emotions came flooding back. Images of what happened nearly a decade ago were still fresh in my mind. It all played out whenever I closed my eyes.

"That's not your fault tho."

His voice was so soothing, I almost smiled in the midst of crying.

"I begged to draw his blood. I saw how he was acting when he came in. I knew better, but I wanted to do it anyway. I messed up earlier in my shift and wanted to prove myself. My child died because I wanted to make myself feel better. For a while, I told myself I didn't want any kids out of fear of the same thing happening again. Then, I had Rhea, and everything changed. Life may have caused you to believe you don't deserve something when, really, it might not be your time to receive it."

"You really believe that?" he asked.

The hopefulness not only in his words, but in his eyes and in his voice, was adorable.

"Yes. I lost my first child because it wasn't my time. You haven't felt loved because no one has been deserving of experiencing yours. The right one will make you feel foolish for doubting love. Trust me."

"I do," he answered. The engine to the car roared, silencing our conversation and starting anew.

"Where are we going?"

"Home. I owe you dick. I gotta pay up 'fore you dip off leaving a glass slipper behind."

We chuckled, and all the heaviness we both felt disappeared. As Nazari pulled off, I connected my phone to the Bluetooth, creating yet another vibe.

NAZARI

Had I not been trying to be a gentleman, I would've fucked Jacelyn the best I could in the front seat of my car. All that shit she said and the way she received my emotions without judgement kept my dick hard. The moment didn't call for a woody, but the way she opened up to me did. Pain tugged at her voice as she talked, vulnerability masking the strength she usually spoke with. In that moment, I remembered what Pops said about a woman trusting a man.

A woman who can see beneath the surface of a man will trust him with more than just her heart. Her secrets will become his, her happiness will become his, her vitality will become his, all without him ever having to ask. She'll blossom at the first sign of his love.

What Jacelyn told me about her miscarriage was her way of blossoming. She allowed for her secret to be mine. The intimacy of it was a turn on, and I wanted nothing more than to return the favor. Getting her in the house, I closed the front door behind us. I yanked at the string keeping the dress pinned to her body. Moving back just enough to watch the dress fall, I took in Jacelyn. Like an art connoisseur, I examined the art that was framed by her skin.

Supple breasts, Hershey kiss nipples. Small waist, two pack at the top, a satisfied pudge leading into wide hips. Thicker thighs, thick calves, buttery soft skin. The major details of Jacelyn were remarkable, the minor ones were even more impressive.

"Nazari, stop!" Jacelyn blushed hard, making the mistake of trying to cover her body. The little bit of space between us was filled in a moment. Removing both of her arms from across her breasts, I seared her lips.

"Ya body is perfect. If I'm gawking, then I'm mesmerizing and appreciating. Never stop me from appreciating what I feel was blessed for me specifically."

I lifted her off her feet, silencing whatever she might've said with a kiss. With her in my arms, I slipped off my loafers and carried her into my bedroom. I walked over to the bed and went to place her down, but she stopped me.

"Eat me under the moonlight."

Her haze-induced stare told me her request wasn't to be denied. I obliged, walking her to the large window. Backing her into it with my chest, I tore her panties off and kicked her legs open. Bowing down before the queen, I clinched her thighs, teasing the inside with my tongue.

"Nazari," she shuddered.

Inhaling deep, I felt victim to her, the scent of her pussy. I brought my tongue to her fold, licking from the clit to the ass. I devoured her, eating her pussy like it was the last meal before death.

"Nazari!"

Jacelyn hummed my name, driving me insane. She'd done it before, but this was different. This wasn't just an outburst of pleasure. There was a need. Our hidden feelings were now surface level and coating the tongue. Hers as she sang my name over and over, amplifying the assault on her pussy. And mine, buried between her legs leaving no crevice untouched. I feasted. Her heavy pants, fingers tracing the parts of my braids, essence coating my lips, I indulged on Jayce, fighting the urge to bend her over and fuck her deep. The sexual tension and anticipation pained my throbbing dick.

The sight of her hardened me.

The taste of her bricked me.

Anything else would've had my dick shattering like glass.

"Nazari, I want dick," she pouted, eyes cascading down as mine lingered upward.

Poking out her bottom lip, she forced my head from between her legs, replacing my tongue with her fingers. I stood up, admiring how pretty she and her pussy was. Slippery and wet, she slowly began grinding against her fingers, putting on a show.

"Don't you wanna fuck me? You promised to fuck me, Nazari. Fuck me," she begged.

Fuck!

Going against what Jacelyn wanted was unlikely. The perfect pout of her lips, the sway of her hips, supple titties, nipples being clasped between her fingers, pussy lips glistening, all of it was so perfectly aligned, saying *no* was far worse than a death sentence. In Jacelyn's presence, I was worse than putty. I was a puppet, and her pleasure was the master.

I stripped my clothes from my body, taking Jacelyn's hand from her sweet pussy and placing it on my dick. She squeezed, massaging the girthy ten inches.

"Damn!" Jacelyn breathed.

She let my dick fall from her hands and sauntered over to the bed. I followed. Lowering myself on top of her, I stroked at her entrance, tipping the head in, then tipping it out.

"Fuck!" we hissed in unison.

I tipped in again and tipped out. A chill swept; eagerness became us. Lifting her legs, Jayce wrapped them around my waist.

I thrusted in.

She locked her legs.

I was home.

I stroked her tenderly, making sure to not slip all the way out. Being outside of Jacelyn was no longer an option. I needed to be inside her; I craved it.

The warmth.

The gush.

The fucking tightness.

Jacelyn's pussy was heaven on earth, a heaven fitted for a king and not the fucking peasant she'd been giving her pussy to.

"Jacelyn!" I demanded, bringing my hand to her throat.

Her lashes fluttered before giving me access to those beautiful brown eyes. For a second, I got lost in them. Completely forgetting what I had to say. I focused on the future I saw, the future I fucking wanted. The fucking future I deserved.

"Jacelyn, I lo—"

Silencing my confession, I leaned forward, taking her nipples into my mouth. Each one I licked, sucked, nibbled until her back arched. I fell deeper inside her.

"Ouuuuu fuck, Nazari!" she gasped, feeling all of me.

I toyed at her breasts, licking and sucking until I felt her walls clamp around me.

"Fuck, this pussy the best," I groaned, then remembered exactly what I had to say.

Taking her legs into the folds of my arms, I bent them back until her knees were touching her ears. That fuck Jayce had been looking for, I gave her. I pumped vigorously, making sure she felt all of me.

"Ouuuuu, Nazari, right there! Keep fucking me just like that! Ouuuuu, just like that!" she encouraged, thrusting towards me the best she could.

Her grip on my dick tightened as her cries turned into screams. Feeling her walls contract, I pulled out, leaving in the tip. Her eyes flew open, a deranged expression contouring her face.

"What?"

"What?" she challenged, visibly pissed. "Nazari, I was about to cum, why would you—"

"I need you to promise me something."

"You want me to... mhmm."

Inch by inch, I dipped back into her, taking my time, swirling my hips so I hit every angle of her pussy... our pussy. I leaned forward, pecking her lips as I told her what the promise was.

"I need you to promise to keep this pussy between me and you."

Eyes fluttering and a slight smile, Jacelyn gazed up at me, falling in rhythm and fucking me back.

"You're so fucking gorgeous Jayce. I need you to make me that promise," I told her, holding back my own need to cry out in pleasure.

"Nazari, I'm—"

"I don't give a fuck 'bout that nigga, girl. All I care about is ya heart and this pussy. I already know your heart belongs to me. Say the same 'bout this pussy Jayce. Tell me it's ours," I begged, not giving a fuck how much of a bitch I might've sounded.

"It yours," she answered.

"What's mine?"

Working her pussy, I caressed her deep. Her shrills vibrating against me.

"This pussy," she affirmed, but that wasn't what I wanted to hear.

"I preciate the ownership, but this ain't about me. When I'm in you, it's not done selfishly. I'm in you 'cause my dick belongs here. You hear me, Jayce, my dick belongs—"

"Here!" she cried out, finishing my sentence. Her pussy pulled taut, securing its hold.

"Ight then," I groaned. "A home ain't shit if just one muthafucka livin' in it. So, this pussy ain't just mine, it's ours. Now, tell me who the pussy belongs to."

"Us. It's ours," she declared breathlessly.

"Good girl, now come ride this dick."

Wrapping Jayce's arms around my neck, I flipped her pretty ass over. Jayce sat up, hands pressed firmly against my chest and started bouncing. I leaned up, freeing her curls from her bun, laid back enjoying the show and how good her pussy felt.

To keep from nutting, I closed my eyes, blocking out how perfect Jacelyn looked riding my dick. The feel of her heated hands left my chest, and her ass slapping against my stomach stopped.

"Nazari! Look me in my eyes, so you can see how this dick makes me act!"

Unable to deny her, I opened my eyes. Slowly, she rocked her hips. Her left clung to my neck as her right gripped at my thigh. Steadying herself, Jacelyn found her groove. Effortlessly, she fucked me, and I loved every minute of it. The way her face became distorted in pleasure overtook me. I couldn't hold back anymore. Taking a hold of her hips, I guided her, weaving her body back and forth like the waves of the ocean.

"Cum on this dick gorgeous. You're almost there, I can feel it. Ouuuuu shit, I like that. I like when you squeeze like that. Fuck!"

Her walls throbbed.

"I'm gonna cum Nazari," she whined, squeezing tighter at my neck.

"Let that shit go," I demand. Grabbing a hold of her waist, I plunged up each time she thrusted down.

One.

Two.

Three.

Three was all it took for her love to come raining down my dick. She leaned forward, forehead sweating and heavy breathing. Holding her tight, I began to slow grind, oozing a nut of my own into the depths of her pussy, silently praying it made a little me.

JACELYN

Squeezing my eyes shut, I fought to fall back to sleep. To spend just a few more hours in the arms of a man who I would've defined as imperfect perfection. Nazari had flaws. We all did but his were a little rougher than most. He was a little banged up thanks to his past but, underneath all the scuff marks, there was a man who knew what he wanted and, despite being afraid, was man enough to go after it. Attentively, he listened. Compassionately, he handled me, allowing me to take the lead but asserting his dominance when needed. Protectively, he assured me that with him, no harm would come my way. Even when his little thot box tried to start shit, he shut it down in an outrageous manner but still protectively. It felt good to be around a man who kept his word, but this wasn't my life. In the real world, I was a mother, a wife, a nurse and maybe a divorcee. I had real life problems that lying up with Nazari weren't going to fix but only make worst.

It was fun while it lasted.

Glancing at Nazari, I smiled. He was sleeping with a grin pointed in my direction. He seemed so peaceful. I leaned forward, kissing along the tattoos on his chest. I took my time knowing this would be the last time. I trailed up his neck, softly lining his jaw, then brought my lips to his.

"I wish it was you. All of it. My husband, Rhea's father, all of it," I spoke against his lips.

Slowly, I pulled away with the intention to sneak out and never see Nazari again. As I swung my legs off the bed, the feel of a strong arm clinching my waist pulled me back.

"Nazari, stop," I giggled. Still holding on, Nazari ran his fingers along my neck, tickling the hell out of me. "You have to stop! Nazari stop! Stop! I can't breathe! Nazari!"

"Try to run out on me like I'm some lame nigga you used for dick and won't be no stopping. Wassup with you?"

The tickling ended, and I was able to finally catch my breath. I took my time before answering Nazari.

"Jacelyn."

Shaking my head, I said nothing. Nazari sucked his teeth and pulled me on to his lap, positioning me so I was straddling and facing him. He leaned back on his headboard, keeping his eyes on me. He glowered at me but said nothing.

"I wasn't trying to hurt your feelings—"

"Who said that's what you did?"

"I can see it Nazari."

"If you can see it, then you could've guessed doing it would've bothered me. Right?" he asked sternly, narrowing his gaze.

"Yeah," I whispered.

"Then, why do it all?"

"I have to get back to my life Nazari. I can't stay here playing pretend with you, no matter how much I want to." I inhaled heavily, knowing what I was going to say next would paint me as a coward. "Leaving is easier than having to say goodbye."

Right as I said it, I watched Nazari's face turn sour.

"I didn't mean it like that. I swear I didn't."

Had I been thinking about Nazari instead of myself, I would've realized how much up and leaving would've bothered him. His hands moved to my waist and, for a second, he lifted me like he was about to toss my ass to the side. It took him a little moment, but he placed me back down and put his hands in mine. His thumbs rubbed the back of my hands, soothing the thumping of my chest.

"I'm trying to do better, you know. Fight for what I want. I want you, Jacelyn. I know that shit comes with a lot, but I can handle it. All I need is for you to let me."

"That's sweet and I wish things were different, but my husband is threatening to take my daughter. If this was just about me, I would blow my life into a million pieces and take a chance on us. But you can't ask me to blow up my life, as well as Rhea's. She doesn't deserve that."

Looking at Nazari in this moment was similar to watching a glass fall from its cabinet and crash against the tiled kitchen floor. Tipping in slow motion, the glass falls. As a reaction, you try to catch it... to secure it. The glass slips from your fingers just as you think you saved it and shatters. Pieces you can and can't see scatter around the floor. In an attempt to not cut yourself, you try to sweep up the mess but, of course, you can't get them all, making the glass impossible to piece back together. The glass was Nazari's heart shattering repeatedly as I denied what we both needed.

"I'm not asking you to blow up nothing I won't fight to piece back together. Rhea is gon' be straight, I promise."

"How do you know?"

"I just know."

Closing my eyes, I shook my head, annoyed that I was even contemplating being with Nazari.

"What if I said you don't have to answer me now? I'll give you some space for you to figure things out, then I'll come get you."

"How much time?"

"However much you need. We gon' figure this out."

I parted my lips, feeling like my heart would leap straight into this man's hands. My whole being tingled with urge to agree.

"I know I have no place in saying this about your daughter, but it's something I learned."

"What is it?"

"A child only gets one childhood. Whatever they experience during this time affects how they interpret the world, love, and trust."

"And this is why I can't—"

"Let me finish. Their experiences include how you maneuver during their younger years. Were you happy, loved, hurt, angry? All children can sense the emotions of a parent, no matter how hard you might try to hide it. I'm a child whose life was blown up. I know what that type of shit can do. I would never ask you to do anything that would hurt Rhea. She's your first priority, I think that's beautiful, more than anything I respect it."

At this point, tears were dribbling down my cheeks. I couldn't take anymore. I leaned forward, placing my head on Nazari's chest. Sniffling, I inhaled the perfect mixture of his natural musk and vanilla, and bourbon. His scent was so damn calming, everything about him was. Nazari brought his thumb to my eyes and wiped away the tears until they stopped. Along with it, he unknowingly wiped away my hesitation.

"Fine. Give me time to figure things out and, then, we can... what would we even—"

I never got a chance to question what we would be. With his body, Nazari spoke to mine. Our tongues dancing. My thighs parted and Nazari fell between my legs, applying pressure at my entrance.

"Ouuuuu," I hissed.

"You're my home and I plan on being your heart. Might fuck around and become the best parts of you," he answered my unasked question.

"As long as I can be the best parts of you."

"You already are."

NAZARI

A Week Later...

"Why every time I see you, you're smiling now? Who are you and what did you do with my brother?"

Coming from behind me, Sariah leaned over my shoulder trying to peek at my phone. I moved it out of her sight, then placed it face down on the counter.

"Man, mind ya business," I told her while laughing.

"I can't, when my big brother is in love."

"Move with that."

I waved Sariah off and started back prepping the packages I had some of my clients picking up today.

"You can try and hide it all you want but I know love when I see it."

I let her words sink in, then shook my head. I wasn't in doubt about my feelings for Jacelyn 'cause they were undeniable. Shit just felt easier, lighter with her around. She was smart, gorgeous, had good pussy and knew how to vibe and laugh at the little shit in life. There wasn't much to not like 'bout Jayce, but calling it love was a bit much.

"How can it be love when she's married to Aidan?"

"What that mean? Love is beautiful, but that doesn't mean it'll be easy. Love is hard and takes effort and fight."

"I get that, but does this shit gotta be so messy?"

Sariah shrugged. "Everyone's love story is different. Yours just so happens to be messy."

"Shit is crazy," I said truthfully.

Those two days with Jayce was some of the most fun I had in a minute. It felt right, a little too right at times but right, nonetheless. Catching her trying to leave fucked me up a little bit. But it was nothing for me to realize she was acting out of fear and not on her feelings for me. After we both agreed she needed space to figure her shit out, I took her to Pops' house for dinner since I still had a few more hours in our forty-eight. The whole time, I sat off to the side watching her interact with my family. Her and Pops kicked it like they were old friends from back in the day. She kept up with all Pops' sports talk, surprising the hell out of me.

Her and Sariah's bonding started off a little rocky. Sariah was playing the protective sister role, and Jayce wasn't going for it. She assured Sariah she had nothing but good intentions for me. After that, whatever snappy shit Sariah sent Jayce's way, Jayce was sending back. Standing on business when it came to me looked good on my baby. Too fucking good 'cause I almost took her ass up to one of them rooms and paid a visit to what I now considered home.

The one interaction that shocked me the most was Cree's. My lil man stepped to Jayce on some mack shit. He was throwing out his best game, talking about Jayce can play the PS5 in his room if she wants.

Cree didn't let no one touch that shit outside of me. I lowkey felt a way but a real nigga never cock blocked. I let him do his thing and just enjoyed the sight of what it looked like to have Jayce in my world.

"What's crazy is you still haven't found out if Rhea is yours or told Jayce about your contacts or who Aidan is to you."

"In due time. I'm handling the Rhea situation today. Everything else will line up when I get them results back."

"Well, you know I have a friend who can rush the results."

"Already a step ahead of you. I gotta drop off the sample later today."

"Nigga, don't be in contact with my friends," she laughed. "It seems like you have everything under control."

"Something like that."

"Have you talked to Tara? Probably not since your hair look like that. She been going off on the bird app, throwing shots and shit."

"Nah, but that's on my agenda for today too."

"I can braid you up if you want. I know you don't like the messy braid look."

"I'm good. You think you can stay here to see these packages off?" I asked, looking at the time on my phone.

"I have to pick up Cree."

"I got him."

"Okay. Make sure you bring him home at a decent time tonight please. I know you like to treat him like he's one of your niggas, but he's not."

"He's the homie for sure," I laughed.

Sariah and I finished getting all the packages together; then, I walked her through the pickup process. After, I grabbed her lunch, then dipped to go see Tara and get this shit over with.

"Aye Tara, open the door!"

After knocking politely on Tara's door a few times and having to deal with her nosey ass neighbors, I got ignorant and started banging on that muthafucka. Shawty was playing games I didn't have time for. From here, I had to scoop Cree and handle the DNA situation.

"I can hear the TV Tara, open the fucking door!"

This time, I kicked the door, hoping it knocked the bitch off track, but I was blessed with something better. A key fell from the top of the threshold and landed at my feet. I picked it up and stuck it into the lock, letting myself into the apartment.

"Oh shit!"

The whiff of the stench was strong as fuck. I tugged at the front of my hoodie, bringing it over my nose and mouth. The apartment smelled like rotten pussy and sour milk. It didn't look any better either. Food containers were thrown around the living room and kitchen. Unidentifiable liquid clung to her floors, leaving patches against the tiles. Empty liquor bottles were tipped over the counter daring funk to blow by just enough for the glass to decorate the floor.

Had I not known the type of woman Tara was, I would've wrote her ass off as a dirty bitch. Tara was clean and, with her doing hair out of her crib, it was mandatory for her to keep her spot hygienic. This shit tho was crazy and anyone coming in here to get braided up had to be begging for pussy.

"Tara!" Her name came out muffled as fuck with my hoodie still over my nose. Figuring she didn't hear me, I walked towards the back of her house to her room.

"Aye, Tara, get up."

Grabbing the blanket from around her, the breeze from the blanket flapping in the air whiffed in my direction, fucking my stomach up even more. Shit smelled worse than the rest of the house.

"Tara, get ya funky ass up!" I shook her until her eyes popped open. Crazily, she stared at me and blinked a few times.

"Nazari?" she whimpered.

"Yeah man. Get up, we need to talk but move slow. Another whiff of whatever I smelled on ya blanket gon' have your carpet drenched in vomit."

"What?" She frowned, offended.

Shit was the truth. Her funky ass blanket fucked my stomach up. Throw up was basically moonwalking on my esophagus.

"Fix your face. My house is a little dirty, but it's not as dirty as you—"

Midsentence, I threw her blanket at her. She shrilled, damn near falling off her bed and proving my point.

"Fuck a little dirty, ya place is fucked up. You good?"

Regardless of what I came here to do, I wasn't 'bout to ignore a cry for help. So many ignored Pops when he was down and letting the crib look just like this. Whatever Tara was going through had to be worse than what Pops was dealt. A heartbreak couldn't have had no one going out this fucking sad. Pops washed his ass; Tara couldn't have seen a shower in days with how disheveled she looked. She was dressed in a dingy wife beater covered in food stains, a thong and a single fucking tube sock that was closer to being brown than it was to white.

As she climbed out of the bed, she tried combing her fingers through her hair, but there was nothing her fingers could do for that mess. On a normal day, Tara kept her hair braided in whatever new style she was trying out; today, her shit was mangled, resembling a wasp nest. Her golden brown complexion was stained with ash on her arms and knees and blotches of dried white patches marred her face.

"I'm so embarrassed that you had to see me like this. Why didn't you call!"

"I've been calling you all fucking day."

"Really, what time is it?"

"One."

"Wow! I slept the day away," she laughed when nothing about this situation called for fucking giggles.

"I'ma ask you one more time 'fore I stop giving a fuck. You good?"

"Uh yeah, I'm just a little—"

Frantically, she was nodding her head and twitching. I didn't want to believe Tara was on something but, shit, that made the most sense.

"Tara, you good? Forreal."

"Honestly, Nazari, I'm not. I'm fucking heart broken and I know you don't care, but how could you—"

"Wait, you're in here smelling pissy with your face resembling a cum rag 'cause I'm not fucking with you no more?"

"Yes! Why else would I let my apartment go to shit?"

Oddly, I stared at Tara, waiting for her to burst out laughing just how she'd done before. What she laughed at earlier wasn't funny. This right here was fucking comical. Ain't no way shawty resembled a fucking dumpster diver 'cause she broke her own heart.

"Yo, you serious?"

"Yea, Nazari! Did you not think seeing you with another woman was going to cause me to spiral?"

"Why would I think that?"

"Why? Nigga, are you dumb?" she barked. "I've been the one sucking you, slurping your kids, fucking you, braiding you, accepting your lack of intimacy, getting these other hoes you tried to fuck out of the way so we could be *us*. I've been riding for two years, being the good lil bitch you needed. I've done it all Nazari. No complaints, no arguing no nothing. I played my role... perfectly. Just to watch you rescue the next bitch and listen to you threaten me. That shit hurts Nazari. You said you would blow my head off for her. For fucking her!"

Glancing around the filthy room, I tried to spot a camera or a phone that was recording this Emmy-worthy performance. Tears cradled the brim of her lower lashes. Her arms frantically waving through the musty air her heavy breathing created. Misery plagued her and she was broken, that much was evident. The blame for all the emotion didn't belong where she was desperately trying to place it.

"I'm not tryin' to clown you, Tara, but you can't be forreal. All that you feel should be felt by someone who was in love. From how you speak, how could you love me when I never gave you anything to love? From the day we linked up, I told you sex was all it was. It wasn't even 'posed to be that at first. I hit you to get braids; you pushed up on me wanting to fuck."

"You didn't deny me."

I laughed humorlessly. "I didn't cause pussy is pussy. You gon' make me hurt your feelings. I'm trying to keep shit cool with us."

"We could never be cool after what you did to me!"

"Fuck it, we're not cool, let me stop tiptoeing around your feelings then. As adults, we both consented to fucking. I can count how many times I took you out and spent time away from your bedroom on two fucking hands Tara. Like you said, you sucked, slurped, fucked and braided. That's it. If that's what you fell in love with, then you need to change your views. On two separate occasions, I told you I was done with the casual sex. You thought saying you're okay with being the side chick was cute. Thought it was gon' get you some brownie points when all it did was get your feelings hurt."

"Okay but why couldn't you make me into the woman you wanted?" Her voice cracked as she asked that pitiful ass question.

Listening to Tara was almost identical to listening to Pops. Both wanted to be the one awarded with affection from their mate, ignoring that there never was love to build on. A relationship was only as strong as the foundation.

"I can't *make* anyone into nothing. You don't make yourself fall in love Tara. That shit just happens."

"And you learned all of that out the fucking blue?" she smacked.

"I did. Love wasn't nothing I saw myself being blessed with. I still don't know if I'll be in it. That's not for me to decide or try to dictate. All I can say is you shouldn't be hurt behind me wanting better for myself. You should want the same for you."

"Better!" She frowned, ignoring all the gems I laid out for her. "You think that married bitch is better than me? I bet your goofy ass didn't even do your due diligence. That hoe been married way before she had her daughter. Yet, you out here claiming her little girl. Baby probably isn't even yours. She looks nothing you."

Everything Tara said was supposed to sting, cause me to act irate and choke her stupid ass unconscious. I took a step towards her and she flinched, confirming my suspicions.

"You got it Tara," I smirked. "Blame me for how you choose to handle things and try to manipulate the situation. Running hoes off was never going to work. I let it slide 'cause the pussy was good. That's all it was Tara, good pussy and talented hands. Get yourself together, ight. There's a nigga out there who's gon' love you for all you have to offer. Find that nigga and go be happy."

Saying all I had to say, I was ready to get the fuck up out of here. I turned towards the door, then felt a tug at the back of my hoodie.

"Nazari, no.... I...I... I love—"

"You don't love 'cause there's nothing here to love. I'm sorry for whatever hurt I caused by not paying more attention to how the rules changed. That's on me, how you choose to behave as a result of your emotions is on you. How I react to your behavior is also on you."

I let my words sink in and took a step. No longer feeling her hold on my hoodie, I dipped from her apartment. At the start of the conversation, I felt bad for Tara. I could've left her alone once I noticed the shift. I ignored it, thinking there would never be anyone else I cared about enough to cut Tara off. God laughed at those plans and brought me a woman I never knew I needed. Jacelyn was home.

JACELYN

"I'M FEELING VERY UNLOVED with how I haven't heard from you since you went on that lil two-day—"

"Not so loud!"

Hushing Dionne, I grabbed a hold of her arm, pulled her over to the side, and glanced over my shoulder.

"Why you acting like the Feds are after you?" she laughed.

I gave her a little chuckle, but what I was going through felt exactly like that. "Aidan has literally been up my ass since I went back home after my little getaway with Nazari."

"Is that why he's been picking Rhea up all week?"

"Yes! He drags me along if I don't have to work and tells me to sit tight in the car."

"And you listen?" Dionne frowned.

"It's not about listening. I'm trying to buy time until I can figure out my next move. I haven't even told you the half: when I was out with Nazari, some cops pulled us over. One took Nazari out of the car and the other handed me a phone."

"What?"

"Girl," I smacked, making sure not to be too loud since we were in the school. Thankfully, Aidan had to run into work for an emergency and couldn't tag along to get Rhea.

"Tell me why it was Aidan on the phone cursing me out, yelling about how he knew I was cheating and that if I wasn't home by the time he got there on Sunday, he was going to take Rhea from me."

"Get the hell out of here." Her focus darted to Rhea, who was at the opposite of end of the classroom playing with Cree. They were the last two kids in the class so, instead of grabbing Rhea to leave, I let her chill until Cree was picked up.

"Yup. He straight blacked on me. Then, when he finally made it home, he had no words. Said absolutely nothing then acted like everything was all good the next morning."

"You sure his momma never had him checked? He seem a little throwed off."

"If she did, I wouldn't know and I don't care. I have other things to worry about."

My eyes lingered over to Cree and my heart swelled. The little boy reminded me so much of Nazari, especially with how he treated Rhea. In the few minutes that I'd been here, I was able to see just how protective Cree was when it came to Rhea. I didn't know if it was a conscious thing or not seeing how Cree was so young but, whenever Rhea moved around the classroom, Cree moved. If she tried to grab something and struggled, then Cree made sure he got whatever Rhea wanted. It was cute, too damn cute.

"Mhmm," Dionne smirked. "So, what's the verdict with Nazari?"

The thought of Nazari alone was enough to make me blush. So, to hear his name, my nerves tickled with excitement.

"Ohhh bit... I almost forgot we're in a school setting. Heffa, don't tell me you done went and fell in love after two days with the man."

"It's not love. I like him though. I like how he handles me. He doesn't ignore the stuff I say that most dudes would probably ignore and, when I think he's ignoring me, he's actually listening. I don't know Dionne. Maybe I'm caught up in what he does because I'm used to the opposite with Aidan. What I like might not even be a big deal forreal."

"Did you tell him about how Aidan treats you?"

"I didn't go into detail. I left things vague."

"Okay, so whatever Nazari is showing you is because that's who he is at his core."

"But, how, when he's never dated anyone forreal?"

"Girl please," Dionne chortled, waving me off. "All these men will say they've never dated or took any woman seriously. As true as it might be, that has nothing to do with what they feel. Mitch told me something similar. He's dated but never went out of his way to try and make a woman feel cared for. She either did or she didn't were his exact words."

I frowned, thinking how entitled some of these men were.

"Exactly," she said about my expression. "But I bet you I receive a morning and night text whenever I don't wake up in his bed. Mitch puts in the effort with me because one, I demand it and, two, he wants to. A man will do all types of things for who they want to do it for. Nazari might be on a learning curve, but I can almost guarantee he wants nothing more than to master the art of Jacelyn Smyth. That's all relationships are, mastering your person and fighting to constantly learn and understand all that they are."

"You're right," I agreed.

"I know. Stop trying to control which way your heart swings. What happened with you and Nazari happened for a reason."

I nodded, fully understanding where she was coming from.

"Alright, Cree, I'm going to call your mother and see where she is. Give me a second."

"Okay."

Dionne walked out of the classroom, and I grabbed my phone from my purse. Unlocking it, I bypassed the missed calls from Aidan and went to my text messages. Starting a new thread, I typed *N* and Nazari's number popped up. Nazari refused to let me leave his father's house without saving his number in my phone. I tried to fight it, scared Aidan would go through my phone. Aidan did check my phone a few times when he thought I wasn't paying attention, but there was nothing for him to find.

Nazari took me needing space too literally. He completely left me alone and created an unhealthy quirk. Anytime my phone chimed or vibrated, my breathing became immured in my chest, pulse racing until I checked if it was him. Each chime or vibration ended in disappointment. Nazari was all I wanted, but how could I be mad when he was giving me what I asked for? The urge to reach out to him haunted me but, today, that urge was going to be satisfied.

Heyy.

I gawked at the screen, impatiently waiting for the text bubble to turn into actual words.

N: Wassup beautiful, you look good asf. Must've known you was gon' see ya man.

I smiled at his message in utter confusion.

What?

N: Turn ya pretty ass around and come see me

His message wasn't even fully read in my mind, as I spun on the heels of my New Balances. Standing there and peeking through the small window, Nazari licked his lips and motioned for me to come to him.

"Rhea, I'll be right outside the door, okay?"

"Yes mommy," she sang, never looking my way.

"She's safe with me, Jayce," Cree chimed.

I all but cried at Cree's chivalry. Holding my composure, I walked out of the classroom and leaned against the door. Pulse racing, heart hammering against my chest. Curling my fingers through the air like he'd done moments before I summoned his body against mine. He didn't disappoint. He took me into his arms with his fragrance lighting a fire within.

"I missed you, Jayce. I need to come home," he growled in my ear.

I shivered, clit pulsing at his request to slide in. "I told you I needed time."

"And I'm trying to respect that. You see I haven't reached out, but it's hard to not miss home when you got these tight ass jeans on."

"Who you wore these for?"

"You."

"How, when you didn't know you was gon' see me?"

"I was hoping I did."

"Good fucking answer."

I smiled briefly, then did what my heart was calling for. Tilting my head, I brushed my lips against his. Kissing him slow, I toyed with him. Pecks in between me sucking the sweet honey taste from his tongue.

"Fuck," he groaned, deepening the kiss.

My eyes fluttered; his hands gripped my ass trying to bring me further into him, but it was impossible.

"Ahem! Y'all do know y'all are in a school, right?"

Dionne clearing her throat took me from my high. Our lips separated, but Nazari wasn't letting me away from his person. We switched our position from chest to chest to my back against his front with one of his arms at my waist and the other around my chest, locking me in place. Dionne beamed in our direction resembling a proud parent.

"Sir, you're late picking up Cree," she said.

"I apologize. I was tying up some loose ends before I come for what's mine." Nazari kissed the side of my neck, tickling me and sending my shoulder upwards.

"Chill, we in a school, you're safe," he whispered to me.

"Mhmm. Well, how are you coming for my girl?" Dionne probed.

"Don't matter, she know how I'm pullin' up."

"Alright now!" she gleamed. "I'll give y'all a minute but make it quick. I have a man of my own. I want to see my man and be hugged up too."

Shifting me away from the door, Nazari still kept me close. He held on to me for dear life as if us being apart would cause him to crumble. Whether it was true or not, I loved that being how it felt. Nothing was better than a man wanting you, even when he didn't need you.

"Where ya ex at?"

"Waiting on me to pick up Rhea, so we can take her to *Launch*."

"He's been chill since being home?"

The way Nazari spoke and chose his words when speaking to me said a lot. They held a kind of possessiveness that I was familiar with it. I could've easily been overthinking things but, something told me if I said anything other than *yes*, Nazari was taking it personally.

"He's been cool. We haven't been talking much, but we play the happy family whenever Rhea is around. Other than that, wherever I go, he goes, outside of me working."

"Do you feel safe?"

"I do."

"Cool. If that nigga gets outta line, let me know."

"I appreciate you wanting to protect me."

"To protect you is a need, not a want. I wanted to ask you something tho."

"What is it?"

"You sure there's no way Rhea could be mine? You said her eye color is a dead giveaway she's your ex's but I just have to ask."

"Why? Does it change how you feel about—"

"Don't start getting in your feelings 'cause either way, I'ma love her like she was mine. I asked 'cause we could do a DNA test and speed up you telling this nigga you want a divorce. He can't take a daughter that's not his."

"She's not yours. Her eyes—"

"Ight. I got it."

Letting me go, Nazari walked into the classroom and, seconds later, he was walking out with Cree.

"Bye Jayce." Cree waved.

"Bye Cree." I matched Cree's smile until my eyes fell on a pair dressed in confliction.

"You aren't going to say bye?" I asked nervously.

"Bye is forever. I plan on seeing you soon, so I'll say see you later." Stillness swept us.

"See you later beautiful," Nazari finally said.

"See you later handsome."

"Jaycee, I already said bye," Cree said, interrupting the moment.

"Yo, you a lil hater. She was calling me handsome, not you," Nazari said.

"Uh huh. I'm handsome."

"Yeah, ight, let's go."

They walked off, and I stayed in the hallway until they were gone. Walking into the classroom, Dionne already had Rhea zipped up and ready to go.

"Come on baby."

The three of us walked out of the school with Dionne making fun of my somber look.

"Fix your face. Soon as you drop you know who, you can be with him anytime you want."

"I don't even know if—"

"I'ma stop you right there, you know and he does too. You might want to hurry up. Nazari doesn't strike me as the type to wait around idly. He makes moves and the way y'all were hugged up, it seems like he's gonna start making moves very soon."

"I got this."

"For Aidan's sake, I hope so." She shrugged. "See you tomorrow Rhea."

"Byee!" Rhea waved, as Dionne walked to her car. "Come on mommy. I wanna see daddy."

"Okay baby."

Getting Rhea buckled into her car seat, I climbed into my car. My phone chimed in the process of me pulling off.

N: We gotta wrap this shit up. Home is where I wanna be. Can't wait much longer.

I read the message and quickly deleted it. Literally as the message swooped off the screen, Aidan's name and picture pulled up. Sighing, I answered the phone, "I'm on my way.

AIDAN KLEIN

BEFORE JACELYN SAID A word, before her breathing was even hearable, I sensed the fucking attitude. Lately, whenever she spoke to me, it was drenched in disgust. Even her saying good morning sounded like *go to hell*. Everything I did within the last week annoyed her, when her hoe ass was the one in the fucking wrong.

"Is the attitude necessary when I'm calling to make sure you still have plans to bring Rhea to the trampoline park?"

"Where else would we go Aidan?"

To fuck on my brother. The thought alone caused me to snarl.

"I don't know Jacelyn, but it seems you love to be anywhere I'm not."

"Please don't start with me, Aidan. Not today," she expressed through clenched teeth, that was probably for the sake of my daughter. "You made your point when you had those cops pull me over and shove a phone in my face. I'm playing the happy wife role. I'm tolerating you being up my ass for the sake of my child. I even went to dinner with your bit... mother. I went to dinner with your mother. Why isn't that enough to get you off my back?"

My sudden control of Jacelyn's life had taken a toll on her. She was frustrated, which I could understand had she not forced my hand. In all the years we'd been married, I'd tried to give Jacelyn the privilege of living her life as she saw fit. Of course, I had demands, but I was flexible when it came to how she implemented them into her daily routine. Unfortunately, all that freedom she'd been blessed with was the reason we were here now.

Jacelyn saw me as a punk; she thought I was chomp and would never put my foot down against her. She saw my tolerance for her as a weakness and chose to part her legs for the first thug willing to bed her. In this situation, Jacelyn had no right to have an attitude. My behavior was the karma of her doing and, as long as she kept getting on her knees to suck *his*, I would toy with her weakness. Threatening to take Rhea away every chance I got until she fell in line. And if she ever wanted to call my bluff, I had a judge on speed dial who would be more than happy to give me full custody for the right price.

"Sweetheart, I can't be on your back if you're willfully laying on it for the next man."

"Kiss my ass Aidan!"

"I would if you—"

"I'll be there in twenty minutes and, when I get there, don't say shit to me!"

A beep signaled she'd ended the call. Leaning my head against my seat, I closed my eyes briefly, then opened them to reach for my phone to call Jacelyn back.

"Let her be."

The sweet gentle voice had been the only thing keeping me calm in the last week. Jacelyn had been infuriating to be around since I had confirmation that she was fucking Nazari. I couldn't stand to be around her. The sight of her was repulsive, yet I held it together for two reasons. One, my mother was close to gathering all she needed to acquire the land and, two, Nazari wasn't taking Jacelyn from me. Call it sibling rivalry. I refused to allow someone so arrogant and haughty to take what was mine. Jacelyn belonged to me in sickness or health, good or bad, in life or death. She was branded with the name Klein. No super thug hoodlum was going to change that.

As a way to keep a balance, I'd been spending more time with Bryn. The little vacation I took for business was spent getting to see what it would be like to live with Bryn and my son, Adrian. The experience was a breath of fresh air. I didn't have to tell Bryn what to do when it came to me. For her, it was natural to cater to her man. Bryn saw my value as a husband and the leader of the household. She treated me like the king I was.

Every night in the past week, I waited until Jacelyn slept to go visit Bryn. She lived fifteen minutes away, making it a quick drive. I would spend the night with the family I created, then bring breakfast home to the family I was obligated to. The back and forth wasn't ideal but, until I warmed Jacelyn up to the idea of Bryn and Adrian living with us, this was just how I had to play it. I was done tiptoeing around Jacelyn's feelings about me having a son. If I could stomach her sleeping with a murderer who I shared a bloodline with, she could stomach me having another family.

"Talk to me, baby." Bryn rubbed her hand across my chest in such a loving and supportive way, I smiled.

"I'm frustrated with the attitude when she's the one who brought us to this point. Had she kept her legs fucking closed, I wouldn't feel so threatened. Nazari isn't a good guy. I'm worried because she's not only jeopardizing Rhea's safety, but yours and Adrian's as well."

"And you're sure she doesn't know that Nazari is your brother? It seems kind of impossible that she—"

"She doesn't know," I gritted, cutting her off.

Her eyes widened and slowly reverted back to size.

"I'm... I'm sorry, I just thought maybe she might've been trying to set you up. I know you care for her, baby, and you have to fulfill certain obligations, but her intentions might not be as novice as you think."

"Nah," I said, shaking my head. "There's no way for her to know. My mom and I don't bring him up and she has no pictures of him around the house."

"Maybe he told her? Why else would she be willing to sacrifice such a great man for a loser?"

"Come here."

Giggling, Bryn brought her face towards mine. I kissed her deep, fondling with her nipples through her button up shirt.

"Ewww!" Adrian spat from the back seat. "Mommy, I need help."

"We have time for that later." Bryn pecked me one last time and went to pull away. I grabbed her by the front of her shirt, reeling her back into me. I wasn't done.

"Okay, that's enough," she laughed. "And Charlotte is calling."

Pecking her one last time, I freed her and answered the phone, "Hello."

"Why am I hearing from your secretary that you've missed three meetings in the past week with prominent clients? Aidan, did I not stress to you enough how important it is for you to keep everyone at the firm happy? Unhappy clients stops the money funnel and if that stops then—"

"Pick what you want me to focus on and stick to it," I blurted, tired of being chastised like a child. "Jacelyn has been with Nazari while I was with Bryn. Since getting back, I've made it my business to keep up with her to limit her down time as a way to keep her from him. I can't focus on her and the firm at the same time."

"Okay, calm down. I see you're under a lot of pressure. Right now, the priority is keeping Jacelyn close. I'll split your clients between some of the other lawyers. In the meantime, allow Jacelyn the room to roam."

"What? Why would I do that?"

"Let her dig her own grave Aidan. We need her land and, with her stepping out on you, she isn't going to just hand it over. The more she spends time with your brother, the eager she'll become to leave. Nazari doesn't strike me as the sharing type. If she wants a divorce, then she has to sign the papers over."

Glancing towards Bryn, she seemed busy in her phone, but I wasn't sure. "I'll be right back," I whispered and stepped out the car. "I don't want a divorce. I'm not making it possible for Nazari to take what's mine."

"Aidan, she's not a shiny toy and y'all are not children. Once we have the land, we don't need her anymore. You'll be free."

"I don't want to be free."

"What about Bryn and Adrian?"

"What about them? They can come live with Jacelyn and me. Rhea would love a sibling."

"Aidan, no woman in her right mind is going to allow you to bring them into a house where another woman lives. Stick to the plan. We'll use divorce and Ashley as a trade for the land if the papers don't come back signed. Then, you can live happily ever after with Bryn. Jacelyn is nothing but a hoe. Bryn should be your focus and who you want to keep happy."

"I know," I sighed.

"Keep your head in the game. We're almost to the finish line."

"Yeah, okay, I gotta go."

"Kiss my—"

Ending the call, I forced a smile on my face as I saw Jacelyn's car pulling into the parking lot. Being a bitch, she glared in my direction and parked closer to the entrance instead of where I was standing. I walked over to her car, opening the back door where Rhea was seated.

"Daddy!"

Slipping her out of the car seat, she clung to me, hugging me tight. Out of this whole situation, Rhea was the greatest thing to come from Jacelyn and me. She was my perfect little princess and filled the void of the child Jacelyn and I lost. Our miscarriage was not to be spoke about by anyone. The mere mention of it put me in a space where temptation was almost too heavy to ward off and giving in would mean senselessly killing Jacelyn the way she killed my child. She swore her actions weren't intentional but, had she listened and kept her ass home, our child would still be alive.

"Why you sad daddy?" Rhea asked sweetly.

I smiled wide, telling her, "I have a surprise for you."

"I love 'prises." She smiled.

"I know."

Closing the door, I held Rhea, waiting for Jacelyn to get out the car. Seeing that she wasn't going anywhere, I walked over and yanked her door open.

"Aidan, will you please—"

"Rhea, tell mommy let's go, so we can jump."

"Let's go mommy! Let's go mommy!"

Jacelyn's face was flustered. Stress and hurt reflected in her teary eyes. She pushed out a smile the same way I had done.

"Alright, baby, here I come."

Staring at me blankly, I guess she thought I was going to leave from the car for her to finish whatever it was she was doing.

"Come on mommy," I encouraged.

Jacelyn rolled her eyes and said, "Dionne, I'll call you back," ending her call. I stepped out of her way, making sure she had room to get out the car and do nothing else.

"Can we go in now?" Rhea asked.

"Yes, baby, come on."

Jacelyn reached for Rhea, but I held her tight.

"We have to go get your surprise first. Okay?"

"Okay daddy. Mommy, daddy got me a 'prise."

"I heard."

Jacelyn was trying her best to keep a happy face but needed to try a little bit harder. The three of us walked across the parking lot towards Bryn's car. I knocked on the window and moved closer to Jacelyn.

"Who's car is—"

"Hey! Jacelyn!"

Bryn got out of the car along with Adrian smiling but, unlike Jacelyn's and mine, her smile seemed authentic.

"Hi," Jacelyn responded dryly.

"Rhea, this is your surprise. I thought you and Adrian could be friends."

"I already have a friend. His name Cree."

Jacelyn snickered. Placing Rhea on her feet, I adjusted her clothes and crotched down in front of her.

"You can have more than one friend sweetheart."

"Okay," she sighed. "Can he come to my party?"

"Oh baby, I don't know if that's—"

"Of course, he can," I answered, trumping whatever bullshit Jacelyn was about to come up with.

"Okay." Rhea walked over to Adrian and grabbed him by the hand. "I'm Rhea."

"Hi Rhea. I'm Adrian."

"Can we go play now?"

"Yes, baby girl."

As we all walked towards the entrance, I noticed Jacelyn lingering behind us. She was taking her time, thumbs moving fast as hell. A part of me felt like the man. I just knew she was dogging my name to Dionne. It felt good to know I'd gotten under her skin, even if it wasn't comparable to how she had got under mine. Still, I wanted her and Bryn to mingle, so I could get a feel of how this house situation would work.

"Jacelyn, you might want to—"

Her head sprang up as I called her name, but all I got was a glimpse of her disgusted expression before my phone ringing caught my attention.

"Y'all go ahead," I spoke out. Jacelyn wasted no time. She grabbed Rhea and walked inside as if Bryn and Adrian weren't with us. The angel Bryn was wouldn't allow her to show out or mistreat Jacelyn in any way. She was a believer in the whole blended family concept. So, she shrugged her shoulders and walked inside. I stood kicking a random pebble as I called the unsaved number back.

"Hello," the woman who answered didn't have a voice I recognized. "Who is this?"

"You don't know me, but my name is Tara and I have information about your wife."

Like the lunch bell ringing signaling that it was time to eat, my ears perked up.

JACELYN

"Mommy, watch me and Adrian!"

I looked towards Rhea displaying the best smile I could muster considering the circumstances. It was enough to appease Rhea who had jumped away with Adrian following behind her. With her out of sight and Aidan wherever the hell he was, I went back to texting Dionne. The amount of audacity Aidan all of a sudden had was astronomical. His little vacation must've provided him with the balls he'd been lacking in this relationship. His behavior was more annoying than anything because who did he think he was and why did he think I was stupid?

Up until this point, I never once would've called Aidan a cheater. The title didn't fit his moniker. He was a family man who put his work before all. There was a time when I questioned Aidan about Bryn, but he swore there was nothing between the two of them. Even then, I didn't truly believe he cheated, but to ignore what was happening here today, would've been me playing blind. What I explained to Dionne, I would never speak out loud because I didn't care enough. If Aidan wanted to play step daddy to hurt me, then so be it. My feelings weren't hurt either way. His little lover wouldn't be getting a rise out of me either. As long as she played her role and didn't speak, I was good.

Dionne: You want me come up there and bust that bitch in her head?

I laughed as I told Dionne there was no need for her to catch a case behind Aidan trying to make me jealous.

"Our kids seem to be having fun."

Bryn came and stood right in front of me, so I couldn't ignore her. I snickered, pressed send on my message, and tucked my phone in the pocket of my jeans.

"Rhea is having fun."

"I'm sorry if me being here is a lot. Aidan was leaving the office at the same time as me and Adrian. He asked did we have plans, then invited us. Had I known my presence would make you comfortable, I would've declined the invitation."

I chuckled at the slight shade. Bryn was a nice nasty type of bitch. She played nice, then said snarky things to see how far she could push you.

"I'm the sorry one. I'm sorry for putting the notion in your head that I actually give a fuck about you."

"Jacelyn, I don't want to start drama. I would love it if our kids could be friends. Great friends even."

"Why?" I frowned.

"Because I... I think it would be good for them. I'm trying to be nice and you're making things difficult."

Bryn hadn't been in my line of sight since she came and stepped her goofy ass in front of me. Now, she had my full attention. The desperation in her voice was telling. Her eyes were fleeting and wet, almost as if they were frightened to look into mine. Then, it was the way her thumbs kept pushing on the back of her fingers as a way to crack her knuckles. Something was there.

"Bryn, if you have something to tell me, then tell me."

"I don't have anything to say."

"Obviously, you do."

"I—"

"What is going on over here?"

Right on time to save his bitch.

Aidan stepped into our space. He loomed behind me, hand on the small of my back.

"Bryn was about to tell me something that's been eating at her. Isn't that right Bryn?"

I couldn't see Aidan, but I didn't have to. His hand on my back went from being feather touch to stiff. My woman's intuition was gnawing at my stomach, but my wife's intuition was screaming for me to not only punch this hoe in the face but to kick Aidan in the balls he recently grew.

"Sooo," I sang out.

"I don't know what Bryn had to say but I would love to hear it," Aidan said.

"Oh, I was just going to say—"

"Daddy!" Rhea's crying was the only thing that could end this conversation, and the heavy breath Bryn thought no one caught proved she was happy that it did.

"What happened Rhea?"

Bypassing me, Rhea ran straight to her father.

"What happened sweetheart?"

"A boy pushed me. I was talking to Cree and, then, somebody pushed me."

"Cree? Who is Cree?" Aidan asked me.

"Friend at school, remember," I answered.

"Cree said he beat the boy up," Rhea continued.

"Sweetheart, you know how I feel about fighting," Aidan said.

"But, he pushed me."

"I know but, sometimes, it's best to move out the way. Just jump elsewhere next time."

If looks could kill, Aidan would've been slumped the moment he told my daughter that bullshit.

"Rhea, if he pushes you again, then push him back and, if that doesn't work, come get me and I'll handle it."

"Okay mommy."

"Jacelyn," Aidan sighed.

I ignored him and grabbed Rhea. Wiping her face, I told her to use her hands how Gramps taught her. She laughed a little and took off running.

"I think I'm going to take Adrian home. It's been a long day," randomly, Bryn spoke as if what she did mattered.

"I'll walk you out," Aidan said, finally letting go of my waist.

"Okay." I shrugged.

"It was nice seeing you again. Adrian, say goodbye to Ms. Jacelyn."

"Bye." He waved politely.

"Bye." I waved.

"I'll be right back."

Aidan leaned over, gave me a kiss and took the hand of Adrian. Watching the three of them leave, an uneasy feeling began to build in my stomach. Adrian didn't have the eyes of Aidan, but I would be stupid to ignore the resemblance. When I turned away, I checked to make sure Rhea was okay and took my phone out of my pocket.

Do you think Aidan would have an outside baby on me?

I sent the question to Dionne, even though I already kind of knew the answer. Doubt wanted to creep in to give me a peace of mind, but there was no use. I knew the truth. Before speaking to Aidan, I needed to know the whole truth.

A numbness sprang from my palm as my phone vibrated. Peering at the screen, I smiled, answering without a second thought, "Hello."

"Aye, why you let ya husband tell Rhea that bullshit 'bout moving out the way?"

Even when irritated, Nazari's tone was so damn soothing. The gnawing feeling in my stomach was now rapid flutters, fluttering upward towards my chest.

"How did you hear that? Where are you? Rhea said Cree wanted to fight the boy, but I thought she was making things up. Are you here?"

"Don't worry 'bout where I am. Hol' up Jayce, give me a second. Aye, next time you push my daughter like that, I'ma fuck you up."

"That's what you paid me to do," a child complained.

"I said a love tap, not a shove. Where ya pops, so I can tell him he gotta teach you the difference?"

"I don't have one," the child answered.

"Damn, my bad lil nigga. Here, take this, it won't make up for his absence but, shit, it'll get you a toy."

Holding in my laughter, I shook my head. So many questions came to mind but only one was important enough to ask.

"Why would you pay a kid to push my child?"

"I paid him to push *our* child to see how much of a bitch ya husband was. Gotta make sure I know what I'm up against, in case I gotta take you against your will."

"What?" I laughed.

"Deadass. Jayce, you playing 'bout leaving this nigga. You should've been done that. Cause if he won't raise hell behind *our* daughter, what's he willing to do about you?"

"You're putting a lot of emphasis on *our*."

"I gotta. To love you is to love her and to love her makes Rhea my daughter. We can speak on changing her last name later."

"What?"

"That shit made your heart burst with love huh?" he chuckled. "Do me a favor. Look up to your left."

Following his directions, Nazari stepped into my line of sight, smirking.

"You look good."

"Thank you."

"You know I'm coming for you, right? You and our daughter."

"What happened to giving me time?"

We were so far away, but his presence was still felt.

"You know how I'm comin' Jayce. Be ready when I pull up."

With that, he ended the call, and Nazari walked away with Cree clinging to his hand.

"Hey, you okay?"

It was funny to me how Aidan could walk up and I not sense his presence. So many years together and this man had little to no effect on me. Yet, someone who'd only recently come into my life left such an impression, I often daydreamed about a life with him.

"Jacelyn."

"I'm fine." I slipped my phone back into my pocket and adjusted my socks. "I'm going to jump with Rhea."

Before Aidan could respond, I was already gone. I grabbed on to my baby and held her hands, as we jumped. For the moment, nothing mattered. I enjoyed the serenity of being with my daughter because it wouldn't be this peaceful forever.

NAZARI

Rhea's birthday...

"Oh, you look handsome."

I smirked at Sariah through the mirror as I adjusted the Amiri distressed sweatshirt. I pulled at the collar, untucked my chain and readjusted the watch on my wrist.

"The least you can say is thank you," Sariah added, coming further into my bedroom.

"Thanks for what? You ain't say shit I don't already know," I joked.

"See, now I take it back. You're ugly and need them braids done."

"Putting me in the same sentence as ugly is crazy. A nigga been handsome, messy braids or not."

"Whatever. Why didn't you let me braid you up?"

"You be busy and shit. Whoever touches my hair, I need them to do so on a consistent basis. I'ma figure it out tho."

I was a week overdue for my two-week braiding session but, with Tara on ice, I had to find a new braider. The way I liked to get my hair braided wasn't ideal for most braiders. I liked to be on a routine with my shit and didn't take well to braiders not being accommodating. I was gon' wear this messy shit one more week; after that, if I didn't find no one, I was just gon' cut the shit off.

"Maybe Jacelyn can braid you up."

"Yeah, maybe." I shrugged.

"Mhm," Sariah smacked. "Why so dry?"

"I'm not. Just waiting on these results to put shit in motion."

"Why when, regardless if she's your daughter or not, you'll still be there for her?"

"I know but, if she's mine, I can do shit how I wanna do it."

"As if you weren't going to do it your way anyway," she laughed.

I laughed too 'cause she wasn't wrong. The DNA test didn't matter for real. Jacelyn and Rhea were going to be a part of my life whether they wanted to or not. The DNA results weren't nothing more than a formality.

"Anyway, Cree has something for you. Cree!"

"Man, I told you not to do nothing extra."

"Hush. You go all out for everyone; you deserve to be celebrated too."

"Happy Birthday Pops!" Cree shouted as he came into the bedroom.

In his hand, he carried a green box with *Rolex* written across in gold.

"Sariah," I started, but she stopped me.

"This is only a fraction of my appreciation for you. All that you do for Cree, how you stepped up and took on the father role when Pops wasn't around to be that for me, the way you protect me, all of it.

Nazari, I appreciate who you are as a brother, father figure, protector, and provider. I love you for life, happy birthday."

Crying wasn't a part of who I was as a man. The only time I ever let a few slip was when I saw Charlotte at the park and the birth of Cree. Each moment was sentimental and changed me in some way. But, this hit different. Emotions flooded me. For the first time in all of my life, I felt loved forreal. I felt like I belonged, and those I love not only needed me but wanted me in their life. The tears fell freely as I scooped Cree into my arms. Together, we sat on the bed with Cree on my lap.

"Whatchu got for me?" I asked him.

"Open it and see. Mommy let me pick."

"Ight, we do it together."

Together, we opened the box, and I was rendered speechless. Sariah had fucked around and copped me a Cosmograph Daytona with the black dial. It was stainless steel with a solid 18K yellow-gold bezel. The watch was crazy fly.

"How did you afford this?"

"I make good money at Seven-Won-Eight and my spade tournaments go crazy. You're not the only one who's hustling," she smirked and dusted off her shoulders.

"Yeah ight."

"Boy, just take off your old watch and put this one on."

"Ight. Thank you, lil man." I squeezed Cree tight until he fussed that I was going to squish him. Coming out of the hug, I dapped him up and told him to finish getting dressed.

"Do you like it?"

I clasped the watch on my wrist and fell in love. "Hell yeah. I love it."

"Good. Does Jacelyn know you and her daughter have the same birthday?"

"Nope. I'll tell her eventually but, for now, it's not important."

"It will be. When are you supposed to get the results again?"

"Early next week."

"Make sure you let me know as soon as you find out."

"That's a given."

"Alright, well, let me finish getting ready, so we can leave. I wanna get there early so I can eat in case we get kicked out."

"Kicked out for what?"

"You acting crazy behind another man's wife!"

"I'm not tripping off that nigga."

"I'm sure, but Aidan isn't going to take kindly to his brother pining over his wife while in his house."

I shrugged, causing Sariah to laugh as she walked out of the room. Aidan being upset didn't have shit to do with me. If the nigga was taking care of home, there wouldn't be room for me to swoop in and find what I didn't realize I needed.

"Hey, so happy y'all could make it!" Jacelyn answered the door genuinely looking excited, but it wasn't the greeting I was looking for. It wasn't personal enough for me.

"Thanks for the invite girl. Your house is beautiful," Sariah complimented, stepping inside. I nudged the fuck out of her. "What, it is a beautiful home," she snickered.

"I wouldn't call it much of a *home* but it is a beautiful residence, so thank you."

Sariah rolled her eyes in my direction, as I winked at Jacelyn. Smiling, she became warm in the cheeks. We lingered, not saying a word but holding the others focus. My eyes traveled south, admiring the way her tights hugged the lower half of her frame. The off-the-shoulder crop sweater she wore looked good too. Trailing back up north, she blushed harder, eyeing me with the same lust and appreciation I did her.

"You look handsome," she mouthed, then took her bottom lip between her teeth.

I blushed. "I miss home."

Jacelyn's eyes became wide. I chuckled. I wasn't mouthing shit. Whoever heard, heard.

"Where is Rhea? I got her a gift," Cree said, interrupting the moment.

"She's out back. You can leave the present over there."

Jacelyn pointed towards the gift table, and Cree took off running. Sariah shifted her gaze between Jayce and me, then went after Cree.

"Nazari," Jayce moaned once I had her in my space.

I held her close, inhaling her warm fragrance and appreciating the peace she naturally brought out of me. I wasn't on ten pulling up to this nigga's spot, but I wasn't on zero either. She took me from where I was and knocked down the guard. With her, nobody else fucking mattered. Whoever felt disrespected had to either speak up or watch from the sideline as I showed my girl just how much I appreciated having her near.

"You smell good," I complimented, tickling her neck with my breath.

"Thank you, but will you stop?" she giggled.

"It's nothing for you to move if that's really what you wanna do."

I paused, swelling my chest with an exhale I refused to let go until she made her move. Jayce didn't move away. We were already close, but she wanted to be closer. She pinned her body to mine, hooking her arms around my waist.

"That's what I thought. I missed you, tho."

"I missed you too."

"Did you put shit in motion?"

"Not yet."

"Then, you couldn't have missed me."

"I did."

"You didn't but it's cool. I'm coming for you, Jayce."

"You keep saying that, but you haven't come yet," she challenged.

"I know. I'm coming tho, so don't get comfortable in this *beautiful home*," I mimicked Sariah.

"Fuck this home," she laughed.

Leaning down, I kissed her on the forehead while whispering, "Good fucking answer."

"Jacelyn, they need you in the kitchen. Nunu is about to drive them cra... oop! Not the two of you hugged up in here for the world to see. You really don't give a fuck about her husband, do you?"

It took Dionne a second to come into view but, once she did, her sly smile got a slight chuckle out of me.

"I don't but, for Jayce's sake, I plan to be respectful... as respectful as I can be," I answered.

"I know that's right," she smacked.

"Go handle business. I'll come find you after I give the birthday girl her gift."

"You can just leave her gift with the others."

"Nah, I got lil mama something special."

"Okay, she's out back."

I kissed Jayce on the forehead and freed her for the moment. Walking past Dionne, she stuck her hand out for a high five. I slapped palms with shawty while shaking my head. Dionne was hell if you let Mitch tell it. Jayce called her the closest thing to a sister she ever had, so to have her approval was cool.

I stepped outside, glancing around the backyard. It was a nice size equipped with all the kiddie shit a child could want or need. Doubt immediately started to set in. Was I selfish for wanting Jacelyn and wanting to uproot Rhea's life? All she knew was a two-parent home and a big ass house for her to reign over. What the fuck was my luxury condo gon' do for her? That shit couldn't compare to what she had here.

"A man in thought is a powerful man, especially when he's contemplating putting the needs of someone else above his own."

Without looking towards the voice, I welcomed the advice. "I'ma always the needs of those I care about before my own."

"Then, you're a good man."

"See, you didn't let me finish. But, with this situation, I want to be selfish. I wanna do what's right for me because it also feels right for the other party. I just wonder if I'm good enough to even step up and be the man I gotta be to make sure both parties know nothing but happiness."

"You contemplating this says a lot. This is your journey, and you must lead if you want others to follow. So, lead with your heart and everything will align how it's supposed to. Love isn't gentle, nor is it easy."

"Thank you."

"No, thank you, young man." The woman rubbed at my arm and took off.

Had that been anyone else, I would've wanted to put a face to the voice. With her, I didn't feel the need. Her advice was sound regardless of who she was in the situation.

Clearing my throat, I walked across the yard and called out for Rhea.

"Yes," she sang happily and ran over.

Looking at her, I felt myself getting choked up. I didn't need a DNA test to prove what I knew in my heart to be true. Rhea was my daughter.

"Happy Birthday Rhea." I smiled.

"Thank you, uh... who are you?"

I chuckled at her forwardness; it reminded me so much of Sariah. "Nazari."

"Nice to meet you, Zari. I'm Rhea. It's my birthday."

Hearing the nickname she gave me set off sparks of happiness from within. "I know. I got this for you." I kneeled in front of her, showing her the black velvet necklace box.

"What is it?"

"Open it and see."

"Okay." She shrugged with the same sass as her momma.

She took the box from me and opened it. Her mouth opened and her already big eyes doubled in size. Her dimples became visible as her face lit up in excitement.

"It's so pretty! Cree, look!" she squealed.

"It matches mine!"

Cree tugged at the gold chain, pulling it from inside his sweatshirt that matched mine. A golden 'C' hung from the gold figaro chain. Cree was right; Rhea's was the same, just with the letter 'R.'

"Ohhhh cool! Put it on! Put it on!"

I laughed and took the chain from the box. Her hair was braided into a ponytail, making it easier to clasp the necklace around her neck.

"Thank you, Zari!"

Without warning, she leaped into my arms, knocking me off balance. I fell back onto the grass, hugging Rhea with as much vigor as she hugged me with.

"Let's go Rhea," Cree said, pulling her away from me. The two of them took off in the direction of the rest of the kids. I got up, dusted myself off, and went to find Jacelyn.

"Hey beautiful."

Her back was towards the back door, blessing me with the greatest view. I snuck up behind and shifted her body towards the right away from the back door opening and buried my face in her neck.

"Stop before someone sees you." She wiggled, trying to break free, stiffening my dick with each sway.

"I don't give a fuck."

"You should. It's Rhea's birthday and I don't want no issues. Everyone here is my people, so they won't say nothing, but Aidan should be back soon."

"His people coming?"

It hadn't dawned on me that Charlotte might've wanted to show up in support of her granddaughter until now.

"Probably not. His mother never shows up to anything that my family and friends put together. But Rhea is going over there once the party is over."

"That's crazy," I said while relief swept me.

Jacelyn just shrugged. Kissing her neck, I sucked then bit down, tugging at her skin.

"Nazari," she shivered.

"I told you I miss home."

"I know, but we can't do this right now."

"Later then?"

"Jacelyn!"

"Oh, my God, that's him. Nazari, let me go."

"Tell me I can come home tonight, and I will."

"Jacelyn!"

"Nazari please," she panicked.

"Tell me," I husked.

"Fine, you can come home tonight," she spoke quickly.

Letting her go, I laughed. Shawty was nervous for all the wrong reasons and was underestimating what she meant to me. Long as I was around, her husband wasn't gon' do shit.

"Kiss me."

"Nazari, no—"

Grabbing her quickly, I kissed her, pulling away as heavy footsteps entered the kitchen.

AIDAN KLEIN

THIS BITCH MUST REALLY think I'm pussy.

The thought crossed my mind, as I peered from around the corner catching a glimpse of Jacelyn and Nazari. I pulled back quick, making sure they didn't see me.

"Aidan, why are you peeking around corners?"

Grabbing Bryn by the wrist, I brought my finger to her mouth, hushing her. Silently, she questioned what was happening.

"Stay here. If you hear a commotion, step in, okay."

She nodded vigorously. I kissed her softly, took a deep breath and walked into the kitchen. By the time either of them acknowledged my presence, they'd ended their lip lock. The expressions they wore were vastly different. Jacelyn's eyes were fleeting, only gracing mine for a moment before looking elsewhere. Her body was even angled towards

Nazari. She was nervous and probably pondering how she was going to get out of this one.

Nazari's expression was what it always was, a look of haughty disdain. His superiority complex might've scared most and, at one point, it scared me. At one point in time, I saw Nazari as untouchable. He had a rougher edge, making him sustainable to harsh environments. Back then, I allowed him to barge into my office and speak to me in any manner he pleased. Unbeknownst to him, I wasn't that man anymore and now was a hell of a time for him to find out.

Snickering under my breath, I stepped further into the kitchen. "Jacelyn, you didn't hear me calling you?"

"I... I didn't. I was um... ah... I was—"

"She was getting the food prepped for the grill," Nazari answered for her.

I jerked my head in his direction in shock at how soft his tone was. Nazari always spoke brassily. This was different. The sweeter tone caused Jacelyn to blush, angering me. I couldn't stand seeing these two within distance of each other. The space between them was enough for another person to fill, but another body wasn't going to block the connection they possessed. A certain synergy lingered between them, a synergy Jacelyn and I never had.

"I'm sorry, but I was asking *my* wife a question. Had she needed a man to answer for her, then I would be the one to do so."

"Nigga, had your ass been here, there would be no reason for your question."

"Funny. Jacelyn, baby, who is your friend?"

"Oh, this is Cree's father, well technically his uncle," Jacelyn stammered. She was stumbling over her words and talking fast, which was something she did when nervous. "Cree is in Rhea's class. Nazari came with his sister."

"Then, why isn't he with his nephew-son and sister?" I snarled, glaring towards Nazari.

The smirk he'd worn since I made my presence known had faded and anger had become him. His nostrils flared and his chest thrusted forward. Jacelyn must've sensed what I did. She stepped in front of him, keeping her distance but still acting in a protective manner.

"Aidan!" she fussed. I looked her way, puzzled at how she thought it was okay to not only chastise me in my own home but in the name of another man. "Nazari, he didn't mean it the way it came out. My husband can get beside himself."

"I don't need you apologizing for me or making excuses. I meant exactly what I said. If Nazari has a problem with it, then we can handle it outside like men."

"Yeah, ight, nigga. The last place you wanna see me is outside," Nazari humorlessly chuckled.

"Outside is exactly where I—"

"This is not happening," Jacelyn spat. "Today is my daughter's birthday and I will not have two grown ass men bickering back and forth."

Annoyed with her need to defend Nazari instead of me, her husband, I lost it.

"Jacelyn, who do you think you're—"

I stepped towards Jacelyn, and that one step was one too many. For Nazari to be as tall as he was, the man was agile on his feet. The one step I took towards my wife, he managed to take four. Peering down at me, I flinched thinking he was about to yank me how I envisioned yanking Jacelyn's disloyal ass. Instead, he spoke low enough for Jacelyn not to hear but loud enough for me to get the message clearly.

"You know how I used to give it up. I know you know 'cause you sent them two goofy ass cops my way. When addressing Jacelyn, your tone needs to be that of a fuckin' mouse. Go above a squeak and you'll find out how quickly I can make a body disappear."

I swallowed hard, poked my chest out and stood firm. "Get the fuck out of my face," I growled.

Humorlessly, Nazari chuckled, leaning further into my space. "What if I fuckin' don't?" he challenged.

"Hey everyone! I hope I'm not interrupting."

Finally.

Bryn walked into the kitchen, moving past a stunned Jacelyn and coming over to where I stood in my face off. She touched my arm, handing me a present. I took it from her and snickered at Nazari.

"Jacelyn, I suggest showing your guest to the door before I have to do it."

I walked quickly towards the sliding doors which led to the backyard. In the distance I could hear Nazari laughing. There was no humor in his tenor, just eeriness I knew I would have to answer to.

"Rhea, come here sweetheart."

Rhea came over with another boy tagging along behind her. "Yes daddy."

"Look what Bryn brought you!" I added extra excitement to my voice, but Rhea didn't seem fazed.

"Okay. Mommy said gifts go on the table." Rhea started to take off, but I stopped her.

"Don't you want to see what it is Rhea?"

"No. I wanna play with Cree. We have matching necklaces."

Happily, Rhea showed me her R pendant sliding across her chain. Cree did the same and my heart clinched.

"Who um... *ahem*, gave you that?" Getting the question out was killing me because even without Rhea telling me, I knew.

"Zari gave it to me," she sang. "Ah, daddy, you're hurting me."

"Aidan, let her go. You're squeezing her." Bryn gently touching my shoulder brought me back.

"I'm sorry baby. Go play."

Rhea took off, and I couldn't see shit but red. Jacelyn wasn't only fucking Nazari, she was bringing him around my fucking daughter.

"Are you okay?" Bryn asked softly.

I could tell she wanted to move in to console me but didn't to maintain optics. "I'm fine. You can go have a seat; I have to make a call."

"Oh okay. Is Charlotte coming? I feel a little weird being here without Adrian."

"You're not the only one here without a child."

"I know, but Jacelyn and I don't really get along. I don't want to be left alone while you're dealing with whatever drama Jacelyn cooked up."

"You won't be alone. I'm right here, okay."

I gave Bryn a reassuring smile, then brought her to where some of the other adults were sitting. Moving off to the side, I began typing away, ready to turn this party up a notch. My goal was to get underneath Nazari's skin by embarrassing Jacelyn in front of her grandparents. Nunu and Gramps' opinions were the only ones that mattered to Jacelyn. So, it was time to show them just what their precious granddaughter had been up to lately.

JACELYN

An hour or so passed and my heart still felt like it was thumping against my throat. When inviting Cree to Rhea's party, it never dawned on me that I was unofficially inviting Nazari as well. Our communication happened within spurts. A day after the trampoline park, Nazari sent a good morning text and, when I was at work, he had lunch and flowers delivered. I tried calling to thank him, but he let my call ring out twice. I thought it was odd how we'd both felt so connected during those two days spent together and, now, we'd barely held a conversation. I missed him, and the space I asked for didn't include ceasing all communication. I felt panicked whenever I didn't hear from Nazari. His absence was similar to the rug being pulled from underneath me and, when I fell, it wasn't his arms I dropped into.

I wanted him.

I needed him.

I craved him.

Seeing him today brightened an already luminescent day. I was happy to be just within distance of this man but, when he pulled me close, I felt ignited. His presence warmed my skin, keeping a permanent pink hue in my cheeks. I was definitely carried away by Nazari's charm. So much so I felt inclined to stand by his side during the kitchen fiasco. Aidan was by far the weaker opponent, yet it was Nazari who I wanted to step in for. The whole situation was too much and, thankfully, neither party had said anything to each other since. They weren't talking to me either, but I would take that if it meant keeping the peace while at Rhea's party.

Rhea was enjoying her day running around with Cree and showing anyone with eyes how the two had matching necklaces. The two together were adorable. They treated each other like siblings. Nunu even joked about Cree being the grandson she always wanted. I was happy everyone seemed so inviting when it came to Nazari and Cree. That was one less thing I had to worry about. My family meant the world to me. Had I listened to their opinion on Aidan years ago, I probably wouldn't be falling in love with one man while in the presence of my husband.

"I'm not trying to start trouble, but don't y'all think it's strange how Aidan's coworker showed up to a kids party without a kid?" Dionne asked, sipping from her cup.

"Weird as hell and why her and Aidan damn near glued at the hip. Anytime he move, she's gawking in his direction, ready to move in unison," Sariah added.

"I'm not trying to add sauce but—"

"I'm pretty sure Aidan is fucking her, and I think her son Adrian might be Aidan's."

"Bitch, what!" In shock, Dionne spit out her drink, garnering a few stares. Quickly, Sariah began patting her back as if Dionne was choking.

"Everything is okay. She was just drinking too fast," Sariah said.

I didn't really care who was looking in our direction because I was fixated on him. Across the yard, Nazari was at the grill with Gramps. They were laughing and bonding in all the ways Aidan never tried to. He always wanted me around his family but never put in the effort with mine.

"Girl, come in the house, so we can finish this conversation in quiet," Sariah said, but I couldn't leave, not now.

I walked over to Aidan and stood right in front of Bryn, blocking her view with my ass. "Don't you think you should be over there by the grill with the rest of the men?" The only guys in attendance were Gramps, Nazari and Aidan.

He glanced towards the grill and scoffed. "For what? You know I don't grill."

"There's a lot of shit a man does that you don't," I murmured and started to walk away.

"What did you just say to me?"

Now on his feet, Aidan was the one standing over me. Lowering his head, he whispered into my ear nastily, "I don't give a fuck about your little bodyguard over there. He's here now but has to leave with the rest of these muthafuckas at the end of the night. Then, you have me to answer to."

Pissed and without thought, I raised my hand, slapping the shit out of Aidan.

"This is a kid's party, can we not do this right now?" Bryn said with worried eyes.

Crazily, my face scrunched into a nasty frown. Who the fuck was this bitch talking to? Turning towards Bryn, I slapped a gasp from her thin ass lips.

"This is marital business! Find you another husband to fuck!" I spat.

"Jacelyn, that's enough!"

I fumed but knew better than to go against what Gramps said. I walked backwards keeping my eyes on the both of them. The kids were still playing as if the commotion never happened. I was thankful. The last thing I wanted was Rhea seeing me getting out of character.

"Jacelyn, are you okay?"

As I walked past Nunu, she grabbed my wrist. Gently, I removed her hand and nodded. Nunu backed away, allowing me to continue my journey in the house.

"What the hell was that?" Dionne asked.

Her and Sariah had followed me into the house and closed the sliding door, so no one else could get in. I couldn't even speak; I was so upset. I stomped over to my little corner bar and grabbed a bottle of tequila and three shot glasses. The girls got the hint and followed me into the living room. I poured us each a shot and passed them out. Silently, we did a three quick shots, throwing them back to back. I sat down and bent forward, trying to bury my head between my legs.

When did life get this complicated?

"You don't have to talk if you're not ready, but we can't stay in here forever. You know the later it gets, the colder it gets," Sariah said.

She was right. Had Rhea been a summer baby, being outside wouldn't have mattered but it was late fall and, surprisingly, we had a nice sixty degree weather day, so I took advantage. Regardless of how I felt, my feelings had to be pushed to the side for my daughter.

"We can go back out," I whispered.

"Sariah and I can handle everything if you want to go lay down," Dionne offered.

"No, it's okay. I'll deal with Aidan later. I'll be fine for a few more hours."

"Well, let's do one more shot for good measure," Sariah giggled.

Dionne and I grabbed our glasses, holding them while Sariah poured the next shot. The three of us tossed them back. I stood up ready to put on a brave face for Rhea's sake but, as I adjusted my clothing, a silhouette appeared in my peripheral. I didn't have to confirm who it was because I knew.

"Um, y'all go outside. I'm gonna go upstairs to change," I told the girls.

I didn't give them time to question me because as I talked, I was already heading towards the stairs. I climbed them two at a time until I reached the second landing. With my back pressed against the wall, I hiccupped unsteady breaths waiting for him to invade my space.

"What the fuck was that out there?"

Nazari's tone was low, but his growl was still present. A mixture of disappointment and hurt lingered in between the space of his exhales and inhales. Seconds was all it took for me to realize I'd somehow hurt his feelings. I reached for his beard to tug at it like I'd always done. Just as quickly, Nazari grabbed my wrist, bringing my hand back to my side.

"What did I do wrong?"

"Why you puttin' hands on another nigga, Jayce?"

"What?" I was confused. "He disrespected me, so I—"

"That's not for you to handle! Any man who gets out of pocket with you is for me to handle."

"Nazari, what were you going to do?"

"Whatever is fucking necessary. You worried about all the wrong shit tho. Had he slapped you back, this conversation wouldn't be happening. You understand that, right? All it would've took was for him to raise his hand at you and I would've—"

"He's my husband, my daughter's father," I cried, refusing to hear what Nazari was alluding too. "You're in *his* house. My family and daughter are here. I can't have my business being aired out when I haven't even figured out what I'm going to do."

"Oh, you don't know what you're going to do?" Nazari nodded and stroked his beard. Taking as many steps as the small staircase landing allowed, Nazari shifted his weight to his back foot. Dark eyes reminiscent of the night sky without the stars loomed over me. Under his watch, I felt so exposed. My inner most thoughts were tatted on my skin for Nazari to bare.

"That's not what I meant. I know what I'm going to do, but things are different now. Aidan might be cheating on me. I like you, I do, but I think he had a baby on me. I'm scared Nazari," I was rambling, rushing to make Nazari understand what I couldn't.

"You don't gotta say shit else Jayce. I get it."

Nazari turned away from me, and my body jolted in his direction. The unseeable attachment I had to this man went deeper than the surface. His emotional waves pierced the skin, plunging into the veins of my heart.

He took a step, I followed.

He inhaled the hurt; I swallowed the pain.

We were too in sync for me to just let him leave like this.

"Nazari!" I tugged at his shirt as a last resort to stop him from walking out the front door.

He paused, fingers gripping the knob but missing the tug needed to open it.

"Don't leave me like this. I should've been clearer with my words, but I'm so confused. I want you, but I'm hurt by what I think is happening with my husband and his coworker."

The tug that was missing was now present. The door opened, despite my attempt at trying to help him understand what I didn't.

He took a step outside, and I took two. His direction was mine, as I followed him to the sidewalk.

"Nazari, please don't leave like this."

He ignored me and went to open his car door. In a last attempt to make things right, I rushed passed him, slamming my body against the car door.

"Jayce move," he chuckled, leaving the humor elsewhere.

"Not until we talk."

"What happened to you not wanting your family to know your business?"

I swallowed hard. "I don't care. I care about you."

Reaching up, I hesitated, scared he was going to stop me from finding comfort. When he didn't, I entangled my fingers into his soft, coarse beard. I tugged, bringing us only a breath apart. The hardened frown of his broke into the handsome grin I loved. Finally, I was able to get back to the steady rhythm of my chest rising and falling. His lips brushed against mine as he spoke so eloquently.

"You're mine Jayce. I mean that in the most possessive way possible. I don't give a fuck if you're not meant to belong to me, we gon' rewrite history until they get it right. You are the best experience I've ever encountered. The only love I wish to fall in over and over is yours. Do you hear me, Jayce? Don't let my words carry you away 'cause they sound sweet. With this heartfelt shit comes the dark parts of me that will do whatever is necessary to make sure no harm comes your way, to ensure no other nigga gets to experience what I already conquered and flagged as mine. When I say you know how I'm comin', that's a warning to let you know all bets are off 'bout you. I'm shootin' shit up 'bout you and a nigga got A1 aim."

"What if you get hurt?"

Nazari swallowed my exhale, then smirked and held my gaze like he'd never done before. In a crisp breezed manner he answered, "Then, I'll cherish the scars the same way I cherish your heart."

I swooned. Flutters flapping away in my stomach quickly rose to that special place in my chest. Nazari gripped my hips, leading me in the sway of our bodies. No melodies, just the heaviness of breathing and angst of our bodies needing to be on top of each other in more ways than one.

"For a married woman, you damn sure don't mind being hugged up with the next bitch man."

Our happy moment ended just as quickly as it started.

"Tara, what the fuck are you doing here?" Nazari asked before I could. He moved to the side but kept his hands on my body.

"I came to celebrate the birthday girl. You left her gift at my house, silly."

The hoe Nazari couldn't shake stepped forward with her arms out holding a gift.

"Tara, get the fuck outta here," Nazari gritted.

"Only if you come with me."

Tara was playing a dangerous game that she wasn't going to win. It seemed like everyone was trying to test me today.

"Bitch, get the fuck away from my house!" I spat.

"You hear that Nazari? She said this is *her house*. So much for her leaving that husband for you. A bougie bitch like her could never be happy with you."

I snarled and tried moving out of Nazari's grasp.

"Bitch, pipe down, a kid's party happening," Tara snickered.

"Yo, calm down and go back inside. I'll handle this."

"No, fuck that! I'm tired of everyone thinking they can play in my fucking face!" I thrusted my body forward, catching both Nazari and Tara off guard.

"Oh shit!" Tara tried running, but it was too late. I grabbed her by her braids and yanked her to the ground.

"Bitch, stop fucking playing with me!" I kicked the hoe repeatedly until Nazari lifted me into the air. I held on to Tara's braids for dear life, trying to rip them shits from her scalp.

"Jayce, you gotta chill, so you don't cause a scene. I'll handle her, ight. Trust me, beautiful."

"You fucking better," I snarled. "Put me down and get that hoe the fuck from around here."

Nazari hesitated when moving from me to Tara. I could tell my harsh tone took him by surprise from how furrowed his brows became. I shrugged because at this point, it was what it was.

"Getcha punk ass up." One hand was all it took for him to pull Tara from the ground. The hoe kept ranting and raving but didn't try to jump my way, not once.

"Man, shut ya ass the fuck up Tara!" Nazari shoved her into the back of his car and eyed me.

"What?" I frowned, over the drama for the day.

"I'm pullin' up on you tonight. Be ready."

"Seeing me should be the last thing you're trying to do. Handle your bitch." I nodded towards the car.

"Handle your husband first."

"Nigga—" I started to curse his rude ass out but stopped myself. He was right.

"Answer when I call tonight."

"Maybe."

I rolled my eyes when, truly, I was fawning over the thought of seeing him and not having to pretend. Nazari blew me a kiss, got in his car and sped off. I heavily exhaled a few times, then went back inside. Everyone was still in the backyard, including Aidan and Bryn. The two weren't sitting close like before, but they were still close enough to hold a conversation. I bypassed them, walking over to Dionne, Sariah and Nunu.

"Jayce, are you okay?" Nunu asked, taking my hand into hers.

"Where did Nazari go?" Sariah quizzed.

"Do I need to cut a bitch?" Dionne whispered harshly.

Shrugging, I shook my head because I didn't have an answer for any of them. Way too much had popped off at a damn kiddie party and brought on more questions than I had answers for.

TARA

"CAN YOU SLOW THE FUCK down!"

My body swerved from the left to right literally mimicking how Nazari was driving. He was cutting in and out of traffic, speeding, and just doing the fucking most. The drinks I'd drunk prior to showing up were playing peek-a-boo with my throat. One minute, it was swirling around in my stomach; then, it was floating upward into my throat but not once did it leave my mouth.

Getting it out probably would've solved all of my problems. Nazari would be forced to slow the hell down and let me out of his car. At that point, I would run for my life and never to be seen the fuck again. Playing with Nazari was a death sentence waiting to happen and, instead of letting go and just dealing with my loss, bitterness talked me into getting revenge.

Finding Jacelyn's husband wasn't an east fete. That bitch was hiding Aidan's fine ass from the world. I had dug as far back on Facebook just to find a picture of her with this man. From there, I pieced shit together. Aidan's fine ass was very receptive to the information I had, and I made sure to tell it all. Down to that nappy headed baby he was claiming actually being Nazari's. I wasn't sure if that part was true but, shit, it didn't matter. No feelings were going unscathed, including an innocent child's. If I hurt, then so would everyone else.

I probably should've thought shit through instead of leading with emotion. Aidan texted asking was I free for the day and, of course, I was since braiding had taken a back seat to my depression. I jumped at the opportunity to stir up some fucking trouble. Aidan wanted me to just show face to piss Jacelyn off and cause a rift between her and Nazari. I agreed, but I had other plans.

Aidan was thinking too little. He wanted to sever the bond between Jacelyn and Nazari; I wanted to demolish any chance at happiness that hoe thought she was going to have. Whether it was with Aidan or Nazari, I was going to crush it. The plan was to go and tell everyone at the party just what a whore Jacelyn actually was. I was well aware of the ass whooping my little speech would've granted me, but what did I care? My heart had already been stomped on and thrown out like yesterday's trash. My war wounds would've healed; the depths of the cuts I planned on slicing Jacelyn with were wounds she had to deal with for life. No makeup could've covered scars of the heart.

Before I could even make it into the house, I was hit with an image so pure and fucking cute that it sickened me. The two of them hugged up against Nazari's car, eyes dancing upon each other. The warmth from their affliction was felt on my skin. I cringed with bitterness tantalizing me. The emotion ran ramped, sparking each nerve. I ran a Hail Mary, needing immediate conflict to rear its head between the two. It was a failed attempt because the only one left hurting was me. My heart and my head were both suffering the pounds of a hammer knocking against them, courtesy of Jacelyn fucking Klein.

"Finally," I exhausted, feeling the car begin to slow down. The gravel the wheels turned onto was bumpy as hell. Frantically, I looked around as the racing of my heart echoed throughout my ears.

"Nazari, where are we?" I screamed. My hysteria was meant with silence. Absolute silence. "Nazari, where the hell are we? Tell me or I'm going to scream as loud as I can."

His eyes cut to the rearview mirror. Those dire ominous specks laid on mine. I parted my lips out of fear and yelled. I shrilled as loud as I could, providing my own ears with a sharp pain. Nazari didn't flinch.

"Yelling won't do shit but make it worse. No one can help you out here Tara."

"Nazari, please don't do this! Please," I begged.

He turned the car off and stepped out, slamming the door behind him. My door opened and, out of fear, I scooted to the opposite side, pulling my knees as close to my chest as I could get them.

"Nazari, get off me!"

He grabbed a hold of my ankle, tugging me towards him. I kicked and wiggled to break free, but it was pointless. I slid across the leather seats right into his arms. His calloused hands choked my wrist. Numbness took over in my fingers as he jerked my body around. He brought me over to a mountain of dirt where you couldn't see anything but more dirt for miles.

"Please let me go," I sobbed.

I knew enough and heard enough about Nazari to know if I was being brought out to the middle of nowhere, my chances of making it back to civilization were slim.

"I own this shit Tara. All of it," he expressed. "I can make it like you never existed with a squeeze."

As if his hold on my wrists couldn't get tighter, he clamped down harder. I winched from pain.

"You hurting me, Nazari, please."

"Nah, don't try and cry your way outta this shit. I tried letting you off with a warning when you tried jumping my girl."

"Your girl?" Disbelief blanketed my face because how could he be so dumb? "She's fucking married with a baby that isn't yours! Aidan isn't one to fuck around with, Nazari! He has connections!"

"That nigga don't got shit but his dick in the mouths of a couple cops. Him nor them mean nothing to me," he chuckled. "I'm kind of offended you think a square ass nigga like him could touch me in anyway."

"You're not invincible Nazari."

"Never said I was, but I can guarantee it won't be that nigga who takes me out."

"You'll go to war with him over a bitch who's been lying to you. Her daughter isn't... Nazari!" I yelped.

His hand had freed my wrists but was now pining at my throat. I gagged on the air being denied access to my lungs.

"Disrespecting Jayce is disrespecting me, Tara. I don't wanna choke ya ass 'cause you a lady and shit, but keep letting ya tongue get beside you and it's gon' become a meal for the mutts."

Thrusting me back, I fell into the dirt. I panted and coughed, welcoming the oxygen.

"Just fucking kill me if that's what you're gonna do!" I shouted, digging my nails into the dirt and throwing it towards Nazari.

"I'm not gon' kill you, Tara. Death would be too easy. I want you to see what a nigga in love looks like. I gotta set an example for your dumbass, so you know what to look for when choosing a nigga."

He was taunting me. The smug smile, the deadly twinkle in his eyes, it was all taunts.

"Then, why bring me here?"

"Look to your right."

I did and saw a shallow hole that had to be at least seven feet deep. Shivering, I shuffled my body as far to the left as Nazari allowed. He stopped me by crouching down and tapping a gun I never seen him pull out against my knee.

"Nazari please," I shrilled.

"I already told you I'm not gon' kill your stupid ass. A lesson needs to be taught and I'm the muthafuckin' teacher. That grave isn't for you. It's for the nigga you ran ya muthafuckin' mouth too."

"How did you—"

"It doesn't matter how, I fucking know. He called you to the house, didn't he?"

"Yes."

"Bitch ass nigga. Look, this how shit gon' go. When I call, you're going to answer and do whatever the fuck I tell you to do. No questions asked, got it."

"Oo... oo.. okay," I trembled.

"Good, now get the fuck up."

"Are you bringing me home?"

"Fuck no. Grab that shovel and start fucking digging."

"For what?" I asked stupidly.

"For if you decide to disobey me, you'll have a place to fucking rest."

I couldn't move. Death loomed over us, but it had become Nazari. His honeyed complexion was no longer vibrant and a murkiness casted over his already sable eyes.

"Aye, Tara, get to digging or you gon' be laid on top of that fuckin' nigga."

I moved. One foot at a time, I grabbed the shovel. Heaping after heaping I dug, barely making a dent in my own fucking grave. Sweat dripping from my forehead burned my eyes each time the shovel was buried under the earth, lifted above and shifted to the side.

"Oh shit!" Cheerfulness exuded Nazari. With his head tilted back, he looked towards the sky mumbling something I couldn't make out.

"What?" I asked nervously.

"I'm a fucking father!"

"Whaa... what? How?"

"I nutted in shawty and made a child. How the fuck else? Don't tell me you need a birds and the bees talk too. Man, bring ya slow ass the fuck on. Gotta drop you off and get shit situated for my family."

As confused as I was, Nazari didn't have to tell me twice. I dropped the shovel and all but flew over to his car and got in the back seat. Whatever Nazari had going on with that bitch was his business. I thought fighting for our love was worth it, but there was nothing like digging your own grave to change your mind. Nothing in this world was worth walking around with death eerily walking alongside you. Nazari was willing to play grim reaper for the one he chose. There was no beating that for me. I lost and I was more than willing to admit defeat, if it meant I could live another day.

JACELYN

Complete and utter chaos.

Crying.

Complete and utter confusion.

Crying.

Complete and utter fucking everything.

Even more fucking crying.

Tears and screaming matches were the highlights of the past two weeks of my life, and I wasn't even a boohoo kind of bitch. I took losses on the chin, wore them like a badge and kept it pushing. With this, I couldn't attack it in the same way. The softer parts of me who still believed in love wouldn't allow it. Nunu told me a long time ago, each time I fall in and out of love, it was best I treated it like a funeral. *Be thankful for the good days, appreciate the great days and mourn the bitter ones.* Every failed attempt at love which you buried were the roots of a new love waiting to blossom. As a teenager, you don't really look into the depths of the lessons you're being taught. What I didn't understand then, I was understanding now. My marriage was a few shovels from being dumped into a shallow grave.

The home which used to bring a sense of comfort now left me restless. It was the battle grounds for the never-ending war between Aidan and me. Since Rhea's party, Aidan had not let up about Nazari and what he meant to me. He fired away question after question. I shot off question after question because I wasn't the only one who'd done wrong in this marriage. As the questions circulated, no answers were told. We each stayed tight-lipped, blaming the other for being less than what the other person needed.

All the yelling, screaming, and ranting was a facade. We both knew the truth would end this marriage, yet we were holding on for our own reasons. His differed vastly from mine, I was sure. I planned on leaving the confines of one guy to run into the arms of another, and I was probably stupid for it. My marriage had been troubled from the start and, still, I stayed. I sucked it up believing Aidan had the potential to be the man I wanted, the man I once loved. That kept me warm and tucked in at night. For the moment, it was enough.

But every once in a while, a chill sweeps from the cracks of the window and brushes against your skin. Needles piercing your skin awakens you in pure shock. That was Nazari. He was the crisp unexpected breeze that I wasn't looking for but appreciated. The fear of being pricked by him existed until you allowed the needle to go beneath the skin and realize it wasn't so bad. Nazari was brass, stoic, and emotional undeveloped in the sense he'd never truly given himself to anyone. He had all the makings of being just another heartbreak to grieve, but he also had all the capabilities of being my strength when I was weak. Nazari was the thread skillfully sowing the cracks across my heart. What he brought to the table was incomparable. More than anything, I believed with everything in me that he was created specifically for me. A man of his magnitude, a chance to be loved by all that he was, was a chance I was willing to take.

I planned on taking things slow with Nazari until Rhea was used to the change. It was important for my heart and soul to be fed, but Rhea was the priority. I'd been wanting to tell Nazari that I was ready if he was. I called, sent DMs, text messages and even rolled by *Ashes 2 Ashes* a few times. On school days when Aidan couldn't make it to pick up Rhea, I stayed around just to see him.

It wasn't until yesterday that I asked Sariah about him. She said he was fine as far as she knew. He called to check in and speak to Cree but, other than that, she hadn't seen much of him either.

Knowing Nazari was alive settled the nerves bubbling in my stomach, but it did nothing for the ache his absence left on my heart. I refused to believe Nazari would butter me up just to leave me stranded. That just wasn't the type of man he was, the type of man I believed him to be.

"Mommy, let's go before daddy comes home." Rhea tugged at the sleeve of my hoodie, trying to lift me from the couch.

"Baby, give me a minute."

"We have to go before daddy come," she complained.

Rhea wasn't one to throw tantrums. She dealt with her emotions as well as any child her age would. A little whining, some tears and pouting. This wasn't her normal behavior when trying to get what she wanted. She was more panicked.

"Why don't you want daddy to come?" I asked. Reaching down, I lifted Rhea onto the couch and sat her beside me.

"He yells a lot, and it hurts my feeling," she pouted.

"You know he's not yelling at you, right?"

"I know, but it hurts. I always feel sad."

"Oh baby." I wrapped Rhea into my arms and kissed her all over her face.

"Mommy stop! Stop mommy!" she giggled.

"Fine but you know I love you, right?"

"Yes."

"And you know daddy loves you?"

"Yeah," she sighed.

"Daddy is just going through a hard time right now. He'll be back to his old self soon."

"Okay. Can we go?"

"Yes, we can go."

Rhea hopped off the couch, and I followed her lead. I grabbed my purse, keys and phone from the coffee table and headed out the door. I buckled Rhea in her seat and passed her the iPad. I climbed into the driver seat and pulled off with music playing from my phone.

Since Aidan and I had been arguing nonstop, I thought it would be good for Rhea to get out the house. My first thought was to drop her off with Nunu and Gramps, but they were busy and wouldn't be able to bring her to school and pick her up her last two days of the week. My last resort was to call Charlotte and see if she was okay with keeping Rhea for a few days. Her ole sour milk ass was more than happy to take Rhea, so I agreed. Charlotte occupied the bottom of my favorite people list, but I refused to stop Rhea from knowing her family.

"Okay, Rhea, I love you."

"I love you too, mommy."

Rhea threw her little arms around my neck, hugging me tight and momentarily relieving the tightness I felt in my chest.

"Okay, Ashley, go to your room and change out of your clothes."

I cringed at Charlotte calling Rhea by her middle. No matter how many times I heard it, it would never sit right with me.

"Okay."

Rhea took off and I turned away from the door, ready to get back in my car. The less Charlotte and I spoke, the better, at least that's how I felt.

"Jacelyn, one second. I wanted to speak to you."

I stopped walking and peered over my shoulder. "I'm kind of in a rush Charlotte."

"Whatever man you're running off to can wait."

Rolling my eyes, I faced Charlotte. She closed her front door and met me in the middle of the walkway. Her expression wasn't pleasant. Her face was twisted and stank, so I matched her energy. I folded my arms across my chest and lowered my eyes into sharp slits.

"What?"

"I don't know what your end game is, but you need to stop all of this chaos you are causing."

"I'm causing chaos," I scoffed. "Whatever Aidan is telling you is a lie, not that it's any of your business."

"Sweetheart, anything to do with Aidan *is* my business. Now, I'm going to keep this brief since you have pressing matters and all. Aidan is your husband. Running around the city flaunting a no-good street thug is bad for his image. Your husband is a pilar of the community and should be treated with grace and care. The game you're playing is a dirty one and, believe me, Jacelyn, cleaning yourself up after the blow back will not be an easy accomplishment. Love your husband, raise your daughter, and die happy knowing someone of Aidan's stature could love a heartless whore like yourself."

Heat rushed through me, tensing my muscles. My hands clenched, making a fist.

"Jacelyn, baby, fighting is a young woman's games. An elderly woman like me loves money."

Charlotte was provoking me. Beating this bitch black and blue was what she wanted.

"Charlotte, if you think so highly of your son, then you marry him. You love him with grace and care. Maybe your marriage will last," I seethed, clawing at the palms of my hands.

"Jacelyn, please," Charlotte laughed. "My marriage wasn't successful because my ex-husband couldn't stand having a powerful woman as a wife. He was much like you, was weak and always needed to cause drama for attention."

"Fuck you, Charlotte!"

I trembled with rage looking at this bitch. My teeth dug into my bottom lip, the bitterness of blood staining my tongue. I shook my head and forced myself to walk. Each step I took in the opposite direction was harder than the last. The urge to knock Charlotte's head off her shoulders was stronger than anything I'd ever felt.

"Fuck!" I exploded.

My fists drummed against the steering wheel and quickly began to throb in pain. I was enraged. Tears skating down my cheeks caused my vision to resemble rain drops on a windowpane. I was hurt and so fucking frustrated that I didn't know what to do or who to call. I just sat crying until tears no longer flowed from my eyes.

Five second inhale.

Three second exhale.

I continued on until the rapid pacing of my heart slowed back to its natural rhythm.

Bzzzt! Bzzzt! Bzzzt!

My eyes darted towards my phone lying on the dash. The N initial overpowered the screen with each ring. I froze.

Bzzzt! Bzzzt! Bzzzt!

The phone wouldn't stop ringing. The call would end and another call was coming through quickly. One after another, this nigga was blowing my phone up. I sniffled, wiped my eyes and swiped my finger across the screen, finally answering. I greeted him with heavy inhales and even heavier exhales. His response was the sharp grinding of his teeth occupied with a single question.

"Who did it?"

NAZARI

"JACELYN IS GOING TO fuck you up," Sariah giggled.

She fluffed a few of the pillows she placed on Rhea's bed, then stepped back to look at her handiwork. In four days, she managed to set up Rhea's Little Mermaid themed room, bathroom and supplied her with a whole new wardrobe. The kitchen was fully stocked with food, drinks, liquor, and every kitchen essential one could think off. I had her set up one of the guest bedrooms, so Jacelyn would have somewhere to sleep in the new two-family home I brought. I would've had Sariah hook up the master bedroom but felt that was something Jayce would want to do. It was important to me that both Rhea and Jacelyn were comfortable here. I wanted them both to take this house and make it into a home they could love and feel safe in.

"Fuck me up for what? I didn't do shit," I finally said.

"Nigga, you've been ghosting her for two weeks. And it doesn't help that you pulled a Houdini right after you showed up to her daughter's birthday party causing chaos."

"I missed enough birthdays with Rhea. I wasn't about to miss another one."

Finding out Rhea was my daughter was what I imagined waking up from a coma felt like.

Confusion.

Happiness.

Fear.

Doubt.

Inadequacies.

All those different feelings washed against my conscience once I read the results for myself. With the paper in my hand, my fingers trembled and my heart went numb. Being a father to Cree was some of the happiest moments in my life. I loved that kid more than I loved any other human on this earth. I clung to him in all the ways my father never clung to me. Protected him with every breath I took, provided by any means. I didn't see how I could love a person any more than I loved Cree.

Now, after five years, I had a daughter. A little lady who needed to be shown all the ways a boy, teenager, boyfriend, man, and husband was supposed to treat her. I was supposed to be her first example of love, but how was I 'posed to do that when I feared what I was supposed to be an example of? Heartbreaks weren't something my bloodline handled with grace. Pops almost killed himself and, if it wasn't for Cree, Sariah probably would've sunken further into depression. Neither of their partners deserved an ounce of the love they had to give, but something like that was only recognizable in hindsight. How was I... a man who's just now willing to take a chance and possibly lose himself in order to experience something beautiful, supposed to teach his daughter the gift of taking risks when it comes to love? How was I supposed to control the urge to revert back to the old me whenever someone made her cry?

Teaching a son to be a man was something I could do. Cree would know the importance of providing, protecting, and standing on his word. He'd know how to treat a woman because Sariah wasn't willing to accept anything less. Teaching a daughter how to be loved was a different journey, one I was ready to embark on but was afraid of the outcome. Mistakes wasn't something I had room to make. I'd already missed out on five years. That's hella days to make up for. I had to do this shit right, for Rhea's future self, I had to get this shit right.

"Nazari, you okay?" Sariah asked, coming to stand in front of me.

I lifted my head and faked like I was rubbing my nose but was really wiping at my eyes. The thoughts of raising a daughter, loving a daughter, had brought tears to my eyes and this wasn't the first time.

"Aww, are you crying?" she pouted.

"Shit gets hella emotional when I start thinking about the kind of father I want to be. Rhea deserves a man who's going to be there for her, Sariah. What if I fuck up with Jacelyn and—"

"I'ma stop you right there," she said sternly. "Your relationship with Jacelyn has nothing to do with your relationship with your daughter. I know you like Jacelyn, you might even love her, but you can't make the two synonymous. Love Jacelyn because she represents whatever peace you might need in life. Love Rhea because she is an extension of you, your legacy, your newfound reason."

"I feel you." I nodded.

Even though I didn't fully understand it, I was learning love had different meanings, different feelings, and way too many possibilities. It couldn't be bound to one definition.

"Good. Stop doubting yourself. You're an amazing father figure to Cree. You'll be just as amazing with Rhea. I mean, look at all that you did in two weeks."

"I hope she likes it. I'm still trying to figure out how to even tell Rhea who I am to her."

"That's not a battle for today. You and Jacelyn will decide that together. For right now, you need to have a conversation with Jacelyn. You owe her the truth about everything. Aidan, Charlotte, your past, Rhea, this new house, all of it Nazari."

"She already knows about the shit I was into."

Taking a step back, Sariah raised her eyebrows in shock. I chuckled.

"Yeah. She seemed to take it well, but only time will tell."

"Well, if she can handle that, then she can handle the rest of this mess."

That what I hoped, but there was no telling how Jacelyn was gon' handle this shit.

"Ight, let me give this big headed girl a call," I told Sariah.

"Okay, and tell my girl to braid you up too," she laughed and left out the bedroom.

I leaned against the wall taking in the bedroom once more. Shit was crazy as hell, but I couldn't have asked to be put in a better situation. Through the dark, I found not one light but two, and I prayed Jacelyn and Rhea both saw the light in me that I saw in them.

Unlocking my phone, I hit call on Jacelyn's number. No answer. I called her a few more times, refusing to give up until she answered. If I had to pull up on her and beg for forgiveness because of my absence, then so be it. She wasn't about to slip away from me now that I had her in my grasp.

Man, answer the fucking phone.

Stress caused my forehead to wrinkle with lines. I hit call again and, this time, on the third ring, she answered. Lifeless breaths took over the call. I closed my eyes envisioning the tears in her eyes courtesy of her faint sniffles. Heat rose through my body, tingling at my chest. My jaw clamped down as I gritted, "Who did it?"

"What do you want Nazari?"

"I want to know who did it?" I asked again.

"Who did what Nazari?" she spat.

"Aye, I didn't do shit to you. I'm tryin' to correct what the next muthafucka did."

"But you did do it Nazari. Where have you been? I told you I needed time to figure things out—"

"And I gave you that!"

"Let me finish!" she barked back. "I needed time to figure things out and, no, I didn't expect you to wait by the phone, but I did think when I sent a text letting you know I chose you, that you would at least respond back with something. I would've been happy with a fucking emoji, but I couldn't even get that. I was ready to blow my life up for you, Nazari, and you couldn't respond?"

"So, you mad I didn't hit you back?"

"I'm mad that I feel so fucking strongly about you, and you don't give a fuck about me!"

I wasn't used to Jayce using such a rigid tone with me. Shit was pissing me off but, since I was in the wrong, I was trying to let her get her shit off. She had every right to be pissed, but to come at me like I hadn't been pining for her ass was crazy.

"What are you even saying right now? Since when I don't give a fuck about Jacelyn? All I been fucking caring about is you."

"Then, where the fuck were you? Where have you been Nazari? Huh? Cause I can tell you where I've been."

"Oh yeah, where you been Jacelyn?" I snickered.

"Arguing and crying with my fucking husband because of the mess you made."

"This shit my fault now?"

"I was fine before I ever met you, Nazari, so what do you think?" she smacked.

"How the fuck were you fine when I met you drunk and emotional in a fucking club? You were crying 'cause your husband don't call you beautiful but you were fine, right?"

"Yes, I was fucking fine! I didn't need you coming into my life and making me feel special. I was fine being ordinary. I didn't ask for everything to tense because I'm within inches of you. I was fine breathing normal like a regular fucking person. I didn't fucking need you sweeping me off my feet and reminding me what love could feel like. I was perfectly fine settling. Nazari, do you hear me? I was fine without you making me feel alive every time your lips touched mine. I was fucking fine before you made me believe that I was home for you because that's what you've become for me, Nazari, and I fucking hate it!" she cried, panting and sniffling uncomfortably.

"You sound dumb ass fuck."

"Fuck you then, Nazari. Leave my dumbass right where I'm at then!"

"Where are you?" I sighed, done with this over the phone shit.

"Don't worry about it."

"Jacelyn, stop fucking playing and tell me where you are."

"No! Go back to acting like I don't exist, and I'll act like I never met you."

Chuckling, I told her, "That's impossible. I'm home to you, beautiful."

"I'll find a new home then," she snickered.

"Yeah, ight. You gon' tell me where you are?"

"Nope."

"Fuck it, you know how I'm coming."

JACELYN

"You fucking him, Jacelyn? Yes or no? It's that fucking simple."

Tucking my bottom lip into my mouth, I bit down as hard as I could until the faint trace of blood lingered on my tongue. My eyes shifted towards the clock on the wall that was mainly for decor but kept the time. It was a quarter to twelve, twelve midnight, and this was the question lingering in Aidan's mind. Not *how long do you plan on sleeping in the guest room* or *how can we fix our marriage?* But am I fucking Nazari?

"Jacelyn, I won't keep asking you. Are you fucking him?"

Are you fucking him?

The answer was simple just like he'd said. Yes. Three letters, one syllable, followed by a period so no further explanation was needed.

That's it, that's all. Yes, I was fucking Nazari, but what was the point in feeding into Aidan's bullshit?

Being honest about sleeping with another man wasn't going to progress this relationship or put divorce on the table, which was the conversation we should've been having. Who slept with who didn't matter; how we would go about splitting amicably for Rhea's sake was the most important thing.

"Aidan," I huffed. "I'm not having this conversation with you. You already pushed Rhea out the door with all your bitching. Do you want to push me out next?"

"Push you out?" he gasped. "You're already out the fucking door Jacelyn. I'm not fucking stupid. How many times do I have to catch you with *Zari* for you to understand that?"

Calling Nazari by the nickname Rhea gave him had Aidan's entire face looking like someone squirted a lemon into his mouth.

"Then, you had the audacity to bring him to our daughter's birthday party where he gifted her a necklace Jacelyn. A fucking necklace."

I stared at Aidan blankly, wondering what the point of all this was.

"If you had such a problem, you should've spoke up?"

"I tried and you stood firm alongside him, Jacelyn."

"The same way you stood firm with Bryn, right?" I snickered. This wasn't the game Aidan wanted to play. The same way he had questions for me, I had questions for him. Only difference was I refrained from asking because I knew the answer would hurt me in some way.

"That was different. Bryn is a coworker of mine. You can't go putting your hands on people because you don't like them, Jacelyn."

It was my turn to scoff because who did Aidan think he was talking to.

"Oh, you think that's funny?"

"I think all of this shit is funny." I shrugged.

"I don't know why you think you can play these mind games with me, Jacelyn."

"What fucking mind games?" I exhausted. "Aidan, I don't want to be with you! I haven't for years. Remember that anniversary dinner I had planned that you missed?"

"Yes," he answered dryly. The lack of remorse for his absence brought a smirk to my face.

"I planned on leaving you the next day. I only stayed because I'd just got done fucking Nazari and you seemed to be apologetic."

"Bitch!" he squealed, shock riddling his face. "I ate your pussy that night."

"Yup," I smirked. "Oh, the condom broke too, so you probably sucked your brother's cum out of me too," I laughed.

"I'm going to fucking kill you," he seethed.

"Aidan, if you put your hands on me, I can promise you, your mother will have to bail you out."

The threat of jail stopped his ass right in his tracks. For a moment, we stared at each other. The two of us had long changed from the vibrant young college kids we once were. The love we once held for the other had faded into something ugly. Years together and responsibilities turned us into people I no longer recognized. I couldn't even put all the blame on Aidan the way I wanted to. This wasn't only his fault; I was part to blame.

Excuses and guilt kept me with a man who I knew couldn't love me the way I wanted to be loved. I fought with myself until I believed I had a good man and needed to accept him for who he was. When that logic went stale, I used Rhea as an excuse. It was like Nunu said, whether Aidan was there or not, Rhea would know love from a father figure. Gramps had been that for me and was willing to be that for my daughter as well. That was all she needed.

"I always knew you were nothing more than a fucking slut."

"Aidan, stay the fuck away from me or—"

"Or what?" he raged and lunged for me, tackling me to the ground.

Quickly, I swung, slapping him as his hands went straight for my throat. I sucked in as much air as I could. My eyes bucked the tighter Aidan squeezed.

"Aidan," I croaked. His fingers kneaded, rubbing against my bones.

"Shut the fuck up!" he growled. "I fucking loved you, Jacelyn, and this is how you fucking repay me! You fuck him! Out of all fucking people, you fuck him!"

Spit flew from Aidan's mouth, slathering my face. Digging my nails into Aidan's wrist, I clawed foolishly thinking it would help.

"Aidan," I whimpered. Tears dimming my sight and causing it to haze.

"I should fucking kill you! I should fucking kill you!"

My head slammed against the carpet each time he jerked me forward by my throat. A strangled scream fell from my lips.

"I hope you told Rhea you love her because Bryn is going to be her new mommy."

Aidan's words were almost incoherent as the life in my body became faint. Eyes fluttering open and shut, I saw quick flashes of what life could've been like with Nazari and Rhea. It was nothing but bliss and laughter.

"Nazari," I mouthed. "I love you."

The truth unfolded, sending Aidan into a fit of hysteria.

"You love him? That's who you fucking love? I hope he's worth dying for!" Aidan's hands clasped at my neck, stealing the breath I had left.

My throat burned and, when my lashes fluttered for what felt like the last time, I saw two blurred silhouettes standing behind Aidan, each one screwing something onto what looked like a gun. I drifted on the verge of being lifeless, Aidan's threats of death surrounding me.

"Please," I spoke, setting my throat on fire.

"Don't fucking beg now, bit—"

Aidan's rage stopped. The threats he promised had been exchanged for grunts of pain. He was now the one doing the pleading. Heavy pants filled the space in the room. I rolled over, gasping for air to bring life back into my lungs. In the midst of a choking fit, my body was propelled from the floor and cradled into the arms of one of the masked men. The faint smell of vanilla and bourbon cleared the dizziness, replaced with a calming sensation.

"You good?"

I nodded.

"Leave that nigga here and let's go," the man holding me demanded.

He smelled so damn good and sounded just like the man I envisioned saving me. I clung to him, whoever he might've been, and buried my face into his hoodie. Tears dribbled down my cheeks as realization set in. Aidan not only tried to kill me, but he'd admitted in so many words that Bryn was who he truly wanted.

"Come on beautiful, time to go home."

I looked up from the masked man's chest and felt so fucking connected to him, it was insane. I brought our faces together and leaned forward, kissing him through the mask. His stare lingered on mine as I pulled away, bringing my face back to his hoodie.

NAZARI

PARKED OUTSIDE THE CRIB I'd purchased for Jacelyn, I couldn't take my eyes off her. The oversized hoodie I gave her from the trunk of my car to keep her warm did little to cover the finger shaped bruises along her neck. I winched each time my eyes traveled from her beautiful tear-stricken face to the painful reminder that my peace was almost stolen from me.

The thoughts that followed were murderous, torturous, excruciating. The shit I wanted to bring to Aidan's door for what he'd done wasn't nothing short of nice and would leave him unidentifiable. His time was coming, that was a fact but, for now, I had to let the urge to snatch that nigga up subside. Bigger shit had to be handled first. I reached over Jacelyn and opened the glove compartment to grab a lighter and my weed box. I grabbed one of my pre rolled blunts, rolled up my mask, let it sit on the top of my head and sparked up.

"I was wondering when you were going to reveal yourself," Jacelyn murmured.

Hearing her scratchy voice had me fucked up. I took another long pull before answering her.

"Had to calm down first, you know?"

"No. No, Nazari, I don't know. Do you want to tell me what the hell that was back there?"

I frowned, wondering how her ass could have an attitude after I saved her from the nigga who was supposed to love her the most in life.

"Don't make that face. You know I'm thankful for what you did. Had you not shown up then—" she shook her head, declining to even acknowledge the thought. "Why did you come with guns and a mask Nazari? I thought you were done with that life."

"I am."

"Then why?"

Leaning back in my seat, I passed Jacelyn the blunt. She needed that shit. It was understandable that she was shaken up. I had patience for that but I wasn't about to have another conversation like the one we had on the phone.

"Aye, I wanna talk to you and shit, but I'm not for you makin' me the villain in your story."

"Wha... what? That's not what I'm doing." She coughed, inhaling the weed harder than necessary.

"Take it easy. This ain't the harsh shit you're used to. My work is smooth, don't gotta do the most."

"Oh okay." She took another pull and handled this second one better. With a softened gaze, she looked at me. "I don't mean to make you the villain of my story."

"Doesn't mean that's not what you're doing. And I get it, I'm easy to blame 'cause I'm the new nigga, but all this shit that's happening isn't on me."

"I know."

"Then, stop placing it on me. The mess isn't mine to wear alone. You played a part in this shit, and I'm happy you did," I smirked, causing her to do the same.

"Why did you come to the house on some kidnapping shit?"

Her question came off jokey, which made me laugh 'cause her ass didn't understand the type of nigga I was at all.

"That's *exactly* what I was on. I'm not playin' with you or about you, Jacelyn. Anytime shit get rough and you try to run left, I'ma be there to snatch you up and bring you back right. I don't gotta problem chasing a woman. Chase your ass to the ends of the earth and back."

"Nazari," she giggled.

"Deadass Jacelyn. I'm not letting you run from the best thing that's happened to the both of us. We all we got, ain't nobody else for you but me, and no one exists outside of you in my world."

"How can you be so sure?"

Cupping her chin, I moved in, speaking against her lips. "How could I not? Shit been a lot more peaceful for me since I spotted you at that spades tournament."

"You think our messy situation is peaceful?" I swiped my tongue across her bottom lip then bit into it and gently tugged.

"Nah, our shit messy as fuck. I'm talking 'bout the peace you've brought to me up here."

Taking my index finger, I tapped against her temple. "Peace of mind is something I didn't get much of in life. 24/7, my mind ran amuck with voices of those I... you know and those who pained me. I struggled with finding peace amongst the chaos because in a twisted way, I didn't deserve it. With you, shit gets silent and I'm able to clear all the muddiness and begin to forgive myself for the mistakes I've made. That's how I can be sure about us. I know shit won't always be sweet with us, but I can say there's no argument, attitude, or hurt that will ever keep me from you. We locked in and I'ma always come for you, Jacelyn. That's a promise."

Inhaling deep, she kissed me intimately. She took my tongue into her mouth, sandwiching between those thick lips. I tongued her back and stopped before I got too lost in finally being back home.

"I got something I need to tell you." My words were whispers against her lips as I pulled back and grabbed the blunt from her hand.

"Okay, but can we go inside. Wait—" she paused and looked out the window, "where are we?"

"Let me get this off my chest, then I'ma tell you."

"Okay."

"Rhea is mine, Jacelyn."

"What?" she scoffed in disbelief.

"Rhea is mine. She's my daughter."

"Nazari, I love that you're willing to go as far as claiming Rhea but, I told you before, Rhea is not yours. She can't be."

"Why, because of eye color?"

"Well yeah."

"Ight, come with me."

We both exited the car and walked up the stone path leading to the front door. I used my key to let us in, then told Jacelyn to wait in the living room area. She agreed, and I went into the bathroom. Quickly, I washed my hands and placed my fingers below my eye to pull the skin down and take out my contact. I did the same on the other side and rubbed the tears away.

Catching my reflection in the mirror, I became stiff. I was my father's son. I resembled that man in every way but my eyes and complexion. Those two things, I received from her. My complexion was a mixture between her pasty ass skin and my Pops' vibrant melanin, but these chestnut hazel green eyes were all fucking her. I hated that shit. I hated anything about me could act as a reminder of that bitch and who she once was to me.

"Nazari, are you okay in there? I'm a little nervous and—"

Hand on the bathroom door handle, I pushed down and tugged. The door opened with Jacelyn looking as beautiful as ever, even with worry plagued against her skin.

"Nazari, I—"

The truth had been discovered, rendering her silent. Shaking her head, she stepped back from me while mouthing the word *no*. I stayed where I was, unsure of how she would feel if I approached her.

"This can't be real. Those aren't your eyes, Nazari. Take those damn contacts out and stop playing with me. Your eyes are dark like coal with the gleam of an obsidian stone. Please take those contacts out and stop playing with me. Stop playing with me, Nazari!" she babbled, hand on her chest.

"Jayce, I'm not playing. Shit is messy but remember what I told you; nothing is gon' keep me from you. Not even you marrying my half-brother."

"You got to be fucking—"

"Oh shit, Jacelyn!"

Rushing towards her, I caught her limp body in my hands right before she hit the floor. "Jacelyn," I whispered.

I brought my hand to her chest just to make sure she was still breathing. Counting ten rise and falls, I was satisfied. I carried her to the guest room and laid her on the bed. Taking off her sneakers, I tucked her in, then went and sat in the corner. Leaving her side wasn't even a thought for me. She'd been through a lot and needed some rest. I was gon' give her that. But the second she woke her ass up, we were finishing this conversation. Too much time had already passed, I didn't have another minute to spare.

"Ugh," Jacelyn groaned loudly, waking me from my light sleep.

I stretched, sat up in the recliner and swiped at my eyes. This muthafucka was comfortable as hell and a good buy on Sariah's part. I tried talking her out of it but, shit, it was proving to be worth every penny.

"You good?" I asked Jacelyn, capturing her attention.

Wide eyed in confusion, she glared at me and, without her having to say a thing, I knew exactly what she was thinking.

"I grabbed you last night from your crib. We talked shit out and I told you Rhea was my daughter. Then, I showed you my—"

"Eyes," she gasped, finishing my sentence.

"Yeah, you fainted, and I brought you up here to sleep that shit off."

"Your fucking eyes!" she gritted and moved from the bed. "Why the fuck would you lie to me, Nazari?"

Angrily, she stood before me, and I couldn't do shit but smirk. The way her t-shirt shaped her body was sexy as fuck. My dick was hard and begging to get back home.

"Why are you laughing? There's nothing funny about... Nazari, get off me!"

In the midst of her bickering, I grabbed her and plopped her directly on my dick. She wiggled her ass against my dick.

"You don't gotta fight me to feel this dick. It's yours. You can get it wherever and whenever," I told her, kissing along her neck.

"Nazari, stop because I'm mad at you. Why would you keep something so important from me?"

Shifting herself, she swung one of her legs over my lap and wrapped her arms around herself.

"I didn't know how to tell you," I told her honestly.

"When did you realize my Aidan was your Aidan?"

"That nigga is not my anything but when I dropped you off that one day after the kickback shit."

"And he never said anything to you about us?"

"He did."

"Okay what?" she probed.

"Told me to leave you alone and we see how that shit worked out."

I pinched her chin, pecking her on the lips. I could've told Jacelyn what I saw when I went to speak to Aidan, but that wasn't my truth to tell.

"Wow, I can't believe you and Aidan are brothers. I feel like such a fucking hoe," she said, shaking her head. "This is too much. I'm sorry Nazari, I—"

Jacelyn went to move away from me, but I pulled her back in. With my fingers back at her chin, I guided her head to my chest.

"Nazari," she bickered, trying to lift her head.

I pulled her right back, locking her head in place. "Shut the fuck up Jayce and listen." After what Jacelyn went through with Aidan, I was trying to keep shit gentle with her. I would never put my hands on her in the way Aidan did, but I needed her to shut up and fucking listen.

"Listen to what Nazari? What else could you have to tell me? Huh? Please let me go. I just want to go home to my daughter," she whimpered.

That fast, Jacelyn went from talking tough to softly crying. "Our daughter, and stop fucking crying. I understand the part I played in hurting you, ight. I should've been honest with you, but I didn't want you running away from me like how you trying to do now. After I say what I need to say, I'll let you go, but the only place your ass running to is another room in this muthafucka. When things get hard, we're not doing the runaway bullshit. We cool off and talk shit out. Ight?"

Sniffling, Jacelyn nodded her head. I shook mine 'cause this girl was a fucking crybaby.

"What did you want me to listen to?" she asked.

"Close your eyes and listen," I whispered. I peered down to make sure she had her eyes closed and, once she did, I did the same and closed mine. The slow yet dominant rhythm of my heart began to dictate her breathing pattern. It was so peaceful, serene even. I didn't know about Jayce, but I was lost in how perfectly sync we'd became.

"You hear that?" I asked, allowing my words to drift from my lips and tickle at her lobe. "I know you hear it 'cause your breathing is matching the beats of my heart. That's what I needed you to hear. You asked me how I could be sure about us, and this is how."

"I hear it," she finally acknowledged.

"Stop allowing circumstances to dictate how you feel about yourself, ight? You far from a hoe. The only thing that nigga counts as in your life is a mistake. Not your husband, not your baby daddy, nothing more than a mistake. This shit between us was gon' happen one way or another Jayce. There was nothing that was gon' keep you from me."

"I believe it."

"Good."

With our eyes still closed, I held Jayce close, finally feeling like I was on the path to something better than what I deserved. Jacelyn was a blessing I was already counting twice each time I said my prayers.

"Wait and don't get mad," she said, fucking up the moment. I opened my eyes, knowing she was about to be on some bullshit. "I know you think because you and Rhea have the same eyes that she's yours, but I feel like we should do a DNA test just to be sure."

The way I laughed, bounced at that shit, bounced Jacelyn's head from my chest.

"You funny as fuck, you know that?"

"I'm not trying to be, I'm just saying."

"What are you saying Jayce? 'Cause it was cool for you to say eye color was enough to determine that Rhea was Aidan's and now that her eyes match mine, you need more proof?"

Clenching my teeth, pain shot through my jaw. A tightness in my throat I'd never felt before began to settle in. Jacelyn, with nothing but innocence on her face, searched mine for a way to fix what she'd broken with the bullshit she'd said, but it was too late. The feeling of inadequacy had already began to topple over my confidence.

"You still trying to be with that nigga?" I gritted.

"I don't want Aidan. Do you not see what the fuck he did to my neck." Her fingers yanked the collar of her shirt, showing her purplish bruises. I leaned forward, kissing along them, pushing my own hurt feelings to the side. "Nazari."

Forcefully, she moved my face from her neck and started playing in my beard. Her gentle tugs had been missed.

"I just want to make sure what you're telling me is the truth because I'm the one who has to find a way to explain this to a four year old. Please know I'm not trying to hurt you. I would never be so careless with the gift you've given me, but I do have to make sure I'm taking all the steps necessary to make sure Rhea... my daughter... our daughter, will be okay."

"Do you listen to me when I talk? And I need you to answer me forreal," I told her.

"Of course I do Nazari. Why would you ask me that?"

"Listen to how you're talking. I told you before nothing in this life that causes you confusion, pain, hurt or anything else is yours to carry alone. I'm here to help you in any way that I can and, when it comes to the ways I can't, I'll learn. That goes for Rhea too. Whatever y'all need me to be, whoever y'all need to be, as long as it doesn't compromise my morals, I'll be that for y'all. Why do you think I bought this house for you?"

"What house?" she asked.

"The house we're in Jacelyn. It's yours, no strings attached. That's where I've been the last two weeks. I found out the results of the DNA test and started putting shit in order for y'all to make that move comfortably."

"Is that why you had that boy push my daughter?" she smacked.

"Yeah. Had to get a strand of her hair. Lil nigga pushed my baby a little too hard tho. I almost had Cree beat his ass," I joked.

"I can't believe you. I can't believe you would do all of this for me... for us."

"Believe it because it's done. I meant what I said Jacelyn, I want you. All that you come with, I want. In every lifetime, in every spiritual plane, all I want is you."

What I said must've hit her deep because once again, her ass was crying. This time, I wiped her tears like I planned to do each and every time.

"Talk to me, Jayce."

"Nazari, you shouldn't have done this. I'm appreciative, but I'm not ready to live with another man. I'm not even sure I want Rhea to live with another man so quickly, especially if she doesn't know who you are."

Jacelyn said what she said with care, but that didn't stop the sting I felt in my chest.

"Did I upset you because that's not what I meant to do?"

"I'm good. You said the right thing. I didn't have intentions on moving in here with you. The same way you're not ready, neither am I. As sure as I am about us, it's still new. I wanna make sure we have room to grow. I also wanna respect Rhea and the time she's gon' need to come to terms with all of this. For right now, we don't even have to tell her I'm her father. We can keep it at me being *Zari* until you feel she's ready."

"Really?" she beamed.

"Yeah. I got a lifetime with you and Rhea, no need to rush shit."

"Thank you," she gleamed, smashing her lips into mine.

"Don't thank me yet."

"Why not?" She frowned.

"I'm cool with taking our relationship slow and the whole Rhea situation, but you gotta get up outta that nigga's crib like yesterday. Have them divorce papers drawn up in the next hour type of shit," I told her seriously. I needed all ties between Jacelyn and that other side severed immediately.

"Nazari, I need at least a week to get my affairs in order."

"What affairs? Let that nigga keep everything. We can get it all back plus some."

"It's not just the items, I also have to tell him about Rhea. By no means does he deserve that conversation, but I'm not going to let his actions dictate how I handle this."

"You said you need a week?"

"Yes."

"Ight. You got twenty-four hours to leave that nigga."

"Nazari." She frowned, but I wasn't trying to hear it.

"Twenty-four fucking hours Jacelyn. Six for the shock to wear off and for you to vent to Dionne. Six to meet up with a lawyer to get these divorce papers drawn up. Six for you to inform this nigga he's not the pappy and have him sign them papers, then six to get your ass back to this house with you and Rhea's stuff. Twenty-four is all I got to spare."

"That's not fair Nazari. You can't ask me to make such a huge life change in twenty-four hours."

"What's not fair is me missing years of Rhea's life. I'm not holding that shit against you, so don't hold this unfairness against me. Don't start not shit Jayce. Twenty-four hours is me being generous; appreciate that shit, handle ya business, then come show a nigga what he been missing."

"And if I don't?" she challenged.

"Then, I'ma have to come get you," I smirked and grabbed the front of her shirt, bringing her face close to mine. Licking my lips, I trailed hers with the tip of my tongue. "And you know how I'm coming 'bout you. Get that nigga buried six feet deep if you want to."

"Fine, twenty-four hours."

"Happy you see it my way," I smirked.

I let her shirt go and grabbed a hold of her hips. Knowing Jayce was about to be mine on some official type shit had me wanting to be deep within her walls. I guided her hips, grinding her pussy along my hardened tool.

"Mhmmm," spilled from her mouth.

Closing her eyes, she groped her titties, tugging at her nipples. My mouth watered watching them firm. I leaned forward, biting and sucking on 'em through her t-shirt. Her back arched, pushing them further into my face. Lifting her shirt, I slathered them both, raking my tongue across and running it back.

"I'm ready for you to come home," she purred.

Standing up, Jacelyn stripped out of her t-shirt and panties, then kneeled in front of me tugging off my sweats and briefs. With her eyes locked on mine, she crawled between my legs and took me into her mouth. Waves of pleasure crashed into me each time her mouth made them crazy ass slurping sounds. Feeling my nut build, I lifted her from her knees and brought her back to my lap.

"Oouuf!" she moaned, as I pressed into her entrance. Slipping my way inside, her pussy warmed my throbbing dick, drawing me further into her depths and welcoming me home.

JACELYN

"I don't know what Nazari did to your ass, but the way you're glowing and limping around this here kitchen has me a little jealous friend," Dionne said.

Turning around, I looked at her, and she was serious as hell.

"Ew! My brother is the reason and I'm not trying to hear none of that. It's bad enough I caught them fucking outside the club," Sariah huffed, shaking her head as if she was trying to erase the memory.

"Whaat!" Dionne squealed.

"Relax because it was five years ago. The night of my anniversary, she walked outside and caught Nazari and me."

"Why you never told me?"

"Why would I? I never thought I would see Nazari again, let alone be with him, and I thought Sariah was his bitch." I shrugged.

"Whatever, all I'm saying is I've never seen you shine so bright friend. Tell me what Nazari put on you, so I can tell this nigga Mitch to step his shit up," Dionne giggled.

"Again, that's my brother," Sariah smacked.

"Oh, my bad girl, cover your ears then," Dionne laughed.

"Let's not act like you're not a guest in my home," Sariah snapped and, for a second, the room stood still.

The three of us had been friendly since Rhea's party, but we were still getting to know each other and seeing how well we meshed. Sariah had a standoff attitude while Dionne was jokey as hell. Sometimes, Dionne got beside herself, and Sariah didn't seem like the type to play like that.

"Come on y'all, let's not start arguing," I said, trying simmer the room.

"Arguing, who's arguing?" Dionne asked.

"No, forreal," Sariah laughed. "Girl, Dionne knows when to take me seriously and when not to. I play all day until I don't but, trust, you'll know when the attitude is real," she explained.

"Oh," I laughed, letting out a sigh of relief. "But to answer your question," I smirked and bit my lip.

"Lawd, let me go to the bathroom. You got five minutes to get whatever freaky shit you gotta say out." Sariah stood from the table and went to the bathroom.

"Okay, bitch, spill."

"Dionne, when I say that man cherished every part of my body all day yesterday. Not a single inch of my body went untouched. That man used his tongue and his dick interchangeably to hit every nerve my body possessed."

"Not him having you locked away in orgasm city," she smacked excitedly.

"It wasn't one sided tho. Best believe that nigga got up this morning with more than just a pep in his step."

"Yes bitch! Let that nigga know not a bitch alive can make him feel how you do," she hyped me up.

"And did!" I smiled proudly.

"I hope y'all done because I'm not trying to hear nothing above PG-13," Sariah spoke.

"I got it all out, come on," I laughed.

Sariah came back into the kitchen and sat at the table. I handed each girl a mimosa, then sat down to eat myself. This morning, I woke up in the arms of a man who felt like home and couldn't have been happier. We talked a little, with Nazari making it clear my twenty-four hours started today. I didn't argue and met his demand with a simple okay. The first thing on my to-do list was meet up with Dionne who insisted that we invited Sariah. When I called, she was making breakfast and invited us over. I was hesitant at first because I didn't know how to take Sariah knowing my personal business, but she was the only one who truly knew Nazari. So, whatever questions I had, she was the best person to get answers from.

"Good because what I want to know is how did you handle the eye reveal. I swear I wish I could've been a fly on the wall for that."

"Eye reveal? What's she talking about Jacelyn?" Dionne asked.

Quickly, I went over the events that happened after Nazari broke into our home, whisking me away. "I fainted. I was so in disbelief that I told him to pop them contacts out," I laughed.

"Why would he hide such pretty eyes?" Dionne quizzed.

"They remind him of his mother," Sariah answered before I could. "Nazari and Charlotte are very estranged. Nazari won't say it, but he holds a lot of resentment for that woman, and I don't blame him. As a mother, I could never imagine leaving Cree just to go and have a baby elsewhere."

"Me either," I sighed. "When he told me everything, I couldn't even bring up Charlotte or the things she's done to me while being with Aidan. The few times he did mention her, he did so with so much disdain, it almost felt vengeful."

I didn't think Nazari had it in him to kill his own mother, but I also wasn't going to put it past him. The young boy within him still needed to be healed. When he was ready, then we could talk about it but, for now, I wasn't going to push; we had enough issues already.

"Yeah, he gets like that. A few times he's broke into her house too."

"What?" Dionne and I gasped.

"Yup. He never hurt her though. He's just struggling with how to deal with all those emotions. Before you, I didn't think he would ever allow himself to feel anything for someone outside of family. Nazari is tough and a true definition of a man but, like everyone else, he needs to be cared for, shown that it's okay for him to let his guard down and be vulnerable. This thing y'all have is new and beautiful. I appreciate you liking, loving, or whatever you feel for my brother because he deserves to be cared for."

"Whatever it is I do for him, he does for me also. I think in ways I may not understand right now, I calm whatever goes on in his head. The madness that he struggles with is always at ease when he's with me. With me, Nazari makes me feel safe enough to be who I am. When he took me on our date to *Duluchi's*, what I had on was so revealing. Aidan would've never allowed me out the house wearing it. Nazari encouraged me and constantly praised how good I look. That meant a lot to me. Nazari just..."

My words trailed off because there was no explanation for what Nazari did for me. He was the lighter needed to ignite the flame that had been burned out within me for so wrong. He was the love I would always be willing to fight for and not because I had to but because I wanted to.

"I'ma need you to stop before I start crying. I don't know if it's this champagne with a drop of juice or what, but I'm ready to boohoo cry. Seeing you happy makes me happy friend. I'm so damn happy you found someone who deserves you and doesn't mind checking you," Dionne sniffled, fanning at her eyes.

"Right because my brother said you got twenty-four to wrap this marriage up," Sariah giggled.

"That man is not playing 'bout you, you hear me," Dionne cheered.

"I'm not playing about him either. Tara better had learned her lesson or I'ma have to toe tag her dumbass."

"We gon' jump that hoe next time for sure!" Dionne cosigned.

"I'm sure Tara learned her lesson after what Nazari did," Sariah smirked.

"Oh, you got tea and didn't say nothing? What he did?" Dionne asked.

"He took her to one of the properties that he owns where he's doing construction and made her dig her own grave."

Sariah said it as if it was the most normal thing in the world. Dionne and I exchanged wide eyed glances and crinkled brows. Sariah saw our reaction and just shrugged.

"Do you think he was going to—"

My phone vibrated against the table, and the name on the screen caused me to lose all train of thought.

"Hey," I sang, happily answering the phone.

"Wassup beautiful. You still at my sister's house?"

"Yeah, why?"

"I got something coming for you in like ten minutes."

My face lit up with excitement. "What is it?"

"Don't worry about it, just make sure you answer the door."

"Okay, but where are you? It sounds like you're outside some-where."

"I am. Handling business so I can make it back to you tonight. Rhea's gon' be at Nunu's house, right?"

"She's with your mot... Charlotte. She's with Charlotte. I have to go pick her up later today. I'm not sure if Aidan made it over there yet, but I don't want her caught up in the drama."

The phone went silent, including Nazari's normally hearty breaths. "Hello?"

"Yeah, I'm here. Let me know how shit go with grabbing Rhea. If you need me to, I can go and scoop her."

I paused. A long, pregnant pause had me in a chokehold. "Jayce."

"Uh, yeah, I'm here. What you said kind of caught me off guard."

"I bet," he chuckled, but his laugh lacked humor. It was dry and scratchy. "Charlotte isn't my favorite person but, to keep you from having to deal with her and Aidan's bullshit, I can grab her for you."

"Um, okay."

"Cool. Go open the door."

"Why can't you just tell me what the surprise is?" I asked and began heading for the door.

"Cause I wanna hear the surprise in your voice."

"Fine. I'm opening it now." I twisted the locks and opened the door.

"Hello, Ms. Smyth. My name is Mrs. Wild; I'm a divorce attorney. A Mr. Caddel told me I would be able to find you."

Stunned, I was left speechless.

"Jayce, you still there?" Nazari asked and, this time, his laughs were filled with humor.

"Yes, I'm Ms. Smyth and you can come in."

"Thank you." Mrs. Wild smiled and walked inside.

Sariah and Dionne both came to usher her into the kitchen.

"Why would you send a lawyer here Nazari?" I asked in a hushed tone.

"I said twenty-four hours Jayce. I wasn't playing. Hit me when you finish, so I can grab that and make sure Aidan signs that shit."

"Nazari, this is—"

"This what needs to be done. We can go back and forth all you want, but the results are gon' be the same. Now, go handle your business so you can bring your ass home to me and braid me up. You worried about me sending a lawyer to handle shit, when your nigga is out here looking crazy."

"No one told you to disappear for two weeks. I could've braided you up then. You ever think about locking your hair?" I asked randomly.

"A few times, but I didn't know anyone who could keep my shit up. Is that what you're tryin' to do?"

"I don't know yet. I guess we'll find out tonight."

"I guess we will. Go handle that shit Jayce."

"Okay."

"I'm not playin' either."

"Neither am I. Twenty-four hours, right?"

"Twenty-four. Make 'em count."

"Okay Nazari," I giggled. I was about to hang up when Nazari called out to me. "What now Nazari?" I asked kiddingly.

"I fucks with you."

"I fucks with you too," I blushed.

"Good 'cause you know how I'm comin' if ya ass try any funny shit."

"I know, bye. I have a divorce to figure out."

"Good fucking answer!" he shouted.

I laughed, ended the call and went into the kitchen. As I sat down, both Sariah and Dionne said, "Twenty-four!"

"Nunu!"

Walking into my grandmother's house, I called out to carrying a manila envelope in my hand. She wasn't in the living room, so I walked into the kitchen where a bunch of papers were sprawled out across the counter. I left my envelope on the island and went to see what all the mess was about. I picked up a few papers and scanned over them.

"Girl, if you would answer the phone, you wouldn't have to sneak into my house and read my papers."

Nunu startled me, as I was heavy in thought after what I'd read.

"Nunu, what is all of this about you having land and someone trying to take it from you?"

I waved the papers I had in my hand, waiting on an explanation. Nunu had always been private about the things she had going on. If it wasn't a need to know situation, then she found no reason for you to know. I always knew Nunu and Gramps had money stashed, but I never thought she would have acres of land.

"Get them papers out of my face." Nunu stashed the papers I had in my hand and cleaned up the ones on the counter. "Like I said, if you answered the phone yesterday, you would know what was going on. Where were you?"

I nibbled on my lip.

"Open your mouth and say something Jayce," she said.

"I was with Nazari," I blurted.

"Okay. Is he controlling and stopping you from answering the phone? If that's the case, I can send Gramps over there to set his fine ass straight."

I laughed at that last comment because Nunu was going to find a way to speak on Nazari's look. "No. Uh, we we're spending time together because—"

The reason why I wasn't answering the phone was simple, but the explanation that had to follow was the hard part.

"Jayce!" Nunu smacked. "Because what?"

"He broke into the house the night prior and caught Aidan choking me. He roughed Aidan up, then brought me to a house that he bought for me and Rhea. And before you ask, he bought us a house because come to find out, Rhea is his daughter."

Nunu's eyelids slowly began to rise, making her eyes bulge, which had me nervous. She brought her hand to her chest, and I just knew I'd said too much.

"Come on Nunu, let me help you have a seat." I reached for her arm, and she swatted my hand away fussing.

"Don't you try and sit me down after telling me all of that bullshit. Girl, if you don't tell me the truth, I'ma go upside your head."

"Nunu, that is the truth. I know it's hard to believe, but it's the truth. I slept with Nazari the night of my anniversary when Aidan never came home for dinner."

"Well, the coochie is just loose, ain't it," Nunu huffed. "If that's the case, why wouldn't you get a DNA test to know for sure?"

Sighing, I made the mistake of tugging at my hoodie and showing Nunu the bruises I still had on my neck.

"Jacelyn Smyth, what the hell happed to your neck?" she roared. Her soft spoken voice had the power of a lion's growl.

"That happened when Aidan choked me. I told you, Nunu."

"No, you mixed that in with all the other bullshit you was spewing. Lord, if this is you trying to take me out, you could've just let me pass peacefully in my sleep."

"Nunu," I complained.

"Jacelyn, baby, this is a lot and, if my heart doesn't stop racing, I just might meet the Lord."

"Okay, let's sit you down."

This time, Nunu didn't object as I grabbed ahold of her and brought her over to the table. After sitting her down, I grabbed a bottle of water from the fridge and brought her some crackers and cheese. She looked at me like she wanted to object but she didn't have a choice. Either she would feed herself or I would stuff it in her mouth. Call me selfish, but I needed my Nunu more than anything right now.

"Okay, I ate some, now explain."

Eating a cracker myself, I went on to explain to Nunu all that Nazari had told me. I kept the part about him being an ex-hitman because her old self did not need to know that. When I was finished, she just looked at me while shaking her head, with eyes filled of disappointment.

"The mess you done made," she finally said, exhaling heavily. "Jacelyn, baby, I love you. I love you more than anything, well outside of Gramps and Rhea, of course, but you're still my heart. And because of that, I can tell you the truth. All of this didn't have to happen if you would've handled your business from the start. I don't know where you got the silly notion that you had to stay with Aidan for Rhea's sake or for whatever reason you made up for yourself. But those reasons are exactly why you are in this situation now. I've never liked Aidan, but I don't have to like him to say he doesn't deserve to raise a daughter for four years and then lose that privilege because her real daddy showed up. I don't know how you're going to handle this, but I know one thing; you better not be moving that man into your house. I'm rooting for Nazari but, from what you tell me, he has a lot of trauma he has to work through. The beginning stages of any relationship are all fun and games, the truth comes out when things get tough. Until you know the both of you are willing to fight tooth and nail for this relationship, y'all need to live separately and date."

"We both agreed to that already. As for Rhea, I have no plans on telling her that Nazari is her father until I feel she is ready."

"Good. As for Aidan, you need to get started on the divorce and file for a restraining order. That boy putting hands on you is no good. You know Gramps has a shotgun out in the shed. One call and he'll pull up and shoot his momma house the fuck up," Nunu grumbled.

"Gramps will not be shooting anything up. I have the divorce papers already drawn up. I just need him to sign them."

"Mhm. When you bring them over there, make sure you take Nazari with you. That boy a little touched, them crazy ones know how to protect they lady."

"What you know about a crazy one Nunu?"

"Everything. Gramps wasn't always the Gramps you knew," she smirked.

"Oh really!"

"Yup, but that's another story for another day."

"Well, tell me about the land."

"The land is yours, actually. Gramps bought a few acres when he found out your mom was pregnant with you. He planned to wait until she got a little more mature to tell her about it, but she passed before he could. I've been keeping the land waiting for the right time to tell you about it. Anyway, for the past few years, a company has been reaching out trying to buy the land. Then, recently, they dropped off an envelope saying that I either had to build on the land or it was going to be taken from me."

"That's illegal I'm sure. Do you know the name of the company?"

"Shell something. It's on them papers over there."

I got up, went to look over the papers and found the name of the company. "*Shellington & Co.*" I mouthed, growing annoyed. "Nunu, I'll handle it."

"How are you going to... Jacelyn!"

"I got it, okay. Please just trust me," I told her.

"Okay," she sighed.

"Nazari is going to drop Rhea off to you. Please be nice to him."

"No promises." She smiled mischievously.

I shook my head, gave her a kiss, and walked out of the home I grew up in and prayed I made it back. *Shellington & Co.* was an LLC Aidan and his mom used when they wanted to do business under an alias. Wasn't no telling if I was going to walk through Nunu's door or a steel door with metal bracelets clamped against my wrists.

NAZARI

BEING PARKED BACK IN front of this house was giving a nigga flash-backs. Last time I was here, I was pulling up on Aidan for advice. That shit was five years ago and, just like then, the nigga was still as dumb as they muthafuckin' came. On the strength of Pops, I pulled up. That was the first and last time I listened to him about seeking advice or anything else from Aidan. Pops wasn't as pissed as I was about Charlotte having another kid. He was more concerned with the bitch saying I do to the next nigga. Even in his drunk state, he would try to convince me into having a brotherly bond with Aidan. As far as I was concerned, that shit was never gon' fly. I might've thought about it once or twice until I realized a bond with Aidan would leave me to compare my life to his, myself to him. Had the question *fuck is it about this corny nigga that made her want to be a mother* when she already had a son who needed her.

Any bond between Aidan and I would've resulted in resentment. Keeping my distance was the best thing I could've done. It made it easier to keep those feelings I wasn't ready to face on lock. And whenever they thought about jumping up, I pulled up over here, snuck inside and stood over the bitch at her bed side. Cold steel waiting to be heated with the pull of the trigger, silencer screwed to the front so not a soul would hear. One, two, shots and the bitch would be dead. So fucking easy. I could've rid the world of a heartless bitch who didn't deserve to breathe. For whatever reason, I stalled each time. Fingers cramping from how tight I held the trigger.

As easily as I crept in, I snuck out leaving the bitch none the wiser that she was within seconds of taking her last breath. Whatever the big man had planned for Charlotte had to be worse than death because to kill a muthafucka came easy to me. Emotional detachment, I was skilled at. I could slump a body and feel no remorse right after. But, with her, shit wasn't easy. Too many times she was blessed with another chance at life and, each time, she neglected to make amends. 2045 Hunters Lane had been remised of my presence for five years and, just as my life was about to take a turn for the better, I was right back at this bitch. Talk about some shit coming full circle.

Getting out my car, I casually walked across the street. I used the pathway leading to the back part of the house. I cleared the gate with ease and continued on the walkway leading to her back door. I slipped my phone from my pocket and leaned against the house. Sending a quick text, I gave the word to cut the cameras. Seconds later, a text came through letting me know it was cool for me to move. Pulling a pocketknife from my pocket, I stuck it against the lock. After jiggling it a few times, the door opened, giving me access yet again.

Nonchalantly, I walked through the kitchen and checked out the bottom floor. It was quiet and empty as hell. I moved towards the stairs taking them two at a time. I checked all rooms, empty. As I bypassed one of the bedrooms, I glanced towards the wall where markings were etched into the paint. Going over, I ran my hands across the letters and cringed. Eighteen marks cascaded up the wall with Aidan's name scratched above all the marks. Beside his name was Rhea's. Below her name was five marks indicating her height. I snarled seeing this shit. With my knife in hand, I scratched out this nigga's name and height marks but left Rhea's. Her relationship with the deadbeat was hers to cherish. I would never take that from her. But when it came to the other nigga, he would never be given grace on my end. It was fuck him and her until my dying day and, if a nigga came back as a rock, it was still going to be fuck them.

Pulling myself away from the wall, I went over to the office I'd barged into the last time I was here. I took a seat at the desk and rummaged all through that bitch. Finding a locked compartment, I jimmied the lock, popping the shit open. Pulling out a file, I flipped it open and pictures of me and folded up letters came spilling out. Pictures of my first day of school, photos of me playing at the park, graduation pics. Important events of my life had been captured and given to this bitch. Taking each photo, I stacked them on top of each other, then unfolded one of the letters.

Dear Charlotte,

I'm better now and because I am I can say this without any ill will or malice. Walking away from me is something I'm able to forgive. The looming question of why no longer haunts me the way it once did. I made peace with your decision in terms of me. What you did to Nazari is unforgivable. Your absence in his life has caused him nothing but harm since the day you left. Your absence has caused him confusion that I wasn't man enough to clear up. Now that he's grown he doesn't wish to know the why because he loathes you, Charlotte. Your son, your first born son is into things that I cannot control. I fear he's able to do what he does because each time he raises his hand and squeezes, he's envisioning your face on the body of someone else. I hope you're clever enough to understand what I'm saying to you. Repeatedly, he ended you, Charlotte; do you understand what that means?

The boy you left is now a man, a tainted man filled with resentment but a man, nonetheless. We as parents failed Nazari. You lacked to show him how a boy is supposed to be loved, so he would be able to receive that love as a man. I failed by showing him just how low a heartbreak can drag a person without showing how high love can also take you. We failed him Charlotte and, if the day comes when he turns that chrome against us, then we have more choice but to accept it. This will be my last letter and the last picture of Nazari I ever send. I used to think sending you these would somehow bring you back to me. I know now where you are is exactly where you're meant to be.

Crumbling the letter, I snatched up the rest of them and stacked them by the pictures. I placed the folder back in the compartment along with something else that would act as a safety net for when I found myself in trouble. Grabbing everything off the desk, I left the office, making sure everything was back to how I left it. I jogged down the stairs and went into the kitchen where I dropped the letters and pictures. Watching them fall against the stainless steel sink, I could feel my heart sinking to the pit of my stomach. I never took Pops for a begging ass nigga but, if the rest of them letters were like the one I read, then that's exactly what he was.

Still, I wasn't gon' hold it against him. He did what he thought was right at the time and what was right now was for all this shit to go up in flames. Memories of me, Charlotte didn't deserve. She wasn't there by choice and, now, she had to live with that. Grabbing I few paper towels, I brought them to the stove and twisted the knob. Catching fire to the tip, I brought it over to the sink.

Woosh!

The flames grew as it brought the contents to ashes. I smirked knowing this bitch would have nothing to remember me by.

"Grandma, it smells burned."

Rhea's squeaky voice traveled through the house loud as hell. Their footsteps grew louder, the closer they got to the kitchen. I glanced back at the sink, making sure nothing was salvageable, then turned the water on to kill the flames.

"Why does it—"

"Zari!" Rhea's screaming happily drowned out whatever Charlotte was about to say. She stared at me in shock, as Rhea wiggled out of her grasp and came running over to me.

"Wassup baby girl." I smiled, picking her up.

"Look, I still have my necklace."

Rhea pulled the chain from being tucked behind her sweater to show me the gift I bought her. I smiled proudly knowing the first gift I gave my daughter, she loved.

"I see. It looks beautiful on you."

"Thank you. Is Cree here too?"

"Nah but you can see him tho. Go upstairs and pack your stuff. Your mommy sent me to come get you."

"Okay. Grandma, I go with Zari," she said excitedly, as I put her back on her feet.

"Ash... Ashley, go upstairs for me please," Charlotte stammered.

"Okay."

Rhea took off the stairs, and I kept my eye on her until she was fully out of sight. Once she was gone, I stepped towards Charlotte.

"What are you doing here?" she asked nervously, staring in my direction.

It felt crazy standing before her looking in the pair of eyes that mirrored mine, only they held a fear mine didn't.

"What you not happy to see your son?" I smirked.

"Aidan is on his way Nazari and, if I don't answer, he'll—"

"He'll what?" I barked, stepping into her personal space. The bitch jumped, backing herself against the wall. I shook my head. "What happened to all the tough shit you used to talk when it came to Jacelyn?" I asked and cupped my hands behind my back.

"I... I don't know what she told you, but it's a lie."

"Still a deceitful ass bitch," I chuckled heartlessly. "Nah, all the shit she told me was facts. You were comfortable talkin' crazy cause the bitch she married wasn't ever going to check you. Luckily, for Jacelyn, I wasn't raised by you, so bitch isn't in my blood. Fuck with Jacelyn in any kind of way again and this conversation is gon' be between you and my friends, Smith and Wesson."

Charlotte swallowed hard and blinked rapidly. "Why are you here?"

"I came to ask you why?"

"Why what?" she asked stupidly.

"Bitch, you know exactly what *why* I'm speaking on," I sneered. My fingers squeezed at her throat with my palm applying enough pressure to let her know I wasn't above strangulation.

"You and your father didn't fit the image I had for my life. I loved your father, but he wasn't the trophy husband I needed in order to be successful in life. He was fun that was never supposed to be more than us bedding one another. You... you were a mistake but, by the time I found out about you, it was too late for me to have an abortion. Then, you were born, and I thought I could turn a ghetto rat into a pristine man, but I couldn't. Your father loved the hustle and bustle of the hood too much. So, I left. I left for a better life for me. Was it selfish, yes, but I would do it again in a heartbeat. As a young boy, you were defiant and, I knew once you got older, I wouldn't be able to control you, mold you into who I needed you to be to fit the Klein aesthetic. Leaving you behind was necessary."

Tears blurred my vision. Every vein in my body strained against my skin. The pounding in my ears blocked out all rational thinking. Murderous thoughts guided the increase of adrenaline I felt ripping through me. Dense breaths escaped me as words alluded me. I applied pressure to Charlotte's throat, ramming the palm of my hand further into her thyroid cartilage. This was the only response I had for the shit she'd said. A wordy response wasn't needed, action was all that was required. I squeezed harder, enjoying the way her eyes popped open wide. Her lips cracked as they stretched each time she attempted to say my name.

"Zari! I'm ready!" Fast small footsteps could be heard getting closer. "Zari!"

Rhea's voice got louder. Opening my eyes, it wasn't Charlotte I saw fighting to keep the little bit of air that was keeping her alive. It was Jacelyn. Flashes of Jacelyn flickered, masking Charlotte's face. I loosened my grip and, as I moved my hands, I watched her skin on her neck pulse and begin to change from the pasty white to ruby red. Her body slid against the wall as her gasps hurriedly tried to fill her lungs with air.

"Zari! I ready," Rhea said, entering the kitchen.

I stepped in front of Charlotte, so Rhea wouldn't have to see her like that. "Okay, go wait for me at the front door."

"Okay. Where's grandma?" she asked.

"She went to the bathroom. I'll tell her you said bye."

"Okay." Rhea shrugged and went to wait for me at the front door.

"You can't take her," Charlotte struggled to say.

Bending down, I smirked. "I can because she's my fucking daughter."

"What?" she choked.

"Rhea is my daughter, not Aidan's. The granddaughter you loved so fucking much came from your mistake."

Charlotte shook her head rapidly like that was going to change the truth. Knowing some shit like this might've happened, I pulled a copy of the DNA test from my pocket and dropped it on the follow. Like a roach, her ass scurried towards it.

"Get out! Get the fuck out!" she gritted after confirming what I told her to be true.

I backed away from her, more than happy to leave. Once again, the big man above had saved her from a life in hell.

Walking up to Nunu's door, I felt nervous like a nigga who was coming to pick up their prom date. Jayce's grandparents meant the world to her and, even though I got the feeling that they fucked with me, I wanted to be sure. Shit was different now that I wasn't just the nigga who wanted to date Jacelyn. I was a father before anything and that came with a different type of responsibility.

"You good down there Rhea?" I was holding her hand and she seemed to be cool, but I wanted to hear from here that she was good.

"Yes. Are you?" she asked, shocking me.

The car ride over here, she was chatty as fuck telling me about her day and how purple and blue were her favorite colors. She was a lighthearted kid who seemed to be happy without needing a reason.

I appreciated that 'cause I knew all too well how easy it was to be anything but happy.

"I'm good, long as you good," I finally told her.

"Then, we good," she giggled.

"That we are," I laughed lightly.

My heart ached at the fact I couldn't tell Rhea who I was to her. I was eager as fuck to step into daddy role. But this shit was a sensitive situation. Soon, I would be able to proudly walk around with my baby girl and smile whenever she called me dad but, for now, I just had to be good with having her in my life anyway I could get her.

Approaching the front door, I knocked once before Nunu opened the door. "Hello." I said, sounding awkward as fuck.

"Hello," Nunu mimicked.

"Rhea, baby, come in here and go tell Gramps about your day," she said, ushering Rhea into the house.

Rhea's little hand left mine, and I swear I almost snatched her back by my side. I'd missed so much of her life, I didn't want to miss anything else, even if it was her spending time with her Gramps. I wanted to be selfish with Rhea.

"I appreciate you bringing her over here," Nunu said.

"She didn't need to be around the chaos, so it was nothing."

"Mhm. Come in here and let me talk to you."

I walked in and followed Nunu into the kitchen. She gestured for me to sit, and I took a seat.

"Would you like something to drink?"

"No, thank you."

"Polite," she smiled, "I like that." She poured herself a glass of lemonade, then came and sat across from me. "I'm going to make this short because I don't have it in me to have one of those drawn out conversations after everything Jacelyn told me about the two of you.

Now, I don't normally condone no mess and I do believe marriage to be a sacred thing. But we both know Aidan is not the right man for her. I won't say you are just because time will definitely tell. Jacelyn is a wonderful woman who deserves the greatest things life has to offer."

"I plan on giving her all of it and then some. Jacelyn has nothing to worry about when it comes to me. Nothing is perfect in life, so troubles are gon' come but, if we can make it through this, then our odds of making it through the rest is looking good."

"You're right. And I believe that you will do right by Jacelyn. Who I'm more concerned about is Rhea. That little girl deserves to have a father in her life who will go to the ends of the earth and back for her. If you're not willing to do that, then you might as well walk away now. Gramps can be the father figure she—"

"Another man already raised my daughter for the first five years of life. Another nigga isn't stepping into that position outside of me. I know what being a father entails. I raise my nephew as my son."

"But this is different. At the end of the night, your nephew can always go back home to his mother. Rhea's home at some point will be yours. There's no giving her back."

"I wouldn't want to. It's probably hard to believe, but I'm willing to do whatever to make sure she's a part of my life. Even if it's not as her knowing I'm her father because she's not ready. I don't have all the answers Nunu, I don't. All of this is new to me but, for Jacelyn and especially Rhea, I'm willing to do *whatever* needs to be done for their happiness. I go hard for my family, and I don't fuck around when it comes to them. Rhea and Jacelyn are now a part of my family. No harm will come their way and, if by chance it does, it'll be dealt with in a manner that will make the next person think twice."

Nodding her head in approval, Nunu smiled, then got up with her arms outstretched for a hug. We shared an embrace, then went to find

Gramps and Rhea upstairs. Nunu took over with Rhea while Gramps and I exchanged words. His speech was less wordy and consisted of *I got guns and know how to use them. Don't be the reason I do.* His threat was clear and direct. I could respect that. I stayed for a little bit just to watch Rhea in her element.

When I got ready to go, I stopped by the kitchen to grab the manila envelope addressed to Jacelyn from the law office that sat on the counter. Getting back in my car, I checked under my seat to make sure my gun was where I needed it to be. It wasn't there. Grabbing my cell, I dialed Jacelyn, only to get her voicemail. I switched my shit into drive, speeding off knowing there was only one place her and my gun could've been.

AIDAN KLEIN

"I JUST DON'T UNDERSTAND why he would storm in here and pistol whip you for no reason?" Bryn complained as she rubbed my shoulders.

The moment Jacelyn was carried out of this house, I made two calls. One of them being to Bryn. My ego was bruised, and I was in need of some tender love and care. Whoever Nazari brought with him was a heavy handed fucker. The gun clobbered into my face and anyway else the gunman devised to aim. The swelling on my face had gone down, but the bruising was all too prominent on my light complexion. I figured I could pop a few Tylenol and sleep it off but, when I woke up, my head felt worse than it did before I went to sleep.

Bryn nagged until I okayed her to bring me to the hospital. Six hours we spent in that muthafucka, just for them to stitch up a gash

I had at the corner of my eye and prescribed me Ibuprofen. It was a waste of fucking time if you asked me.

"He's a thug Bryn, what else would you expect from someone like him?"

"I... I don't even know what to say other than I blame Jacelyn. You don't deserve to be treated like this Aidan. You deserve so much better and, if you would've listened to me, none of this would have happened."

"Bryn, not right fucking now!" I barked.

"Then when Aidan? We don't need Jacelyn's family land and, if Charlotte wants it that bad, then she can figure out how to get it herself. Look what you've had to endure all in the name of property. It's absurd! We have a son, Aidan. Adrian should be able to call you poppa or dad."

"Don't I fucking provide and spend as much time as I can with him?"

"Yes but—"

"That's the problem Bryn, you keep trying to add a but where one doesn't belong. As a father, I do what I'm supposed to do. The situation we're in isn't ideal, but it's the best I can do right now."

Moving from behind me, Bryn came and stood in front of me. Her slim frame was the complete opposite of Jacelyn's. She was thin with the slightest of curves and barely enough ass for me to hold on to. I wasn't too much of a fan, but she was presentable. When she walked into a room, men weren't eyeing her lustfully. Her body didn't command attention the way Jacelyn's did when the spotlight was supposed to be on me. Bryn was a pretty girl who looked good on my arm. My mother was pleased with her, and she checked all the boxes.

More importantly, she was easily manipulated. It didn't take much for me to sweet talk her into doing everything I wanted her to do, including stopping Adrian from calling me any form of daddy. Shit was just easy with Bryn and less of a headache. It was cool, but I wasn't ready to let go of Jacelyn. At the start, I couldn't wait to get rid of her; now that she was slipping away from me on her own cognizance, I wanted to hold on.

"Aidan, how much longer do you think I'm going to wait around for you? For years, I've sat idly waiting for you to divorce Jacelyn. I listened to all the promises you made. I've beared your child and still you—"

"So, Adrian is yours."

Jacelyn's calm voice was chilling. Bryn quickly moved to the side of me, as I stood up. In the doorway, Jacelyn stood arms folded across her chest but wore a look of contentment.

"Jacelyn, what are you—"

"Aidan this isn't the time for you to speak. You've done that shit enough," she said in such a calm manner.

Nothing about her seemed angered or even bothered by what she'd just heard. Unfolding her arms, she reached behind her, pulling a gun from wherever she had it tucked. Her finger clicked off the safety and, then, she aimed. From me to Bryn, the gun shifted. Jacelyn took a step forward, and we took two back. She smirked and aimed at Bryn, giving me a sense of relief that I wasn't her target.

"Bryn, I have some questions for you."

"Uh okay," Bryn said nervously.

"How long?"

"It started around the time I began working at the firm. So, before you two were married."

"And your son?"

Bryn glanced towards me. I kept my eyes on Jacelyn.

"He's seven and he's Aidan's."

"Seven huh?" she huffed, licking her lips. "Seven is how old our child would've been if I hadn't—"

The pain the truth inflicted on her was enough to silence Jacelyn. She tucked her bottom lip between her teeth and bit down, shaking her head uncontrollably.

"Get the fuck downstairs," she murmured.

"Jacelyn, let me—"

"Get the fuck downstairs now!" she shouted.

Startled, Bryn and I both shuffled past Jacelyn. Once downstairs, Jacelyn directed us to the living room. We both sat at the couch; Jacelyn stood before us with a gun being held by her unsteady hand. I swallowed hard, not wanting to believe Jacelyn had the balls to pull the trigger.

"Jacelyn, just let me explain please," I begged.

"Shut the fuck up!" she screamed.

Her hand swung so fast, I never saw the gun coming. I felt that bitch though. The blow reopened the gash I just had stitched.

"Ahh fuck!" I groaned, blood dribbling into my eye.

"Oh, my God!" Bryn hollered.

"Bitch, shut the fuck up!" Jacelyn demanded. "You know I actually felt sorry for you, Aidan. I felt fucking guilty about cheating while being married to you. I even felt guilty about it after I learned you and Nazari were brothers."

She knows.

Nazari had finally let the cat out the bag, and Jacelyn was still willing to be with him. The ace I'd been holding waiting on the right time to use was gone. I only had one play left, and I prayed it came through in the nick of time.

"I was going to give up my chance at happiness to stay with you. I was doing it all for Rhea but, still, I was willing to put up with all of your bullshit! And this is how you fucking repay me?"

"I don't love her, Jacelyn," I tried to explain.

Bryn gasped and, from the corner of my eye, I could see the tears beginning to well.

"I don't give a fuck if you did. The two of you probably deserve each other. What I'm talking about is this."

Digging in her pocket, she pulled out a piece of paper and tossed it at me.

"Read," she demanded.

I scanned over the letter that was from my shell company.

"How could you try and steal something from my fucking grand-mother?"

Is that what she's fucking mad about, land?

"You're mad about land, Jacelyn? Some fucking land is the reason you're pointing a gun at me," I gritted. I stumbled as I raised up from the couch but, once I was on my feet, I walked towards her.

"Back the fuck up!"

"Or what? You're not going to pull that trigger. I'm Rhea's father. How would you explain to her that you killed her father Jacelyn, huh?"

Seeing the dumbfounded look on her face, I smirked. She hadn't thought this the fuck through; if she had, she would've brought Nazari along to protect her stupid ass.

"Back up Aidan! I'm warning you!" her voice trembled.

"Bryn, go in the kitchen and get this bitch a fucking cookie. Is that what you want Jacelyn? A cookie for your poor fucking efforts as a wife. You think you're the only one who was putting up with shit they didn't deserve? I never fucking loved you. You were a fuck, a bitch that got my dick hard and kept my nut warm. I married you because of the fucking land. I planned on stealing it from that old bitch right after she signed it over to you."

"How could you?" she murmured.

"What's yours is mine, right," I scoffed.

The calm act Jacelyn had tried to put on was gone. The brown hue in her eyes glistened from the tears that were now falling.

I fucking broke her!

"See, you chose the wrong muthafucka, Jacelyn, and now you have to pay for your mistakes."

Backing her into a wall, the gun pressed against my chest as Jacelyn and I stood eye to eye.

"Aidan, back the fuck up," she gritted.

"If you're going to shoot then fucking—"

The front door swung open, drawing our attention to the last person I expected to see back in my fucking house.

"Jayce, the fuck you doing?" Nazari barked, slamming the door behind him. "Give me that shit!"

Walking over, he shoved me out the way and snatched the gun from Jacelyn. With his hand on her chin, he told her, "How many fuckin' times do I gotta tell you any man who gets out of pocket with you is for me to handle?"

"But he—"

"I don't wanna hear no fucking buts. Who's your nigga?"

"You," she sulked.

"Ight, then let your nigga handle this shit."

"Okay," she mumbled.

Smirking, Nazari kissed her, completely ignoring the rest of us in the room.

"Aidan, get up and let's go," Bryn said, coming over and trying to help me off the floor.

"Nah, you can go bring your ass back to that couch. Me and this nigga got some shit to talk about."

Nazari kneeled down, tossing an envelope and a pen my way.

"Sign 'em now."

"I'm not signing shi... ahh... ahh... okay... okay!"

Nazari yanked me forward by my throat, then stuffed the gun into my mouth. "Move faster nigga," he threatened.

I could barely see as I scribbled my name on papers I didn't read.

"Good doing business with you," Nazari smirked, shoving me away from him. He picked up the papers and handed them to. "I need to feel at home," he told her.

She smiled as if he'd just recited the perfect soliloquy in her honor. Jayce clung to him proudly. Getting up, I followed them towards the door.

"Jacelyn, are you really leaving me to be with this thug?" I asked.

"Aidan, I'm leaving because you and I are done. You've been cheating on me and lying to me for years. What's left to hold on to?" she asked without glancing in my direction.

"What about Rhea?"

Chuckling humorlessly, Nazari peered over his shoulder. "Rhea is mine, you don't gotta worry about her; she good just like her momma."

"Jacelyn!"

"Nigga, what I just say?" he growled.

"He committed a murder and he's going to jail! Jacelyn, do you hear me? He's going to jail!"

Without a doubt, I knew I was embarrassing myself. Not once but twice Nazari had bruised me in honor of *my* wife. Jacelyn made it clear she was done with me, but I couldn't let go. Even with Bryn here, I couldn't just let her leave with him and be fucking happy. Turning around, they both faced me. Jacelyn wore a look of pity, not only for me but Bryn as well. Nazari smirked arrogantly.

"Aye nigga, pipe the fuck down. I'm not going nowhere 'cause I didn't do shit. To answer ya other question tho, yeah, I'ma thug, nigga but with ya bitch—"

"Nazari!" Jacelyn spat.

"You know I ain't mean it like that, chill."

"I don't care how you meant it, watch your mouth."

"Ight. Ight. God damn, she can be aggy. But like I was saying, yeah, I'ma thug but with ya wife I get gentle... well ya ex-wife. Better?" He eyed Jacelyn exuding nothing but love and affection. She clamored.

"Yes," she giggled.

"See, she already got a nigga softening up and shit."

"Jacelyn, he's never going to change."

"She know the streets ain't for me. I love bein' her baby."

The two shared a kiss and walked out of the front door, slamming it behind them.

"Aidan!" Bryn called out once I was off the floor.

I ignored her and rushed towards the window. As I looked out, red and blue lights lined the street, all stopping in front of my house. One by one, cops jumped out of their vehicles, guns all aimed at Nazari. The other call I made after Nazari and his goon ran into my home was to my officer friends. Their little pop-ups on him wasn't enough. I wanted him arrested, even if they couldn't hold him for long. I needed Jacelyn to realize that as long as I was able to breathe, her and Nazari would never be happy.

"Aidan, what did you do?" Bryn gasped, rushing to my side.

"Nazari Caddel, you are under arrest for the murder of Creedence Leighton Sr."

As the cops moved in on Nazari, Jacelyn glanced back towards the house she used to consider home. We caught eyes, and I smirked.

"I fucking won."

EPILOGUE
NAZARI

*A **YEAR** & A day later...*

The cold air breezed past me as I walked through the metal door. Hearing it *cling* against the concrete wall was a sound I'd never forget but also one I was grateful for. Being in a cell block was some shit I hated. Nothing was worse than having to sit the fuck down. But the *cling* I heard today was the same *cling* I heard six years ago when I vowed to never come back to this place. I guess that's why muthafuckas said never to say never. Soon as you tried to move on from something, life always had a funny way of bringing you back. I might've ended up back here today but, when I walked of this bitch, wasn't no coming back. This was the last time for sure.

"You sure you wanna do this shit? You can always do the regular normal shit and be done with it," Mitch said, as I stepped into my hazmat suit.

Adjusting the skully I had sitting at the top of my head, I told him, "This the only way to make sure she never runs her fucking mouth. We gon' chop this nigga up, so there's enough pieces of him to send her ass each muthafucking year. It'll be a reminder of what she lost and the monster she created."

"Ight, nigga, you on you diabolical psychological, shit. That fucking year up top didn't change shit about you."

Mitch was wrong. The year I spent locked up changed more about than what the eye could see. The night those punk ass cops tackled me to the ground and threw them cuffs on my wrists was the start of my change. Jacelyn's piercing screams bounced throughout my ears for the first few weeks. I couldn't shake the fear that laced her voice or the stress etched on her face each time she appeared in court.

That's when I realized my presence and freedom was bigger than me. For me, home was between Jacelyn thighs; for her, it was my presence and I'd selfishly robbed her of that comfort. I say selfishly cause there was no one to blame but myself. As a man, it was my job to stay one step aged of Aidan's bitch ass. He managed to get one over on me and, on everything I love, it was his last time.

The murder charge didn't stick, and I never thought it would. There was no one way I would go down for Creedence Sr.'s murder, but there was someone else who would pray the price.

Before they sentenced me and all the other bullshit, I had Jacelyn drop a letter to Charlotte for me. In the letter, I made it clear that if Aidan didn't drop the battery charges they tried to tack on to my shit, she would go to jail for multiple murders, Creedence Sr.'s included. All those times I snuck into her crib to kill her ass but couldn't, I made sure to leave something behind. Throughout her property was evidence waiting to be found for all of the kills I'd ever committed. Assuming her arrogance wouldn't allow her to believe me, I made sure to put in the letter for her to check her locked compartment of her desk. What I left behind the day I found those pictures and letters was Creedence's phone, and Charlotte's number was the last one in the call history.

The murder and battery charges were dropped, leaving me to serve a year for having a non-registered firearm. I did that year like it was nothing, making sure none of my family came to see me, Jacelyn and Rhea included. They were all pissed but wasn't nothing they could do. I needed this time to get my shit together. Sariah and Pops worked at *Ashes 2 Ashes* holding it down for me, and Jacelyn held shit down in other ways. Just cause I was losing a year of my life didn't mean I wanted the same for them.

The year of sitting my ass down was needed, it gave me time to fully deal with my demons. I did some therapy in that bitch and realized I would never fully be able to give myself to Jacelyn and be who I needed to be for my family unless I rid myself of the fear I held. My therapist had his way of how I should do it, and I had mine. This was mine.

"Where Tara at?" I asked Mitch.

"She in there with that nigga."

I nodded, then walked through another. "Aye!" I called out.

"Nazari," Tara mouthed, turning around, "I... I did everything you told me to do. I acted like I was Bryn and called him from her phone after I stole it."

Tara looked like the Tara I used to fuck. She was well put together and was looking like she was back taking care of herself. I was happy 'bout that. In our situation, Tara made me the villain of her story, and I deserved that. Whatever hurt I caused her was unintentional, but I was still going to take accountability for it.

"I 'preciate that."

"No problem, can I go now?"

She was leery, and I could understand why. This wasn't a place you wanted to be for long unless death was your destination.

"Yeah, but I wanted to apologize."

"Oh no, Nazari, you don't have to," she said, waving her hand.

"I do. I know what we agreed on when we first started fucking around. Shit was 'posed to be light and it was, but I can't act like you were delusional for feeling how you felt. We had good times together and, even tho they weren't love on my part, it might've been that for you. I just wanted to apologize for keeping you around for so long, knowing shit was changin' and I wasn't willing to change too."

"I appreciate that Nazari."

I could see her eyes starting to get teary, so I nodded for her to leave. Giving Tara a sentimental moment and her ass taking it further than it needed to wasn't some shit I wanted to deal with. She did like I asked, answered the phone, and followed my instructions perfectly. Our slate was now clean and never to be messy again.

I waited until Tara was gone to walk over to the metal butcher table. Lying across it was a strapped down Aidan. Hanging above him was an electric bone saw. I peeled the tape from his mouth and tapped a few times to wake his stupid ass up.

"Ugh," he groaned groggily.

"Wakey wakey, muthafucka, it's time to pay up," I smirked.

It took a minute for Aidan's eyes to adjust to the dim lighting. Once they did, they were plagued with fear, amusing me.

"Na... Na... Nazari," he stammered. Thrusting his body, he moved from left to right trying to free himself from the clamps. It was pointless and would only make this shit hurt ten times more.

"Please, I'm sorry! Everything was Charlotte's idea. I swear to God I never meant to—"

"Whether it was her idea or not, you played your fuckin' part. That lil cop stunt you pulled cost me a year with my fuckin' daughter after you robbed me of five."

"I'm sorry," he gulped anxiously.

"Keep that shit 'cause this shit is going to be more of an apology than your words ever could be."

Pulling down my mask, I turned on the machine and began to lower it towards his body. My therapist wanted me to deal with my fear by forgiving those who caused it. Charlotte was never going to be the recipient of my forgiveness. The hurt and pain I had to live with because of her absence was now hers to bare. She left me without a mother and, now, I was leaving her without a son.

"Ah shit, I almost forgot!"

Jogging back into the crib, I grabbed the two bouquets of flowers then walked out to my car, sitting them on the passenger next to the three jewelry boxes I already had in the car. As I drove, nervousness began to take over. I was still a handsome ass nigga, but I looked scruffy as fuck and didn't know how Jacelyn was going to take me. In her eyes, I still wanted to be the nigga who did nothing but make her smile. We stayed in contact through emails and phone calls but wasn't nothing like being face to face with the one you love.

A year behind bars put a lot of shit in perspective for me, and my feelings for Jacelyn was at the top of the list. A nigga had never been swept but that was exactly what Jacelyn did. I thought I was the one who had her tripping and falling in love, but it was the other way around. On some love at first sight type shit was the only way for me to put it.

That night at the club, she sparked the love bug. Running into her again after all those years was fate telling me that a nigga was ready. I was ready to face everything I'd been avoiding for so long. I loved that girl and couldn't wait to tell her that shit. We hadn't said the words and, the one time she tried, I stopped her. Saying something like that for the first time in a courtroom wasn't ideal for me; plus, I wanted to be the first one to say it. Feeling all giddy and shit just thinking about my baby, I called her on FaceTime.

"Nazari?" she answered, sounding puzzled as fuck.

"Wassup beautiful. You good?"

"Oh, my God, Nazari!" she belted.

I laughed at her dramatic her ass. "Chill and don't start crying and shit."

"I'm... I'm... I'm not crying, I just can't believe it's you," she said, getting choked up and fanning her eyes.

"Man, get yourself together and give the phone to my baby girl."

"Rhea! Someone wants to talk to you!" Jacelyn called out.

Waiting for Rhea to appear on the screen had my stomach feeling crazy. Six months into my year, Jacelyn told me she explained to Rhea that I was her father. I was pissed at first because I wanted to be there to have that conversation. Since it was done, there wasn't much I could do but respect Jayce's decisions. Every day since, I wondered how our first father and daughter conversation would go. Now, a nigga was about to find out.

"Zari!" she squealed into the phone.

Her smile was infectious, and I caught myself smiling just as wide as she was.

"Wassup baby girl?" I asked.

"Nothing. I'm playing with Cree."

"Yeah? Where my little man at?"

Cree being at Jayce's crib wasn't a coincidence. I had Mitch fill Sariah in and make sure my son would be at the crib when I made it over there. For the first few days, I wanted to spend time with my kids and the love of my life.

"Wassup Pops?" Cree said, coming into the camera.

"You been doing right by ya moms and Jayce, right?" I asked.

"Yes, and I been keeping Rhea safe just like you said."

"My boy," I smirked. "Ight, I'ma see y'all soon. I love you."

"Love you too, Pops," Cree said.

"Love you too, Zari Pops," Rhea sang, warming my heart in ways I didn't know was possible.

"Not you about to cry," Jacelyn joked, coming back onto the phone.

"I just might fuckin' around with them. Hearing that hits different from them," I said honestly.

"What if I said it, would it hit different for me too?"

"I love you, Jacelyn," I told her before she could get hers off.

"No fair Nazari! I wanted to tell you first," she pouted, poking out her bottom lip.

"Be easy. You can tell me first when I pull up. I'm ten minutes away."

"How did you even get out? I thought you had a month left."

"Nah beautiful. I got out a day ago and had Mitch grab me. There was something I needed to handle before I saw my family."

"Do I even want to know?"

Deep down, Jayce knew what I did. We'd had one coded conversation that ended with her saying she didn't want me to kill the nigga and me saying I was gon' do what I needed to.

"Nah, you don't cause it doesn't concern you."

"Fine," she sighed.

"Fix your face. How's Nunu?" I asked to change the convo.

"Getting on my nerves. The medical center she's allowing me to build on the land is supposed to be mine, but she goes up there every day trying to tell the builders what to do. Gramps took her on vacation to put her mind on something else."

"Nunu is hell," I laughed.

Charlotte's other condition for staying out of jail was her leaving Nunu and her land alone. There were enough casinos in the world without her trying to add another. Jayce opening a medical center was more fitting anyway.

"Aye, come meet me outside," I told Jayce and ended the call.

I pulled up minutes later, and she came running out of the door and leaped into my arms. Her hands tangled in my messy ass ponytail.

"We gotta do something about this," she said, inhaling deeply.

"Loc me up. I'm ready."

"Sayless!"

Kissing her deeply, I palmed her ass I held her, missing everything about her.

"I love you," she groaned against my lips.

"I love you."

Everything I thought I was incapable of, Jacelyn was pulling out of me. All that I feared, she showed me there was no reason to. By simply being her, she was turning me into a better man. It was forever up about Jacelyn. Any nigga who tried to jeopardize that, had no choice but to come correct. 'Cause it wasn't a secret how I was coming bout mine.

Kelly KIMBERLY Catalog

Completed Series:

The Deception Of Love 1-3

Trinity 1-2

Jealous 1-2

Ain't Nothing Like A Brooklyn B*tch 1-3

Falling For A Real Nigga 1-4

All She Wanted Was A Rider 1-3

She Was A Good Girl Till She Knew Me 1-4

A Boss & His Chick: Superbox set (A Thug's Blessing 1-3)

Lay My Heart On The Line For You 1-2

The Trillest Love Story Ever Told 1-4

Love & The Come Up 1-3

Till This Hood Love Do Us Part 1-3

She's My Lil Hood Thang 1-2

Match my loyalty 1-2

He got me in my feelings 1-2

Always Us, Never Them

Still Us, Never Them

A Rich Hood Nigga Wifed Me 1-3

The Bride of a St. Rowe Millionaire 1-2

Catch My Gaze

Catch My Gaze: Bonus Scenes

Catch My Love

You Know How I'm Coming

You Know How I'm Coming 2

Shorts:

Santa Baby: An East Coast Christmas Story

Phour A.M. In Brooklyn

Summer Vibes In Brooklyn

Poison

Standalones:

A Player's Prayer: Baltimore's Most Wanted

Gunz & Laci (Paperback Only)

Rich Dreams, Hood Nightmares

Incomplete Series:

She Gotta Be The Dopest To Ride W/ The Coldest 1-2

Young, Pretty & Hood

Baby, I Just Need A Thug

Ridin' For My Mr, Thuggin' For My Mrs 1-2

DMFU: Don't Fxck Me Up, Don't Let Me Down

Made in the USA
Middletown, DE
26 November 2025

22228182R00146